The Czar's attendants understood instantly. The invasion was to go ahead. Shortly yet another prize would be wrested from the Turks and Teutons. They exchanged smiles as the observation car reached the bridge.

Which swayed, and then lurched.

The ambassador blurted something incomprehensible, but did his best to remain impassive. So did the Czar. So did their respective retinues—but not for long.

The bridge tilted, and the observation car with it. The Czar lost his balance and fell sidelong to the floor of the nacelle, shouting. Horrified, the engine-driver pushed his regulator wide open, hoping against hope to drag the tail of the train clear of the bridge before—

Too late.

Tor Books by Robert Silverberg

Across a Billion Years
Beyond the Gate of Worlds (editor)
Collision Course
Conquerors from the Darkness
The Gate of Worlds
Hawksbill Station
In Another Country
Invaders from Earth
Master of Life and Death
Next Stop the Stars
Sailing to Byzantium
The Silent Invaders
Time of the Great Freeze

Robert
Silverberg,
John Brunner,
Chelsea
Quinn Yarbro

A TOM DOHERTY ASSOCIATES BOOK
NEW YORK

This is a work of fiction. All the characters and events portrayed in this book are fictitious, and any resemblance to real people or events is purely coincidental.

BEYOND THE GATE OF WORLDS

A Tor Book
Published by Tom Doherty Associates, Inc.
49 West 24th Street
New York, N.Y. 10010

Cover art by Ken Kelly

ISBN: 0-812-55444-2

First edition: January 1991

Printed in the United States of America

0 9 8 7 6 5 4 3 2 1

Contents

INTRODUCTION

The three novellas in this book trace their ancestry to my novel *The Gate of Worlds*, which I wrote in 1966: an exuberant alternate-universe story which I intended, originally, as the first volume of a trilogy. Science-fiction trilogies weren't as fashionable then as they later became, but the theme of *The Gate of Worlds* seemed to me to be worthy of extended exploration.

For one reason and another, though, I never got around to writing Volume Two (which would have taken place in the vastly different Africa of my alternate universe) or Volume Three (which would have been set in South America). Eventually the whole project faded from my mind, until one morning in a hotel room in Barcelona in the spring of 1988, when I suddenly found myself thinking that it might be a good idea to call in a couple of my colleagues and get together to finish this unfinished business out of 1966. Which has now been done, in the volume you're holding at this moment.

Every alternate-universe story has its jumping-off point—the place at which the alternate universe diverges from the world we actually inhabit. For this one, the point of divergence lies in the year 1348, when the Black Death ravaged Europe, killing some 25 percent of the population. In my original novel I simply made the plague a little worse, so that three-quarters of the people of Europe perished and the survivors, shocked and dazed, were left in no condition to defend themselves against the powerful Ottoman Turks, who had survived the Black Death nicely and were about to launch a war of imperialist conquest against Europe.

The Gate of Worlds takes place, therefore, in a vastly altered twentieth century. Because of the depopulation of Europe in medieval times and the Turkish conquest that followed, the Renaissance and the European maritime expansion had never taken place. The great Mesoamerican cultures of the New World had been left undisturbed, so that Incas still ruled in most of South America and Aztecs held Mexico and Central America, with most of North America inhabited only by scattered American Indian tribes. In Africa it was the same story: the indigenous black Islamic empires of medieval times, Mali and Songhay and Ghana and the rest, had survived into the modern era as independent states. Europe was a sorry land, a Turkish-speaking backwater (even Shakespeare had written his plays in Turkish!) in which the Turks, now decadent, still held sway after a fashion over Spain, Italy, and France; England had lately won its independence, but was in poor shape economically; in Central Europe an entity called the Teutonic States was gradually taking form. Russia, still under the rule of the Czar, was a major imperial nation, but (with the Turks in command of Europe) the Russians had looked the other way, toward the Orient, and had established protectorates over Japan and China.

Technology, in my imagined alternate world, lagged behind the level of ours. There were no airplanes yet, nor telephones, and electricity was still a novelty. The railroad had come into use, and so had the automobile, but cars were few and far between, and the fuel they burned was coal, not petroleum.

That was the background against which I sent the young hero of *The Gate of Worlds*, Dan Beauchamp, out from sleepy twentieth-century England to win fame and fortune in Aztec America. And that too was the background I offered Jim Brunner and Chelsea Quinn Yarbro for their companion stories in this new volume.

I took twentieth-century Africa for my sector, and wrote "Lion Time in Timbuctoo." Brunner wanted to examine European geopolitics against the altered world background, and produced "At the Sign of the Rose." Quinn Yarbro's concern was the strange and stylized Inca culture of Peru, in "An Exaltation of Spiders." Collaboration of this sort is fraught with all sorts of perils; but I think most of them have been surmounted here. And I'm grateful to Mr. Brunner and Ms. Yarbro for their willingness to enter into a world of the imagination which, after all, was not originally of their creation.

—Robert Silverberg

Lion Time in Timbuctoo

By Robert Silverberg

IN THE DRY STIFLING DAYS OF EARLY SUMMER THE EMIR lay dying, the king, the imam, Big Father of the Songhay, in his cool dark mud-walled palace in the Sankoré quarter of Old Timbuctoo. The city seemed frozen, strange though it was to think of freezing in this season of killing heat that fell upon you like a wall of hot iron. There was a vast stasis, as though everything were entombed in ice. The river was low and sluggish, moving almost imperceptibly in its bed with scarcely more vigor than a sick weary crocodile. No one went out of doors, no one moved indoors, everyone sat still, waiting for the old man's death and praying that it would bring the cooling rains.

In his own very much lesser palace alongside the Emir's, Little Father sat still like all the rest, watching and waiting. His time was coming now at last. That was a sobering thought. How long had he been the prince of the realm? Twenty years? Thirty? He had lost count. And now finally to rule, now to be the one who cast the omens and uttered the decrees and welcomed the caravans and took the high seat in the Great Mosque. So much toil, so much responsibility; but the Emir was not yet dead. Not yet. Not quite.

"Little Father, the ambassadors are arriving."

In the arched doorway stood Ali Pasha, bowing, smiling. The vizier's face, black as ebony, gleamed with sweat, a dark moon shining against the lighter darkness of the vestibule. Despite his name, Ali Pasha was pure Songhay, black as sorrow, blacker by far than Little Father, whose blood was mixed with that of would-be conquerors of years gone by. The aura of the power that soon would be his was glistening and crackling around Ali Pasha's head like midwinter lightning: for Ali Pasha was the future Grand Vizier, no question of it. When Little Father became king, the old Emir's officers would resign and retire. An Emir's ministers did not hold office beyond his reign. In an earlier time they would have been lucky to survive the old Emir's death at all.

Little Father, fanning himself sullenly, looked up to meet his vizier's insolent grin.

"Which ambassadors, Ali Pasha?"

"The special ones, here to attend Big Father's funeral. A Turkish. A Mexican. A Russian. And an English."

"An English? Why an English?"

"They are a very proud people, now. Since their independence. How could they stay away? This is a very important death, Little Father."

"Ah. Ah, of course." Little Father contemplated the fine wooden Moorish grillwork that bedecked the doorway. "Not a Peruvian?"

"A Peruvian will very likely come on the next riverboat, Little Father. And a Maori one, and they say a Chinese. There will probably be others also. By the end of the week the city will be filled with dignitaries. This is the most important death in some years."

"A Chinese," Little Father repeated softly, as though Ali Pasha had said an ambassador from the Moon was coming. A Chinese! But yes, yes, this was a very important death. The Songhay Empire was no minor nation. Songhay controlled the crossroads of Africa; all caravans journeying between desert north and tropical south must pass through Songhay. The Emir of Songhay was one of the grand kings of the world.

Ali Pasha said acidly, "The Peruvian hopes that Big Father will last until the rains come, I suppose. And so he takes his time getting here. They are people of a high country, these Peruvians. They aren't accustomed to our heat."

"And if he misses the funeral entirely, waiting for the rains to come?"

Ali Pasha shrugged. "Then he'll learn what heat really is, eh, Little Father? When he goes home to his mountains and tells the Grand Inca that he didn't get here soon enough, eh?" He made a sound that was something like a laugh, and Little Father, experienced in his vizier's sounds, responded with a gloomy smile.

"Where are these ambassadors now?"

"At Kabara, at the port hostelry. Their riverboat has just come in. We've sent the royal barges to bring them here."

"Ah. And where will they stay?"

"Each at his country's embassy, Little Father."

"Of course. Of course. So no action is needed from

me at this time concerning these ambassadors, eh, Ali Pasha?"

"None, Little Father." After a pause the vizier said, "The Turk has brought his daughter. She is very handsome." This with a rolling of the eyes, a baring of the teeth. Little Father felt a pang of appetite, as Ali Pasha had surely intended. The vizier knew his prince very well, too, "Very handsome, Little Father! In a white way, you understand."

"I understand. The English, did he bring a daughter too?"

"Only the Turk," said Ali Pasha.

"Do you remember the Englishwoman who came here once?" Little Father asked.

"How could I forget? The hair like strands of fine gold. The breasts like milk. The pale pink nipples. The belly-hair down below, like fine gold also."

Little Father frowned. He had spoken often enough to Ali Pasha about the Englishwoman's milky breasts and pale pink nipples. But he had no recollection of having described to him or to anyone else the golden hair down below. A rare moment of carelessness, then, on Ali Pasha's part; or else a bit of deliberate malice, perhaps a way of testing Little Father. There were risks in that for Ali Pasha, but surely Ali Pasha knew that. At any rate it was a point Little Father chose not to pursue just now. He sank back into silence, fanning himself more briskly.

Ali Pasha showed no sign of leaving. So there must be other news.

The vizier's glistening eyes narrowed. "I hear they will be starting the dancing in the marketplace very shortly."

Little Father blinked. Was there some crisis in the

king's condition, then? Which everyone knew about but him?

"The death dance, do you mean?"

"That would be premature, Little Father," said Ali Pasha unctuously. "It is the life dance, of course."

"Of course. I should go to it, in that case."

"In half an hour. They are only now assembling the formations. You should go to your father, first."

"Yes. So I should. To the Emir, first, to ask his blessing; and then to the dance."

Little Father rose.

"The Turkish girl," he said. "How old is she, Ali Pasha?"

"She might be eighteen. She might be twenty."

"And handsome, you say?"

"Oh, yes. Yes, very handsome, Little Father!"

There was an underground passageway connecting Little Father's palace to that of Big Father; but suddenly, whimsically, Little Father chose to go there by the out-of-doors way. He had not been out of doors in two or three days, since the worst of the heat had descended on the city. Now he felt the outside air hit him like the blast of a furnace as he crossed the courtyard and stepped into the open. The whole city was like a smithy these days, and would be for weeks and weeks more, until the rains came. He was used to it, of course, but he had never come to like it. No one ever came to like it except the deranged and the very holy, if indeed there was any difference between the one and the other.

Emerging onto the portico of his palace, Little Father looked out on the skyline of flat mud roofs before him, the labyrinth of alleys and connecting passageways, the towers of the mosques, the walled mansions of the nobility. In the hazy distance rose the huge modern buildings of the New City. It was late afternoon, but that brought no relief from the heat. The air was heavy, stagnant, shimmering. It vibrated like a live thing. All day long the myriad whitewashed walls had been soaking up the heat, and now they were beginning to give it back.

Atop the vibration of the air lay a second and almost tangible vibration, the tinny quivering sound of the musicians tuning up for the dance in the marketplace. The life dance, Ali Pasha had said. Perhaps so; but Little Father would not be surprised to find some of the people dancing the death dance as well, and still others dancing the dance of the changing of the king. There was little linearity of time in Old Timbuctoo; everything tended to happen at once. The death of the old king and the ascent of the new one were simultaneous affairs, after all: they were one event. In some countries, Little Father knew, they used to kill the king when he grew sick and feeble, simply to hurry things along. Not here, though. Here they danced him out, danced the new king in. This was a civilized land. An ancient kingdom, a mighty power in the world. He stood for a time, listening to the music in the marketplace, wondering if his father in his sickbed could hear it, and what he might be thinking, if he could. And he wondered too how it would feel when his own time came to lie abed listening to them tuning up in the market for the death dance. But then Little Father's face wrinkled in annoyance at his own foolishness. He would rule for many years; and when the time came to do the death dance for him out there he would not care at all. He might even be eager for it.

Big Father's palace rose before him like a mountain.

Level upon level sprang upward, presenting a dazzling white façade broken only by the dark butts of the wooden beams jutting through the plaster and the occasional grillwork of a window. His own palace was a hut compared with that of the Emir. Implacable blue-veiled Tuareg guards stood in the main doorway. Their eyes and foreheads, all that was visible of their coffee-colored faces, registered surprise as they saw Little Father approaching, alone and on foot, out of the aching sunblink of the afternoon; but they stepped aside. Within, everything was silent and dark. Elderly officials of the almost-late Emir lined the hallways, grieving soundlessly, huddling into their own self-pity. They looked toward Little Father without warmth, without hope, as he moved past them. In a short while he would be king, and they would be nothing. But he wasted no energy on pitying them. It wasn't as though they would be fed to the royal lions in the imperial pleasure-ground, after all, when they stepped down from office. Soft retirements awaited them. They had had their greedy years at the public trough; when the time came for them to go, they would move along to villas in Spain, in Greece, in the south of France, in chilly remote Russia, even, and live comfortably on the fortunes they had embezzled during Big Father's lengthy reign. Whereas he, he, he, he was doomed to spend all the days in this wretched blazing city of mud, scarcely even daring ever to go abroad for fear they would take his throne from him while he was gone.

The Grand Vizier, looking twenty years older than he had seemed when Little Father had last seen him a few days before, greeted him formally at the head of the Stairs of Allah and said, "The imam your father is resting on the porch, Little Father. Three saints and one of the Tijani are with him."

"*Three* saints? He must be very near the end, then!"

"On the contrary. We think he is rallying."

"Allah let it be so," said Little Father.

Servants and ministers were everywhere. The place reeked of incense. All the lamps were lit, and they were flickering wildly in the conflicting currents of the air within the palace, heat from outside meeting the cool of the interior in gusting wafts. The old Emir had never cared much for electricity.

Little Father passed through the huge, musty, empty throne room, bedecked with his father's hunting trophies, the twenty-foot-long crocodile skin, the superb white oryx head with horns like scimitars, the hippo skulls, the vast puzzled-looking giraffe. The rich gifts from foreign monarchs were arrayed here too, the hideous Aztec idol that King Moctezuma had sent a year or two ago, the brilliant feather cloaks from the Inca Capac Yupanqui of Peru, the immense triple-paneled gilded painting of some stiff-jointed Christian holy men with which the Czar Vladimir had paid his respects during a visit of state a decade back, and the great sphere of ivory from China on which some master craftsman had carved a detailed map of the world, and much more, enough to fill half a storehouse. Little Father wondered if he would be able to clear all this stuff out when he became Emir.

In his lifetime Big Father had always preferred to hold court on his upstairs porch, rather than in this dark, cluttered, and somehow sinister throne room; and now he was doing his dying on the porch as well. It was a broad square platform, open to the skies but hidden from the populace below, for it was at the back of the palace facing toward the distant river and no one in the city could look into it.

The dying king lay swaddled, despite the great heat, in a tangle of brilliant blankets of scarlet and turquoise and lemon-colored silk on a rumpled divan to Little Father's left. He was barely visible, a pale sweaty wizened face and nothing more, amid the rumpled bedclothes. To the right was the royal roof-garden, a mysterious collection of fragrant exotic trees and shrubs planted in huge square porcelain vessels from Japan, another gift of the bountiful Czar. The dark earth that filled those blue-and-white tubs had been carried in panniers by donkeys from the banks of the Niger, and the plants were watered every evening at sunset by prisoners, who had to haul great leather sacks of immense weight to this place and were forbidden by the palace guards to stumble or complain. Between the garden and the divan was the royal viewing-pavilion, a low structure of rare satin-smooth woods upon which the Emir in better days would sit for hours, staring out at the barren sun-hammered sandy plain, the pale tormented sky, the occasional wandering camel or hyena, the gnarled scrubby bush that marked the path of the river, six or seven miles away. The cowrie-studded ebony scepter of high office was lying abandoned on the floor of the pavilion, as though nothing more than a cast-off toy.

Four curious figures stood now at the foot of the Emir's divan. One was the Tijani, a member of the city's chief fraternity of religious laymen. He was a man of marked Arab features, dressed in a long white robe over droopy yellow pantaloons, a red turban, a dozen or so strings of amber beads. Probably he was a well-to-do merchant or shopkeeper in daily life. He was wholly absorbed in his orisons, rocking back and forth in place, crooning indefatigably to his hundred-beaded rosary, working hard to efface the Emir's sins and make him fit for Paradise. His voice was thin as feathers from overuse, a low eroded murmur which scarcely halted even for breath. He acknowledged Little Father's arrival with the merest flick of an eyebrow, without pausing in his toil.

The other three holy men were marabouts, living saints, two black Songhay and a man of mixed blood. They were weighted down with leather packets of grigri charms hanging in thick mounds around their necks and girded by other charms by the dozen around their wrists and hips, and they had the proper crazy glittering saint-look in their eyes, the true holy baraka. It was said that saints could fly, could raise the dead, could make the rains come and the rivers rise. Little Father doubted all of that, but he was one who tended to keep his doubts to himself. In any case the city was full of such miracle-workers, dozens of them, and the tombs of hundreds more were objects of veneration in the poorer districts. Little Father recognized all three of these: he had seen them now and then hovering around the Sankoré Mosque or sometimes the other and greater one at Dyingerey Ber, striking saint-poses on one leg or with arms outflung, muttering saint-gibberish, giving passersby the saint-stare. Now they stood lined up in grim silence before the Emir, making cryptic gestures with their fingers. Even before Big Father had fallen ill, these three had gone about declaring that he was doomed shortly to be taken by a vampire, as various recent omens indisputably proved—a flight of owls by day, a flight of vultures by night, the death of a sacred dove that lived on the minaret of the Great Mosque. For them to be in the palace at all was remarkable; be in the presence of the king was astounding. in the royal entourage must be at the point of tion, Little Father concluded.

He knelt at the bedside.

"Father?"

The Emir's eyes were glassy. Perhaps he was becoming a saint too.

"Father, it's me. They said you were rallying. I know you're going to be all right soon."

Was that a smile? Was that any sort of reaction at all?

"Father, it'll be cooler in just a few weeks. The rains are already on the way. Everybody's saying so. You'll feel better when the rains come."

The old man's cheeks were like parchment. His bones were showing through. He was eighty years old and he had been Emir of Songhay for fifty of those years. Electricity hadn't even been invented when he became king, nor the motorcar. Even the railroad had been something new and startling.

There was a clawlike hand suddenly jutting out of the blankets. Little Father touched it. It was like touching a piece of worn leather. By the time the rains had reached Timbuctoo, Big Father would have made the trip by ceremonial barge to the old capital of Gao, two hundred miles down the Niger, to take his place in the royal cemetery of the Kings of Songhay.

Little Father went on murmuring encouragement for another few moments, but it was apparent that the Emir wasn't listening. A stray burst of breeze brought the sound of the marketplace music, growing louder now. Could he hear that? Could he hear anything? Did he care? After a time Little Father rose, and went quickly from the palace.

In the marketplace the dancing had already begun. They had shoved aside the booths of the basket-weavers and the barbers and the slipper-makers and the charm-peddlers, the dealers in salt and fruit and donkeys and rice and tobacco and meat, and a frenetic procession of dancers was weaving swiftly back and forth across the central square from the place of the milk vendors at the south end to the place of the wood vendors at the north when Little Father and Ali Pasha arrived.

"You see?" Ali Pasha asked. "The life dance. They bring the energy down from the skies to fill your father's veins."

There was tremendous energy in it, all right. The dancers pounded the sandy earth with their bare feet, they clapped their hands, they shouted quick sharp punctuations of wordless sound, they made butting gestures with their outflung elbows, they shook their heads convulsively and sent rivers of sweat flying through the air. The heat seemed to mean nothing to them. Their skins gleamed. Their eyes were bright as new coins. They made rhythmic grunting noises, *oom oom oom*, and the whole city seemed to shake beneath their tread.

To Little Father it looked more like the death dance than the dance of life. There was the frenzied stomp of mourning about it. But he was no expert on these things. The people had all sorts of beliefs that were mysteries to him, and which he hoped would melt away like snowflakes during his coming reign. Did they still put pressure on Allah to bring the rains by staking small children out in the blazing sun for days at a time outside the tombs of saints? Did they still practice alchemy on one another, turning wrapping paper into banknotes by means of spells? Did they continue to fret about vampires and djinn? It was all very embarrassing. Songhay was a modern state; and yet there was all this nonsense still going on. Very likely the old Em liked it that way. But soon things would change.

The close formation of the dancers opened abruptly, and to his horror Little Father saw a group of foreigners standing in a little knot at the far side of the marketplace. He had only a glimpse of them; then the dance closed again and the foreigners were blocked from view. He touched Ali Pasha's arm.

"Did you see them?"

"Oh, yes. Yes!"

"Who are they, do you think?"

The vizier stared off intently toward the other side of the marketplace, as though his eyes were capable of seeing through the knot of dancers.

"Embassy people, Little Father. Some Mexicans, I believe, and perhaps the Turks. And those fair-haired people must be the English."

Here to gape at the quaint tribal dances, enjoying the fine barbaric show in the extravagant alien heat.

"You said they were coming by barge. How'd they get here so fast?"

Ali Pasha shook his head.

"They must have taken the motorboat instead, I suppose."

"I can't receive them here, like this. I never would have come here if I had known that they'd be here."

"Of course not, Little Father."

"You should have told me!"

"I had no way of knowing," said Ali Pasha, and for once he sounded sincere, even distressed. "There will be punishments for this. But come, Little Father. Come: to your palace. As you say, they ought not find you here this way, without a retinue, without your regalia. This evening you can receive them properly."

Very likely the newly arrived diplomats at the upper end of the marketplace had no idea that they had been for a few moments in the presence of the heir to the throne, the future Emir of Songhay, one of the six or seven most powerful men in Africa. If they had noticed anyone at all across the way, they would simply have seen a slender, supple, just-barely-still-youngish man with Moorish features, wearing a simple white robe and a flat red skullcap, standing beside a tall, powerfully built black man clad in an ornately brocaded robe of purple and yellow. The black man might have seemed more important to them in the Timbuctoo scheme of things than the Moorish-looking one, though they would have been wrong about that.

But probably they hadn't been looking toward Little Father and Ali Pasha at all. Their attendance was on the dancers. That was why they had halted here, en route from the river landing to their various embassies.

"How tireless they are!" Prince Itzcoatl said. The Mexican envoy, King Moctezuma's brother. "Why don't their bones melt in this heat?" He was a compact copper-colored man decked out grandly in an Aztec feather cape, golden anklets and wristlets, a gold headband studded with brilliant feathers, golden earplugs and noseplugs. "You'd think they were glad their king is dying, seeing them jump around like that."

"Perhaps they are," observed the Turk, Ismet Akif.

He laughed in a mild, sad way. Everything about him seemed to be like that, mild and sad: his droopy-lidded melancholic eyes, his fleshy downcurved lips, his sloping shoulders, even the curiously stodgy and inappropriate European-style clothes that he had chosen to wear in this impossible climate, the dark heavy woolen suit, the narrow gray necktie. But wide cheekbones and a broad, authoritative forehead indicated his true strength to those with the ability to see such things. He too was of royal blood, Sultan Osman's third son. There was something about him that managed to be taut and slack both at once, no easy task. His posture, his expression, the tone of his voice, all conveyed the anomalous sense of self that came from being the official delegate of a vast empire which—as all the world knew—had passed the peak of its greatness some time back and was launched on a long irreversible decline. To the diminutive Englishman at his side he said, "How does it seem to you, Sir Anthony? Are they grieving or celebrating?"

Everyone in the group understood the great cost of the compliment Ismet Akif was paying by amiably addressing his question to the English ambassador, just as if they were equals. It was high courtesy: it was grace in defeat.

Turkey still ruled a domain spanning thousands of miles. England was an insignificant island kingdom. Worse yet, England had been a Turkish province from medieval times onward, until only sixty years before. The exasperated English, weary of hundreds of years of speaking Turkish and bowing to Mecca, finally had chased out their Ottoman masters in the first year of what by English reckoning was the twentieth century, thus becoming the first of all the European peoples to regain their independence. There were no Spaniards here today, no Italians, no Portuguese, and no reason why there should be, for their countries all still were Turkish provinces. Perhaps envoys from those lands would show up later to pay homage to the dead Emir, if only to make some pathetic display of tattered sovereignty; but it would not matter to anyone else, one way or the other. The English, though, were beginning once again to make their way in the world, a little tentatively but nevertheless visibly. And so Ismet Akif had had to accommodate himself to the presence of an English diplomat on the slow journey upriver from the coast to the Songhay capital, and everyone agreed he had managed it very well.

Sir Anthony said, "Both celebrating *and* grieving, I'd imagine." He was a precise, fastidious little man with icy blue eyes, an angular bony face, a tight cap of red curls beginning to shade now into gray. "The king is dead, long live the king—that sort of thing."

"*Almost* dead," Prince Itzcoatl reminded him.

"Quite. Terribly awkward, our getting here before the fact. Or *are* we here before the fact?" Sir Anthony glanced toward his young chargé d'affaires. "Have you heard anything, Michael? Is the old Emir still alive, do you know?"

Michael was long-legged, earnest, milky-skinned, very fair. In the merciless Timbuctoo sunlight his golden hair seemed almost white. The first blush of what was likely to be a very bad sunburn was spreading over his cheeks and forehead. He was twenty-four and this was his first notable diplomatic journey.

He indicated the flagpole at the eastern end of the plaza, where the black and red Songhay flag hung like a dead thing high overhead.

"They'd have lowered the flag if he'd died, Sir Anthony."

"Quite. Quite. They do that sort of thing here, do they?"

"I'd rather expect so, sir."

"And then what? The whole town plunged into mourning? Drums, chanting? The new Emir paraded in the streets? Everyone would head for the mosques, I suppose." Sir Anthony glanced at Ismet Akif. "We would too, eh? Well, I could stand to go into a mosque one more time, I suppose."

After the Conquest, when London had become New Istanbul, the worship of Allah had been imposed by law. Westminster Abbey had been turned into a mosque, and the high pashas of the occupation forces were buried in it alongside the Plantagenet kings. Later the Turks had built the great golden-domed Mosque of Ali on the Strand, opposite the Grand Palace of Sultan Mahmud. To this day perhaps half the English still embraced Islam, out of force of habit if nothing else, and Turkish was still heard in the streets nearly as much as English. The conquerors had had five hundred years to put their mark on England, and that could not be undone overnight. But Christianity was fashionable again among the English well-to-do, and had never really been relinquished by the poor, who had kept their underground chapels through the worst of the Islamic persecutions. And it was obligatory for the members of the governing class.

"It would have been better for us all," said Ismet Akif gravely, "if we had not had to set out so early that we would arrive here before the Emir's death. But of course the distances are so great, and travel is so very slow—"

"And the situation so explosive," Prince Itzcoatl said.

Unexpectedly Ismet Akif's bright-eyed daughter Selima, who was soft-spoken and delicate-looking and was not thought to be particularly forward, said, "Are you talking about the possibility that King Suleiyman of Mali might send an invasion force into Songhay when the old man finally dies?"

Everyone swung about to look at her. Someone gasped and someone else choked back shocked laughter. She was extremely young and of course she was female, but even so the remark was exceedingly tactless, exceedingly embarrassing. The girl had not come to Songhay in any official capacity, merely as her father's traveling companion, for he was a widower. The whole trip was purely an adventure for her. All the same, a diplomat's child should have had more sense. Ismet Akif turned his eyes inward and looked as though he would like to sink into the earth. But Selima's dark eyes glittered with something very much like mischief. She seemed to be enjoying herself. She stood her ground.

"No," she said. "We can't pretend it isn't likely. There's Mali, right next door, controlling the coast. It stands to reason that they'd like to have the inland territory too, and take total control of West African trade. King Suleiyman could argue that Songhay would be better off as part of Mali than it is this way, a landlocked country."

"My dear—"

"And the prince," she went on imperturbably, "is supposed to be just an idler, isn't he, a silly dissolute playboy who's spent so many years waiting around to become Emir that he's gone completely to ruin. Letting him take the throne would be a mistake for everybody. So this is the best possible time for Mali to move in and consolidate the two countries. You all see that. That's why we're here, aren't we, to stare the Malians down and keep them from trying it? Because they'd be too strong for the other powers' comfort if they got together with the Songhayans. And it's all too likely to happen. After all, Mali and Songhay have been consolidated before."

"Hundreds of years ago," said Michael gently. He gave her a great soft blue-eyed stare of admiration and despair. "The principle that the separation of Mali and Songhay is desirable and necessary has been understood internationally since—"

"Please," Ismet Akif said. "This is an unfortunate discussion. My dear, we ought not indulge in such speculations in a place of this sort, or anywhere else, let me say. Perhaps it's time to continue on to our lodgings, do you not all agree?"

"A good idea. The dancing is becoming a little repetitious," Prince Itzcoatl said.

"And the heat," Sir Anthony said. "This unthinkable diabolical heat—"

They looked at each other. They shook their heads, and exchanged small smiles.

Prince Itzcoatl said quietly to Sir Anthony, "An unfortunate discussion, yes."

"Very unfortunate."

Then they all moved on, in groups of two and three, their porters trailing a short distance behind bowed under the the great mounds of luggage. Michael stood for a moment or two peering after the retreating form of Selima Akif in an agony of longing and chagrin. Her movements seemed magical. They were as subtle as Oriental music: an exquisite semitonal slither, an enchanting harmonious twang.

The love he felt for her had surprised and mortified him when it had first blossomed on the riverboat as it came interminably up the Niger from the coast, and here in his first hour in Timbuctoo he felt it almost as a crucifixion. There was no worse damage he could do to himself than to fall in love with a Turk. For an Englishman it was virtual treason. His diplomatic career would be ruined before it had barely begun. He would be laughed out of court. He might just as well convert to Islam, paint his face brown, and undertake the pilgrimage to Mecca. And live thereafter as an anchorite in some desert cave, imploring the favor of the Prophet.

"Michael?" Sir Anthony called. "Is anything wrong?"

"Coming, sir. Coming!"

The reception hall was long and dark and cavernous, lit only by wax tapers that emitted a smoky amber light and a peculiar odor, something like that of leaves decomposing on a forest floor. Along the walls were bowers of interwoven ostrich and peacock plumes, and great elephant tusks set on brass pedestals rose from the earthen floor like obelisks at seemingly random intervals. Songhayans who might have been servants or just as easily high officials of the court moved among the visiting diplomats bearing trays of cool lime-flavored drinks, musty wine, and little delicacies fashioned from a bittersweet red nut.

The prince, in whose name the invitations had gone forth, was nowhere in sight so far as any of the foreigners could tell. The apparent host of the reception was a burly jet-black man of regal bearing clad in a splendid tawny robe that might actually have been made of woven lion skins. He had introduced himself as Ali Pasha, vizier to the prince. The prince, he explained, was at his father's bedside, but would be there shortly.

The prince was deeply devoted to his father, said Ali Pasha; he visited the failing Emir constantly.

"I saw that man in the marketplace this afternoon," Selima said. "He was wearing a purple and yellow robe then. Down at the far side, beyond the dancers, for just a moment. He was looking at us. I thought he was magnificent, somebody of great importance. And he is."

A little indignantly Michael said, "These blacks all look alike to me. How can you be sure that's the one you saw?"

"Because I'm sure. Do all Turks look alike to you too?"

"I didn't mean—"

"All English look alike to us, you know. We can just about distinguish between the red-haired ones and the yellow-haired ones. And that's as far as it goes."

"You aren't serious, Selima."

"No. No, I'm not. I actually can tell one of you from another most of the time. At least I can tell the handsome ones from the ugly ones."

Michael flushed violently, so that his already sunburned face turned flaming scarlet and emanated great waves of heat. Everyone had been telling him how handsome he was since his boyhood. It was as if there was nothing to him at all except regularly formed features and pale flawless skin and long athletic limbs. The notion made him profoundly uncomfortable.

She laughed. "You should cover your face when you're out in the sun. You're starting to get cooked. Does it hurt very much?"

"Not at all. Can I get you a drink?"

"You know that alcohol is forbidden to—"

"The other kind, I mean. The green soda. It's very good, actually. Boy! Boy!"

"I'd rather have the nut thing," she said. She stretched forth one hand—her hand was very small, and the fingers were pale and perfect—and made the tiniest of languid gestures. Two of the black men with trays came toward her at once, and, laughing prettily, she scooped a couple of the nutcakes from the nearer of the trays. She handed one to Michael, who fumbled it and let it fall. Calmly she gave him the other. He looked at it as though she had handed him an asp.

"Are you afraid I've arranged to have you poisoned?" she asked. "Go on. Eat it! It's good! Oh, you're so absurd, Michael! But I do like you."

"We aren't supposed to like each other, you know," he said bleakly.

"I know that. We're enemies, aren't we?"

"Not any more, actually. Not officially."

"Yes, I know. The Empire recognized English independence a good many years ago."

The way she said it, it was like a slap. Michael's reddened cheeks blazed fiercely.

In anguish he crammed the nutcake into his mouth with both hands.

She went on, "I can remember the time when I was a girl and King Richard came to Istanbul to sign the treaty with the Sultan. There was a parade."

"Yes. Yes. A great occasion."

"But there's still bad blood between the Empire and England. We haven't forgiven you for some of the things you did to our people in your country in Sultan Abdul's time, when we were evacuating."

"*You* haven't forgiven *us*—?"

"When you burned the bazaar. When you bombed

that mosque. The broken shopwindows. We were going away voluntarily, you know. You were much more violent toward us than you had any right to be.''

''You speak very directly, don't you?''

''There were atrocities. I studied them in school.''

''And when you people conquered us in 1490? Were you gentle then?'' For a moment Michael's eyes were hot with fury, the easily triggered anger of the good Englishman for the bestial Turk. Appalled, he tried to stem the rising surge of patriotic fervor before it ruined everything. He signaled frantically to one of the tray-wielders, as though another round of nutcakes might serve to get the conversation into a less disagreeable track. ''But never mind all that, Selima. We mustn't be quarreling over ancient history like this.'' Somehow he mastered himself, swallowing, breathing deeply, managing an earnest smile. ''You say you like me.''

''Yes. And you like me. I can tell.''

''Is that all right?''

''Of course it is, silly. Although I shouldn't allow it. We don't even think of you English as completely civilized.'' Her eyes glowed. He began to tremble, and tried to conceal it from her. She was playing with him, he knew, playing a game whose rules she herself had defined and would not share with him. ''Are you a Christian?'' she asked.

''You know I am.''

''Yes, you must be. You used the Christian date for the year of the conquest of England. But your ancestors were Moslem, right?''

''Outwardly, during the time of the occupation. Most of us were. But for all those centuries we secretly continued to maintain our faith in—'' She was definitely going to get him going again. Already his head was beginning to pound. Her beauty was unnerving enough; but this roguishness was more than he could take. He wondered how old she was. Eighteen? Nineteen? No more than that, surely. Very likely she had a fiancée back in Istanbul, some swarthy mustachioed fez-wearing Ottoman princeling, with whom she indulged in unimaginable Oriental perversions and to whom she confessed every little flirtation she undertook while traveling with her father. It was humiliating to think of becoming an item of gossip in some perfumed boudoir on the banks of the Bosporus. A sigh escaped him. She gave him a startled look, as though he had mooed at her. Perhaps he had. Desperately he sought for something, anything, that would rescue him from this increasingly tortured moment of impossible intimacy; and, looking across the room, he was astounded to find his eyes suddenly locked on those of the heir apparent to the throne of Songhay. "Ah, there he is," Michael said in vast relief. "The prince has arrived."

"Which one? Where?"

"The slender man. The red velvet tunic."

"Oh. Oh, yes. *Him.* I saw him in the marketplace too, with Ali Pasha. Now I understand. They came to check us out before we knew who they were." Selima smiled disingenuously. "He's very attractive, isn't he? Rather like an Arab, I'd say. And not nearly as dissolute looking as I was led to expect. Is it all right if I go over and say hello to him? Or should I wait for a proper diplomatic introduction? I'll ask my father, I think. Do you see him? Oh, yes, there he is over there, talking to Prince Itzcoatl—" She began to move away without a backward look.

Michael felt a sword probing in his vitals.

"Boy!" he called, and one of the blacks turned to

him with a somber grin. "Some of that wine, if you please!"

On the far side of the room Little Father smiled and signaled for a drink also—not the miserable palm wine, which he abhorred and which as a good Moslem he should abjure anyway, but the clear fiery brandy that the caravans brought him from Tunis, and which to an outsider's eyes would appear to be mere water. His personal cupbearer, who served no one else in the room, poured until he nodded, and slipped back into the shadows to await the prince's next call.

In the first moments of his presence at the reception Little Father had taken in the entire scene, sorting and analyzing and comprehending. The Turkish ambassador's daughter was even more beautiful than Ali Pasha had led him to think, and there was an agreeable slyness about her that Little Father was able to detect even at a distance. Lust awoke in him at once and he allowed himself a little smile as he savored its familiar throbbing along the insides of his thighs. The Turkish girl was very fine. The tall fair-haired young man, probably some sort of subsidiary English official, was obviously and stupidly in love with her. He should be advised to keep out of the sun. The Aztec prince, all done up in feathers and gold, was arrogant and brutal and smart, as Aztecs usually were. The Turk, the girl's father, looked soft and effete and decadent, which he probably found to be a useful pose. The older Englishman, the little one with the red hair who most likely was the official envoy, seemed tough and dangerous. And over there was another one who hadn't been at the market-place to see the dancing, the Russian, no doubt, a big man, strong and haughty, flat face and flat sea-green eyes and a dense little black beard through which a glint of gold teeth occasionally showed. He too seemed dangerous, physically dangerous, a man who might pick things up and smash them for amusement, but in him all the danger was on the outside, and with the little Englishman it was the other way around. Little Father wondered how much trouble these people would manage to create for him before the funeral was over and done with. It was every nation's ambition to create trouble in the empires of Africa, after all: there was too much cheap labor here, too much in the way of raw materials, for the pale jealous folk of the overseas lands to ignore, and they were forever dreaming dreams of conquest. But no one had ever managed it. Africa had kept itself independent of the great overseas powers. The Pasha of Egypt still held his place by the Nile, in the far south the Mambo of Zimbabwe maintained his domain amidst enough gold to make even an Aztec feel envy, and the Bey of Marrakesh was unchallenged in the north. And the strong western empires flourished as ever, Ghana, Mali, Kongo, Songhay—no, no, Africa had never let itself be eaten by Turks or Russians or even the Moors, though they had all given it a good try. Nor would it ever. Still, as he wandered among these outlanders Little Father felt contempt for him and his people drifting through the air about him like smoke. He wished that he could have made a properly royal entrance, coming upon the foreigners in style, with drums and trumpets and bugles. Preceded as he entered by musicians carrying gold and silver guitars, and followed by a hundred armed slaves. But those were royal prerogatives, and he was not yet Emir. Besides, this was a solemn time in Songhay, and such pomp was unbefitting. And the foreigners would very likely look upon it as the vulgarity of a barbarian, anyway, or the quaint grandiosity of a primitive.

Little Father downed his brandy in three quick gulps and held out the cup for more. It was beginning to restore his spirit. He felt a sense of deep well-being, of ease and assurance.

But just then came a stir and a hubbub at the north door of the reception hall. In amazement and fury he saw Serene Glory entering, Big Father's main wife, surrounded by her full retinue. Her hair was done up in the elaborate great curving horns of the scorpion style, and she wore astonishing festoons of jewelry, necklaces of gold and amber, bracelets of silver and ebony and beads, rings of stone, earrings of shining ivory.

To Ali Pasha the prince said, hissing, "What's *she* doing here?"

"You invited her yourself, Little Father."

Little Father stared into his cup.

"I did?"

"There is no question of that, sir."

"Yes. Yes, I did." Little Father shook his head. "I must have been drunk. What was I thinking of?" Big Father's main wife was young and beautiful, younger, indeed, than Little Father himself, and she was an immense annoyance. Big Father had had six wives in his time, or possibly seven—Little Father was not sure, and he had never dared to ask—of whom all of the earliest ones were now dead, including Little Father's own mother. Of the three that remained, one was an elderly woman who lived in retirement in Gao, and one was a mere child, the old man's final toy; and then there was this one, this witch, this vampire, who placed no bounds on her ambitions. Only six months before, when Big Father had still been more or less healthy, Serene Glory had dared to offer herself to Little Father as they returned together from the Great Mosque. Of course he desired her; who would not desire her? But the idea was monstrous. Little Father would no more lay a hand on one of Big Father's wives than he would lie down with a crocodile. Clearly this woman, suspecting that the father was approaching his end, had had some dream of beguiling the son. That would not happen. Once Big Father was safely interred in the royal cemetery Serene Glory would go into chaste retirement, however beautiful she might be.

"Get her out of here, fast!" Little Father whispered.

"But she has every right—she is the wife of the Emir—"

"Then keep her away from me, at least. If she comes within five feet of me tonight, you'll be tending camels tomorrow, do you hear? Within *ten* feet. See to it."

"She will come nowhere near you, Little Father."

There was an odd look on Ali Pasha's face.

"Why are you smiling?" Little Father asked.

"Smiling? I am not smiling, Little Father."

"No. No, of course not."

Little Father made a gesture of dismissal and walked toward the platform of audience. A reception line began to form. The Russian was the first to present his greetings to the prince, and then the Aztec, and then the Englishman. There were ceremonial exchanges of gifts. At last it was the turn of the Turk. He had brought a splendid set of ornate daggers, inlaid with jewels. Little Father received them politely and, as he had with the other ambassadors, he bestowed an elaborately carved segment of ivory tusk upon Ismet Akif. The girl stood shyly to one side.

"May I present also my daughter Selima," said Ismet Akif.

She was well trained. She made a quick little ceremonial bow, and as she straightened her eyes met Little Father's, only for a moment, and it was enough. Warmth traveled just beneath his skin nearly the entire length of his body, a signal he knew well. He smiled at her. The smile was a communicative one, and was understood and reciprocated. Even in that busy room those smiles had the force of thunderclaps. Everyone had been watching. Quickly Little Father's gaze traversed the reception hall, and in a fraction of an instant he took in the sudden flicker of rage on the face of Serene Glory, the sudden knowing look on Ali Pasha's, the sudden anguished comprehension on that of the tall young Englishman. Only Ismet Akif remained impassive; and yet Little Father had little doubt that he too was in on the transaction. In the wars of love there are rarely any secrets amongst those on the field of combat.

Every day there was dancing in the marketplace. Some days the dancers kept their heads motionless and put everything else into motion; other days they let their heads oscillate like independent creatures, while scarcely moving a limb. There were days of shouting dances and days of silent dances. Sometimes brilliant robes were worn and sometimes the dancers were all but naked.

In the beginning the foreign ambassadors went regularly to watch the show. But as time went on, the Emir continued not to die, and the intensity of the heat grew and grew, going beyond the uncomfortable into the implausible and then beyond that to the unimaginable, they tended to stay within the relative coolness of their own compounds despite the temptations of the daily show in the plaza. New ambassadors arrived daily, from the Maori Confederation, from China, from Peru finally, from lesser lands like Korea and Ind and the Teutonic States, and for a time the newcomers went to see the dancing with the same eagerness as their predecessors. Then they too stopped attending.

The Emir's longevity was becoming an embarrassment. Weeks were going by and the daily bulletins were a monotonous succession of medical ups and downs, with no clear pattern. The special ambassadors, unexpectedly snared in an ungratifying city at a disagreeable time of year, could not leave, but were beginning to find it an agony to stay on. It was evident to everyone now that the news of Big Father's imminent demise had gone forth to the world in a vastly overanticipatory way.

"If only the old bastard would simply get up and step out on his balcony and tell us he's healthy again, and let us all go home," Sir Anthony said. "Or succumb at last, one or the other. But this suspension, this indefiniteness—"

"Perhaps the prince will grow weary of the waiting and have him smothered in a pillow," Prince Itzcoatl suggested.

The Englishman shook his head. "He'd have done that ten years ago, if he had it in him at all. The time's long past for him to murder his father."

They were on the covered terrace of the Mexican embassy. In the dreadful heat-stricken silence of the day the foreign dignitaries, as they awaited the intolerably deferred news of the Emir's death, moved in formal rotation from one embassy to another, making ceremonial calls in accordance with strict rules of seniority and precedence.

"His Excellency the Grand Duke Alexander Petrovitch," the Aztec majordomo announced.

The foreign embassies were all in the same quarter of New Timbuctoo, along the grand boulevard known as the Street of All Nations. In the old days the foreigners had lived in the center of the Old Town, in fine houses in the best native style, palaces of stone and brick covered with mauve or orange clay. But Big Father had persuaded them one by one to move to the New City. It was undignified and uncomfortable, he insisted, for the representatives of the great overseas powers to live in mud houses with earthen floors.

Having all the foreigners' dwellings lined up in a row along a single street made it much simpler to keep watch over them, and, in case international difficulties should arise, it would be ever so much more easy to round them all up at once under the guise of "protecting" them. But Big Father had not taken into account that it was also very much easier for the foreigners to mingle with each other, which was not necessarily a good idea. It facilitated conspiracy as well as surveillance.

"We are discussing our impatience," Prince Itzcoatl told the Russian, who was the cousin of the Czar. "Sir Anthony is weary of Timbuctoo."

"Nor am I the only one," said the Englishman. "Did you hear that Maori ranting and raving yesterday at the Peruvian party? But what can we do? What can we do?"

"We could to Egypt go while we wait, perhaps," said the Grand Duke. "The Pyramids, the Sphinx, the temples of Karkak!"

"Karnak," Sir Anthony said. "But what if the old bugger dies while we're gone? We'd never get back in time for the funeral. What a black eye for us!"

"And how troublesome for our plans," said the Aztec.

"Mansa Suleiyman would never forgive us," said Sir Anthony.

"Mansa Suleiyman! Mansa Suleiyman!" Alexander Petrovich spat. "Let the black brigand do his own dirty work, then. Brothers, let us go to Egypt. If the Emir dies while we are away, will not the prince be removed whether or not we happen to be in attendance at the funeral?"

"Should we be speaking of this here?" Prince Itzcoatl asked, plucking in displeasure at his earplugs.

"Why not? There is no danger. These people are like children. They would never suspect—"

"Even so—"

But the Russian would not be deterred. Bull-like, he said, "It will all go well whether we are here or not. Believe me. It is all arranged, I remind you. So let us go to Egypt, then, before we bake to death. Before we choke on the sand that blows through these miserable streets."

"Egypt's not a great deal cooler than Songhay right now," Prince Itzcoatl pointed out. "And sand is not unknown there either."

The Grand Duke's massive shoulders moved in a ponderous shrugging gesture.

"To the south, then, to the Great Waterfalls. It is winter in that part of Africa, such winter as they have. Or to the Islands of the Canaries. Anywhere, anywhere at all, to escape from this Timbuctoo. I fry here. I sizzle here. I remind you that I am Russian, my friends. This is no climate for Russians."

Sir Anthony stared suspiciously into the sea-green eyes. "Are you the weak link in our little affair, my dear Duke Alexander? Have we made a mistake by asking you to join us?''

''Does it seem so to you? Am I untrustworthy, do you think?''

''The Emir could die at any moment. Probably will. Despite what's been happening, or not happening, it's clear that he can't last very much longer. The removal of the prince on the day of the funeral, as you have just observed, has ben arranged. But how can we dare risk being elsewhere on that day? How can we even *think* of such a thing?'' Sir Anthony's lean face grew florid; his tight mat of graying red hair began to rise and crackle with inner electricity; his chilly blue eyes became utterly arctic. ''It is *essential* that in the moment of chaos that follows, the great-power triumvirate we represent—the troika, as you say—be on hand here to invite King Suleiyman of Mali to take charge of the country. I repeat, Your Excellency: *essential.* The time factor is critical. If we are off on holiday in Egypt, or anywhere else—if we are so much as a day too late getting back here—''

Prince Itzcoatl said, ''I think the Grand Duke understands that point, Sir Anthony.''

''Ah, but does he? Does he?''

''I think so.'' The Aztec drew in his breath sharply and let his gleaming obsidian eyes meet those of the Russian. ''Certainly he sees that we're all in it too deep to back out, and that therefore he has to abide by the plan as drawn, however inconvenient he may find it personally.''

The Grand Duke, sounding a little nettled, said, ''We are traveling too swiftly here, I think. I tell you, I hate this filthy place, I hate its impossible heat, I hate its blowing sand, I hate its undying Emir, I hate its slippery lecherous prince. I hate the smell of the air, even. It is the smell of camel shit, the smell of old mud. But I am your partner in this undertaking to the end. I will not fail you, believe me.'' His great shoulders stirred like boulders rumbling down a slope. ''The consolidation of Mali and Songhay would be displeasing to the Sultan, and therefore it is pleasing to the Czar. I will assist you in making it happen, knowing that such a consolidation has value for your own nations as well, which also is pleasing to my royal cousin. By the Russian Empire from the plan there will be no withdrawal. Of such a possibility let there be no more talk.''

''Of holidays in Egypt let there be no more talk either,'' said Prince Itzcoatl. ''Agreed? None of us likes being here, Duke Alexander. But here we have to stay, like it or not, until everything is brought to completion.''

''Agreed. Agreed.'' The Russian snapped his fingers. ''I did not come here to bicker. I have hospitality for you, waiting outside. Will you share vodka with me?'' An attaché of the Russian Embassy entered, bearing a crystal beaker in a bowl of ice. ''This arrived today, by the riverboat, and I have brought it to offer to my beloved friends of England and Mexico. Unfortunately of caviar there is none, though there should be. This heat! This heat! Caviar, in this heat—impossible!'' The Grand Duke laughed. ''To our great countries! To international amity! To a swift and peaceful end to the Emir's terrible sufferings! To your healths, gentlemen! To your healths!''

''To Mansa Suleiyman, King of Mali and Songhay,'' Prince Itzcoatl said.

''Mansa Suleiyman, yes.''

''Mansa Suleiyman!''

"What splendid stuff," said Sir Anthony. He held forth his glass, and the Russian attaché filled it yet again. "There are other and perhaps more deserving monarchs to toast. To His Majesty King Richard the Fifth!"

"King Richard, yes!"

"And His Imperial Majesty Vladimir the Ninth!"

"Czar Vladimir! Czar Vladimir!"

"Let us not overlook His Highness Moctezuma the Twelfth!"

"King Moctezuma! King Moctezuma!"

"Shall we drink to cooler weather and happier days, gentlemen?"

"Cooler weather! Happier days! And the Emir of Songhay, may he soon rest in peace at last!"

"And to his eldest son, the prince of the realm. May he also soon be at rest," said Prince Itzcoatl.

Selima said, "I hear you have vampires here, and djinn. I want to know all about them."

Little Father was aghast. She would say anything, anything at all.

"Who's been feeding you nonsense like that? There aren't any vampires. There aren't any djinn either. Those things are purely mythical."

"There's a tree south of the city where vampires hold meetings at midnight to choose their victims. Isn't that so? The tree is half white and half red. When you first become a vampire you have to bring one of your male cousins to the meeting for the others to feast on."

"Some of the common people may believe such stuff. But do you think *I* do? Do you think we're all a bunch of ignorant savages here, girl?"

"There's a charm that can be worn to keep vampires

from creeping into your bedroom at night and sucking your blood. I want you to get me one."

"I tell you, there aren't any vamp—"

"Or there's a special prayer you can say. And while you say it you spit in four directions, and that traps the vampire in your house so he can be arrested. Tell me what it is. And the charm for making the vampire give back the blood he's drunk. I want to know that too."

They were on the private upstairs porch of Little Father's palace. The night was bright with moonlight, and the air was as hot as wet velvet. Selima was wearing a long silken robe, very sheer. He could see the shadow of her breasts through it when she turned at an angle to the moon.

"Are you always like this?" he asked, beginning to feel a little irritable. "Or are you just trying to torment me?"

"What's the point of traveling if you don't bother to learn anything about local customs?"

"You *do* think we're savages."

"Maybe I do. Africa is the Dark Continent. Black skins, black souls."

"My skin isn't black. It's practically as light as yours. But even if it were—"

"You're black *inside*. Your blood is African blood, and Africa is the strangest place in the world. The fierce animals you have, gorillas and hippos running around everywhere, giraffes, tigers—the masks, the nightmare carvings—the witchcraft, the drums, the chanting of the high priests—"

"Please," Little Father said. "You're starting to drive me crazy. I'm not responsible for what goes on in the jungles of the tropics. This is Songhay. Do we seem uncivilized to you? We were a great empire when you

Ottomans were still herding goats on the steppes. The only giraffe you'll see in this city is the stuffed one in my father's throne room. There aren't any gorillas in Songhay, and tigers come from Asia, and if you see a hippo running, here or anywhere, please tell the newspaper right away." Then he began to laugh. "Look, Selima, this is a modern country. We have motorcars here. We have a stock exchange. There's a famous university in Timbuctoo, six hundred years old. I don't bow down to tribal idols. We are an Islamic people, you know."

It was lunacy to have let her force him onto the defensive like this. But she wouldn't stop her attack.

"Djinns are Islamic. The Koran talks about them. The Arabs believe in djinn."

Little Father struggled for patience.

"Perhaps they did five hundred years ago, but what's that to us? In any case we aren't Arabs."

"But there are djinn here, plenty of them. My head porter told me. A djinni will appear as a small black spot on the ground and will grow until he's as big as a house. He might change into a sheep or a dog or a cat, and then he'll disappear. The porter said that one time he was at the edge of town in Kabara, and he was surrounded by giants in white turbans that made a weird sucking noise at him."

"What is this man's name? He has no right filling your head with this trash. I'll have him fed to the lions."

"Really?" Her eyes were sparkling. "Would you? What lions? Where?"

"My father keeps them as pets, in a pit. No one is looking after them these days. They must be getting very hungry."

"Oh, you *are* a savage! You are!"

Little Father grinned lopsidedly. He was regaining some of the advantage, he felt. "Lions need to be fed now and then. There's nothing savage about that. *Not* feeding them, that would be savage."

"But to feed a servant to them?"

"If he speaks idiotic nonsense to a visitor, yes. Especially when the visitor is an impressionable young girl."

Her eyes flashed quick lightning, sudden pique. "You think I'm impressionable? You think I'm silly?"

"I think you are young."

"And I think you're a savage underneath it all. Even savages can start a stock exchange. But they're still savages."

"Very well," Little Father said, putting an ominous throb into his tone. "I admit it. I am the child of darkness. I am the pagan prince." He pointed to the moon, full and swollen, hanging just above them like a plummeting polished shield. "You think that is a dead planet up there? It is alive, it is a land of djinn. And it must be nourished. So when it is full like this, the king of this land must appear beneath its face and make offerings of energy to it."

"Energy?"

"Sexual energy," he said portentously. "Atop the great phallic altar, beneath which we keep the dried umbilicus of each of our dead kings. First there is a procession, the phallic figures carried through the streets. And then—"

"The sacrifice of a virgin?" Selima asked.

"What's wrong with you? We are good Moslems here. We don't countenance murder."

"But you countenance phallic rites at the full moon?"

He couldn't tell whether she was taking him seriously or not.

"We maintain certain pre-Islamic customs," he said. "It is folly to cut oneself off from one's origins."

"Absolutely. Tell me what you do on the night the moon is full."

"First, the king coats his entire body in rancid butter—"

"I don't think I like that!"

"Then the chosen bride of the moon is led forth—"

"The fair-skinned bride."

"Fair-skinned?" he said. She saw it was a game, he realized. She was getting into it. "Why fair-skinned?"

"Because she'd be more like the moon than a black woman would. Her energy would rise into the sky more easily. So each month a white woman is stolen and brought to the king to take part in the rite."

Little Father gave her a curious stare. "What a ferocious child you are!"

"I'm not a child. You do prefer white women, don't you? One thing you regret is that I'm not white enough for you."

"You seem very white to me," said Little Father. She was at the edge of the porch now, looking outward over the sleeping city. Idly he watched her shoulder blades moving beneath her sheer gown. Then suddenly the garment began to slide downward, and he realized she had unfastened it at the throat and cast it off. She had worn nothing underneath it. Her waist was very narrow, her hips broad, her buttocks smooth and full, with a pair of deep dimples at the place where they curved outward from her back. His lips were beginning to feel very dry, and he licked them thoughtfully.

She said, "What you really want is an Englishwoman, with skin like milk, and pink nipples, and golden hair down below."

Damn Ali Pasha! Was he out of his mind, telling such stuff to her? He'd go to the lions first thing tomorrow!

Amazed, he cried, "What are you talking about? What sort of madness is this?"

"That is what you want, isn't it? A nice juicy golden-haired one. All of you Africans secretly want one. Some of you not so secretly. I know all about it."

No, it was inconceivable. Ali Pasha was tricky, but he wasn't insane. This was mere coincidence.

"Have you ever had an Englishwoman, prince? A true pink and gold one?"

Little Father let out a sigh of relief. It was only another of her games, then. The girl was all mischief, and it came bubbling out randomly, spontaneously. Truly, she would say anything to anyone. Anything.

"Once," he said, a little vindictively. "She was writing a book on the African empires and she came here to do some research at our university. Our simple barbaric university. One night she interviewed me, on this very porch, a night almost as warm as this one. Her name was—ah—Elizabeth. Elizabeth, yes." Little Father's gaze continued to rest on Selima's bare back. She seemed much more frail above the waist than below. Below the waist she was solid, splendidly fleshly, a commanding woman, no girl at all. Languidly he said, "Skin like milk, indeed. And rosy nipples. I had never even imagined that nipples could be like that. And her hair—"

Selina turned to face him. "My nipples are dark."

"Yes, of course. You're a Turk. But Elizabeth—"

"I don't want to hear any more about Elizabeth. Kiss me."

Her nipples *were* dark, yes, and very small, almost like a boy's, tiny dusky targets on the roundness of her breasts. Her thighs were surprisingly full. She looked far more voluptuous naked than when she was clothed. He hadn't expected that. The heavy thatch at the base of her belly was jet black.

He said, "We don't care for kissing in Songhay. It's one of our quaint tribal taboos. The mouth is for eating, not for making love."

"Every part of the body is for making love. Kiss me."

"You Europeans!"

"I'm not European. I'm a Turk. You do it in some peculiar way here, don't you? Side by side. Back to back."

"No," he said. "Not back to back. Never like that, not even when we feel like reverting to tribal barbarism."

Her perfume drifted toward him, falling over him like a veil. Little Father went to her and she rose up out of the night to him, and they laughed. He kissed her. It was a lie, the thing he had told her, that Songhayans did not like to kiss. Songhayans liked to do everything: at least this Songhayan did. She slipped downward to the swirl of silken pillows on the floor, and he joined her there and covered her body with his own. As he embraced her he felt the moonlight on his back like the touch of a goddess's fingertips, cool, delicate, terrifying.

On the horizon a sharp dawn-line of pale lavender appeared, cutting between the curving grayness above and the flat grayness below. It was like a preliminary announcement by the oboes or the French horns, soon to be transformed into the full overwhelming trumpet blast of morning. Michael, who had been wandering through Old Timbuctoo all night, stared eastward uneasily as if he expected the sky to burst into flame when the sun came into view.

Sleep had been impossible. Only his face and hands were actually sunburned, but his whole body throbbed with discomfort, as though the African sun had reached him even through his clothing. He felt the glow of it behind his knees, in the small of his back, on the soles of his feet.

Nor was there any way to escape the heat, even when the terrible glaring sun had left the sky. The nights were as warm as the days. The motionless air lay on you like burning fur. When you drew a breath you could trace its path all the way down, past your nostrils, past your throat, a trickle of molten lead descending the forking paths into your lungs and spreading out to weigh upon every individual air sac inside you. Now and then came a breeze, but it only made things worse: it gave you no more comfort than a shower of hot ashes might have afforded. So Michael had risen after a few hours of tossing and turning and gone out unnoticed to wander under the weird and cheerless brilliance of the overhanging moon, down from the posh Embassy district into the Old Town somehow, and then from street to street, from quarter to quarter, no destination in mind, no purpose, seeking only to obliterate the gloom and misery of the night.

He was lost, of course—the Old Town was complex enough to negotiate in daylight, impossible in the dark—but that didn't matter. He was somewhere on the western side of town, that was all he knew. The moon was long gone from the sky, as if it had been devoured, though he had not noticed it setting. Before him the ancient metropolis of mud walls and low square flat-roofed buildings lay humped in the thinning darkness, a gigantic weary beast slowly beginning to stir. The thing was to keep on walking, through the night and into the dawn, distracting himself from the physical discomfort and the other, deeper agony that had wrapped itself like some voracious starfish around his soul.

By the faint light he saw that he had reached a sort of large pond. Its water looked to be a flat metallic green. Around its perimeter crouched a shadowy horde of water-carriers, crouching to scoop the green water into goatskin bags, spooning it in with gourds. Then they straightened, with the full bags—they must have weighed a hundred pounds—balanced on their heads, and went jogging off into the dawn to deliver their merchandise at the homes of the wealthy. Little ragged girls were there too, seven or eight years old, filling jugs and tins to bring to their mothers. Some of them waded right into the pool to get what they wanted. A glowering black man in the uniform of the Emirate sat to one side, jotting down notations on a sheet of yellow paper. So this was probably the Old Town's municipal reservoir. Michael shuddered and turned away, back into the city proper. Into the labyrinth once more.

A gray, sandy light was in the sky now. It showed him narrow dusty thoroughfares, blind walls, curving alleyways leading into dark cul-de-sacs. Entire rows of houses seemed to be crumbling away, though they were obviously still inhabited. Underfoot everything was sand, making a treacherous footing. In places the entrances to buildings were half-choked by the drifts. Camels, donkeys, horses wandered about on their own. The city's mixed population—veiled Tuaregs, black Sudanese, aloof and lofty Moors, heavy-bearded Syrian traders, the whole West African racial goulash—was coming forth into the day. Who were all these people? Tailors, moneylenders, scribes, camel-breeders, masons, bakers, charm-sellers, weavers, bakers—necromancers, sages, warlocks, perhaps a few vampires on their way home from their night's toil—Michael looked around, bewildered, trapped within his skull by the barriers of language and his own disordered mental state. He felt as though he were moving about under the surface of the sea, in a medium where he did not belong and could neither breathe nor think.

"Selima?" he said suddenly, blinking in astonishment.

His voice was voiceless. His lips moved, but no sound had come forth.

Apparition? Hallucination? No, no, she was really there. Selima glowed just across the way like a second sun suddenly rising over the city.

Michael shrank back against an immense buttress of mud brick. She had stepped out of a doorway in a smooth gray wall that surrounded what appeared to be one of the palaces of the nobility. The building, partly visible above the wall, was coated in orange clay and had elaborate Moorish windows of dark wood. He trembled. The girl wore only a flimsy white gown, so thin that he could make out the dark-tipped spheres of her breasts moving beneath it, and the dark triangle at her thighs. He wanted to cry. Had she no shame? No. No. She was indifferent to the display, and to everything around her; she would have walked completely naked through this little plaza just as casually as she strode through in this one thin garment.

"Selima, where have you spent this night? Whose palace is this?"

His words were air. No one heard them. She moved serenely onward. A motorcar appeared from somewhere, one of the five or six that Michael had seen so far in this city. A black plume of smoke rose from the vent of its coal-burning engine, and its two huge rear wheels slipped and slid about on the sandy track. Selima jumped up onto the open seat behind the driver, and with great booming exhalations the vehicle made its way through an arched passageway and disappeared into the maze of the town.

An embassy car, no doubt. Waiting here for her all night?

His soul ached. He had never felt so young, so foolish, so vulnerable, so wounded.

"Effendi?" a voice asked. "You wish a camel, effendi?"

"Thank you, no."

"Nice hotel? Bath? Woman to massage you? Boy to massage you?"

"Please. No."

"Some charms, maybe? Good grigri. Souvenir of Timbuctoo."

Michael groaned. He turned away and looked back at the house of infamy from which Selima had emerged.

"That building—what is it?"

"That? Is palace of Little Father. And look, look there, effendi—Little Father himself coming out for a walk."

The prince himself, yes. Of course. Who else would she have spent the night with, here in the Old Town? Michael was engulfed by loathing and despair. Instantly a swarm of eager citizens had surrounded the prince, clustering about him to beg favors the moment he showed himself. But he seemed to move through them with the sort of divine indifference that Selima, in her all-but-nakedness, had displayed. He appeared to be enclosed in an impenetrable bubble of self-concern. He was frowning, he looked troubled, not at all like a man who had just known the favors of the most desirable woman in five hundred miles. His lean sharp-angled face, which had been so animated at the official reception, now had a curiously stunned, immobile look about it, as though he had been struck on the head from behind a short while before and the impact was gradually sinking in.

Michael flattened himself against the buttress. He could not bear the thought of being seen by the prince now, here, as if he had been haunting the palace all night, spying on Selima. He put his arm across his face in a frantic attempt to hide himself, he whose Western clothes and long legs and white skin made him stand out like a meteor. But the prince wasn't coming toward him. Nodding in an abstracted way, he turned quickly, passed through the throng of chattering petitioners as if they were ghosts, disappeared in a flurry of white fabric.

Michael looked about for his sudden friend, the man who had wanted to sell him camels, massages, souvenirs. What he wanted now was a guide to get him out of the Old Town and back to the residence of the English ambassador. But the man was gone.

"Pardon me—" Michael said to someone who looked almost like the first one. Then he realized that he had spoken in English. Useless. He tried in Turkish and in Arabic. A few people stared at him. They seemed to be laughing. He felt transparent to them. They could see his sorrow, his heartache, his anguish, as easily as his sunburn.

Like the good young diplomat he was, he had learned a little Songhay too, the indigenous language. "Town talk," they called it. But the few words he had seemed all to have fled. He stood alone and helpless in the plaza, scuffing angrily at the sand, as the sun broke above the mud rooftops like the sword of an avenging angel and the full blast of morning struck him. Michael felt blisters starting to rise on his cheeks. Agitated flies began to buzz around his eyes. A camel, passing by just then, dropped half a dozen hot green turds right at his feet. He snatched one out of the sand and hurled it with all his strength at the bland blank mud-colored wall of Little Father's palace.

Big Father was sitting up on his divan. His silken blankets were knotted around his waist in chaotic strands, and his bare torso rose above the chaos, gleaming as though it had been oiled. His arms were like sticks and his skin was three shades paler than it once had been and cascades of loose flesh hung like wattles from his neck, but there was the brilliance of black diamonds in his glittering little eyes.

"Not dead yet, you see? You see?" His voice was a cracked wailing screech, but the old authoritative thunder was still somewhere behind it. "Back from the edge of the grave, boy! Allah walks with me yet!"

Little Father was numb with chagrin. All the joy of his night with Selima had vanished in a moment when word had arrived of his father's miraculous recovery. He had just been getting accustomed to the idea that he soon would be king, too. His first misgivings about the work involved in it had begun to ebb; he rather liked the idea of ruling, now. The crown was descending on him like a splendid gift. And here was Big Father sitting up, grinning, waving his arms around in manic glee. Taking back his gift. Deciding to live after all.

What about the funeral plans? What about the special ambassadors who had traveled so far, in such discomfort, to pay homage to the late venerable Emir of Songhay and strike their various deals with his successor?

Big Father had had his head freshly shaved and his beard had been trimmed. He looked like a gnome, ablaze with demonic energies. Off in the corner of the porch, next to the potted trees, the three marabouts stood in a circle, making sacred gestures at each other with lunatic vigor, each seeking to demonstrate superior fervor.

Hoarsely Little Father said, "Your Majesty, the news astonishes and delights me. When the messenger came, telling of your miraculous recovery, I leaped from my bed and gave thanks to the All-Merciful in a voice so loud you must have heard it here."

"Was there a woman with you, boy?"

"Father—"

"I hope you bathed before you came here. You come forth without bathing after you've lain with a woman and the djinns will make you die an awful death, do you realize that?"

"Father, I wouldn't think of—"

"Frothing at the mouth, falling down in the street, that's what'll happen to you. Who was she? Some nobleman's wife as usual, I suppose. Well, never mind. As long as she wasn't mine. Come closer to me, boy."

"Father, you shouldn't tire yourself by talking so much."

"Closer!"

A wizened claw reached for him. Little Father approached and the claw seized him. There was frightening strength in the old man still.

Big Father said, "I'll be up and around in two days. I want the Great Mosque made ready for the ceremony of thanksgiving. And I'll sacrifice to all the prophets and saints." A fit of coughing overcame him for a space, and he pounded his fist furiously against the side of the divan. When he spoke again, his voice seemed weaker, but still determined. "There was a vampire upon me, boy! Each night she came in here and drank from me."

"She?"

"With dark hair and pale foreign skin, and eyes that eat you alive. Every night. Stood above me, and laughed, and took my blood. But she's gone now. These three have imprisoned her and carried her off to the Eleventh Hell." He gestured toward the marabouts. "My saints. My heroes. I want them rewarded beyond all reckoning."

"As you say, Father, so will I do."

The old man nodded. "You were getting my funeral ready, weren't you?"

"The prognosis was very dark. Certain preparations seemed advisable when we heard—"

"Cancel them!"

"Of course." Then, uncertainly: "Father, special envoys have come from many lands. The Czar's cousin is here, and the brother of Moctezuma, and a son of the late Sultan, and also—"

"I'll hold an audience for them all," said Big Father in great satisfaction. "They'll have gifts beyond anything they can imagine. Instead of a funeral, boy, we'll have a jubilee! A celebration of life. Moctezuma's brother, you say? And who did the Inca send?'' Big Father laughed raucously. ''All of them clustering around to see me put away underground!'' He jabbed a finger against Little Father's breast. It felt like a spear of bone. ''And in Mali they're dancing in the streets, aren't they? Can't contain themselves for glee. But they'll dance a different dance now.'' Big Father's eyes grew somber. ''You know, boy, when I really do die, whenever that is, they'll try to take you out too, and Mali will invade us. Guard yourself. Guard the nation. Those bastards on the coast hunger to control our caravan routes. They're probably already scheming now with the foreigners to swallow us the instant I'm gone, but you mustn't allow them to—ah—ah—ah—''

''Father?''

Abruptly the Emir's shriveled face crumpled in a frenzy of coughing. He hammered against his thighs with clenched fists. An attendant came running, bearing a beaker of water, and Big Father drank until he had drained it all. Then he tossed the beaker aside as though it were nothing. He was shivering. He looked glassy-eyed and confused. His shoulders slumped, his whole posture slackened. Perhaps his ''recovery'' had been merely the sudden final upsurge of a dying fire.

''You should rest, Majesty,'' said a new voice from the doorway to the porch. It was Serene Glory's ringing contralto. ''You overtax yourself, I think, in the first hours of this miracle.''

Big Father's main wife had arrived, entourage and all. In the warmth of the morning she had outfitted herself in a startling robe of purple satin, over which she wore the finest jewels of the kingdom. Little Father remembered that his own mother had worn some of those necklaces and bracelets.

He was unmoved by Serene Glory's beauty, impressive though it was. How could Serene Glory matter to him with the memory, scarcely two hours old, of Selima's full breasts and agile thighs still glistening in his mind? But he could not fail to detect Serene Glory's anger. It surrounded her like a radiant aura. Tension sparkled in her kohl-bedecked eyes.

Perhaps she was still smoldering over Little Father's deft rejection of her advances as they were riding side by side back from the Great Mosque that day six months earlier. Or perhaps it was Big Father's unexpected return from the brink that annoyed her. Anyone with half a mind realized that Serene Glory dreamed of putting her own insipid brother on the throne in Little Father's place the moment the old Emir was gone, and thus maintaining and even extending her position at the summit of power. Quite likely she, like Little Father, had by now grown accustomed to the idea of Big Father's death and was having difficulty accepting the news that it would be somewhat postponed.

To Little Father she said, "Our prayers have been answered, all glory to Allah! But you mustn't put a strain on the Emir's energies in this time of recovery. Perhaps you ought to go."

"I was summoned, lady."

"Of course. Quite rightly. And now you should go to the mosque and give thanks for what has been granted us all."

Her gaze was imperious and unanswerable. In one sentence Serene Glory had demoted him from imminent king to wastrel prince once again. He admired her gall. She was three years younger than Little Father, and here she was ordering him out of the royal presence as though he were a child. But of course she had had practice at ordering people around: her father was one of the greatest landlords of the eastern province. She had moved amidst power all her life, albeit power of a provincial sort. Little Father wondered how many noblemen of that province had spent time between the legs of Serene Glory before she had ascended to her present high position.

He said, "If my royal father grants me leave to go—"

The Emir was coughing again. He looked terrible.

Serene Glory went to him and bent close over him, so the old man could smell the fragrance rising from her breasts, and instantly Big Father relaxed. The coughing ceased and he sat up again, almost as vigorous as before. Little Father admired that maneuver too. Serene Glory was a worthy adversary. Probably her people were already spreading the word in the city that it was the power of her love for the Emir, and not the prayers of the three saints, that had brought him back from the edge of death.

"How cool it is in here," Big Father said. "The wind is rising. Will it rain today? The rains are due, aren't they? Let me see the sky. What color is the sky?" He looked upward in an odd straining way, as though the sky had risen to such a height that it could no longer be seen.

"Father," Little Father said softly.

The old man glared. "You heard her, didn't you? To the mosque! To the mosque and give thanks! Do you want Allah to think you're an ingrate, boy?" He started coughing once again. Once again he began visibly to descend the curve of his precarious vitality. His withered cheeks began to grow mottled. There was a feeling of impending death in the air.

Servants and ministers and the three marabouts gathered by his side, alarmed.

"Big Father! Big Father!"

And then once more he was all right again, just as abruptly. He gestured fiercely, an unmistakable dismissal. The woman in purple gave Little Father a dark grin of triumph. Little Father nodded to her gallantly: this round was hers. He knelt at the Emir's side, kissed his royal ring. It slipped about loosely on his shrunken finger. Little Father, thinking of nothing but the pressure of Selima's dark, hard little nipples against the palms of his hands two hours before, made the prostration of filial devotion to his father and, with ferocious irony, to his stepmother, and backed quickly away from the royal presence.

Michael said, distraught, "I couldn't sleep, sir. I went out for a walk."

"And you walked *the whole night long*?" Sir Anthony asked, in a voice like a flail.

"I didn't really notice the time. I just kept walking, and by and by the sun came up and I realized that the night was gone."

"It's your mind that's gone, I think." Sir Anthony, crooking his neck upward to Michael's much greater height, gave him a whipcrack glare. "What kind of calf are you, anyway? Haven't you any sense at all?"

"Sir Anthony, I don't underst—"

"Are you in *love*? With the Turkish girl?"

Michael clapped his hand over his mouth in dismay. "You know about that?" he said lamely, after a moment.

"One doesn't have to be a mind reader to see it, lad. Every camel in Timbuctoo knows it. The pathetic look on your face whenever she comes within fifty feet of you—the clownish way you shuffle your feet around, and hang your head—those occasional little groans of deepest melancholy—" The envoy glowered. He made no attempt to hide his anger, or his contempt. "By heaven, *I'd* like to hang your head, and all the rest of you as well. Have you no sense? Have you no sense whatsoever?"

Everything was lost, so what did anything matter? Defiantly Michael said, "Have you never fallen unexpectedly in love, Sir Anthony?"

"With a *Turk*?"

"Unexpectedly, I said. These things don't necessarily happen with one's political convenience in mind."

"And she reciprocates your love, I suppose? That's why you were out walking like a moon-calf in this miserable parched mudhole of a city all night long?"

"She spent the night with the crown prince," Michael blurted in misery.

"Ah. Ah, now it comes out!" Sir Anthony was silent for a while. Then he glanced up sharply, his eyes bright with skepticism. "But how do you know that?"

"I saw her leaving his palace at dawn, sir."

"Spying on her, were you?"

"I just happened to be there. I didn't even know it was his palace, until I asked. He came out himself a few minutes later, and went quickly off somewhere. He looked very troubled."

"He should have looked troubled. He'd just found out that he might not get to be king as quickly as he'd like to be."

"I don't understand, please, sir."

"There's word going around town this morning that the Emir has recovered. And had sent for his son to let him know that he wasn't quite as moribund as was generally believed."

Michael recoiled in surprise.

"Recovered? Is it true?"

Sir Anthony offered him a benign, patronizing smile.

"So they say. But the Emir's doctors assure us that it's nothing more than a brief rally in an inevitable descent. The old wolf will be dead within the week. Still, it's rather a setback for Little Father's immediate plans. The news of the Emir's unanticipated awakening from his coma must rather have spoiled his morning for him."

"Good," said Michael vindictively.

Sir Anthony laughed.

"You hate him, do you?"

"I despise him. I loathe him. I have nothing but the greatest detestation for him. He's a cynical amoral voluptuary and nothing more. He doesn't deserve to be a king."

"Well, if it's any comfort to you, lad, he's not going to live long enough to become one."

"What?"

"His untimely demise has been arranged. His stepmother is going to poison him at the funeral of the old Emir, if the old Emir ever has the good grace to finish dying."

"What? What?"

Sir Anthony smiled.

"This is quite confidential, you understand. Perhaps I shouldn't be entrusting you with it just yet. But you'd have needed to find out sooner or later. We've organized a little coup d'etat."

"What? What? What?" said Michael helplessly.

"Her Highness the Lady Serene Glory would like to

put her brother on the throne instead of the prince. The brother is worthless, of course. So is the prince, of course, but at least he does happen to be the rightful heir. We don't want to see either of them have it, actually. What we'd prefer is to have the Mansa of Mali declare that the unstable conditions in Songhay following the death of the old Emir have created a danger to the security of all of West Africa that can be put to rest only by an amalgamation of the kingdoms of Mali and Songhay under a single ruler. Who would be, of course, the Mansa of Mali, precisely as your young lady so baldly suggested the other day. And that is what we intend to achieve. The Grand Duke and Prince Itzcoatl and I. As representatives of the powers whom we serve."

Michael stared. He rubbed his cheeks as if to assure himself that this was no dream. He found himself unable to utter a sound.

Sir Anthony went on, clearly and calmly.

"And so Serene Glory gives Little Father the deadly cup, and then the Mansa's troops cross the border, and we, on behalf of our governments, immediately recognize the new combined government. Which makes everyone happy except, I suppose, the Sultan, who has such good trade relationships with Songhay and is on such poor terms with the Mansa of Mali. But we hardly shed tears for the Sultan's distress, do we, boy? Do we? The distress of the Turks is no concern of ours. Quite the contrary, in fact, is that not so?" Sir Anthony clapped his hand to Michael's shoulder. It was an obvious strain for him, reaching so high. The fingers clamping into Michael's tender sunburned skin were agony. "So let's see no more mooning over this alluring Ottoman goddess of yours, eh, lad? It's inappropriate for a lovely blond English boy like yourself to be lusting after a Turk, as you know very well. She's nothing but a little slut, however she may seem to your infatuated eyes. And you needn't take the trouble to expend any energy loathing the prince, either. His days are numbered. He won't survive his evil old father by so much as a week. It's all arranged."

Michael's jaw gaped. A glazed look of disbelief appeared in his eyes. His face was burning fiercely, not from the sunburn now, but from the intensity of his confusion.

"But sir—sir—"

"Get yourself some sleep, boy."

"Sir!"

"Shocked, are you? Well, you shouldn't be. There's nothing shocking about assassinating an inconvenient king. What's shocking to me is a grown man with pure English blood in his veins spending the night creeping pitifully around after his dissolute little Turkish inamorata as she makes her way to the bed of her African lover. And then telling me how heartsore and miserable he is. Get yourself some sleep, boy. Get yourself some sleep!"

In the midst of the uncertainty over the Emir's impending death the semiannual salt caravan from the north arrived in Timbuctoo. It was a great, if somewhat unexpected, spectacle, and all the foreign ambassadors, restless and by now passionately in need of diversion, turned out despite the heat to watch its entry into the city.

There was tremendous clamor. The heavy metal-studded gates of the city were thrown open and the armed escort entered first, a platoon of magnificent black warriors armed both with rifles and with scimitars. Trumpets brayed, drums pounded. A band of fierce-looking hawk-nosed fiery-eyed country chieftains in flamboyant robes came next, marching in phalanx like conquerors. And then came the salt-laden camels, an endless stream of them, a tawny river, strutting absurdly along in grotesque self-important grandeur with their heads held high and their sleepy eyes indifferent to the throngs of excited spectators. Strapped to each camel's back were two or three huge flat slabs of salt, looking much like broad blocks of marble.

"There are said to be seven hundred of the beasts," murmured the Chinese ambassador, Li Hsiao-ssu.

"One thousand eight hundred," said the Grand Duke Alexander sternly. He glowered at Li Hsiao-ssu, a small, fastidious-looking man with drooping mustachios and gleaming porcelain skin, who seemed a mere doll beside the bulky Russian. There was little love lost between the Grand Duke and the Chinese envoy. Evidently the Grand Duke thought it was presumptuous that China, as a client state of the Russian Empire, as a mere vassal, in truth, had sent an ambassador at all. "One thousand eight hundred. That is the number I was told, and it is reliable. I assure you that it is reliable."

The Chinese shrugged. "Seven hundred, three thousand, what difference is there? Either way, that's too many camels to have in one place at one time."

"Yes, what ugly things they are!" said the Peruvian, Manco Roca. "Such stupid faces, such an ungainly stride! Perhaps we should do these Africans a favor and let them have a few herds of llamas."

Coolly Prince Itzcoatl said, "Your llamas, brother, are no more fit for the deserts of this continent than these camels would be in the passes of the Andes. Let them keep their beasts, and be thankful that you have handsomer ones for your own use."

"Such stupid faces," the Peruvian said once more.

Timbuctoo was the center of distribution for salt throughout the whole of West Africa. The salt mines were hundreds of miles away, in the center of the Sahara. Twice a year the desert traders made the twelve-day journey to the capital, where they exchanged their salt for the dried fish, grain, rice, and other produce that came up the Niger from the agricultural districts to the south and east. The arrival of the caravan was the occasion for feasting and revelry, a time of wild big-city gaiety for the visitors from such remote and placid rural outposts.

But the Emir of Songhay was dying. This was no time for a festival. The appearance of the caravan at such a moment was evidently a great embarrassment to the city officials, a mark of bad management as well as bad taste.

"They could have sent messengers upcountry to turn them back," Michael said. "Why didn't they, I wonder?"

"Blacks," said Manco Roca morosely. "What can you expect from blacks."

"Yes, of course," Sir Anthony said, giving the Peruvian a disdainful look. "We understand that they aren't Incas. Yet despite that shortcoming they've somehow managed to keep control of most of this enormous continent for thousands of years."

"But their colossal administrative incompetence, my dear Sir Anthony—as we see here, letting a circus like this one come into town while their king lies dying—"

"Perhaps it's deliberate," Ismet Akif suggested. "A much-needed distraction. The city is tense. The Emir's been too long about his dying; it's driving everyone crazy. So they decided to let the caravan come marching in."

"I think not," said Li Hsiao-ssu. "Do you see those municipal officials there? I detect signs of deep humiliation on their faces."

"And who would be able to detect such things more acutely than you?" asked the Grand Duke.

The Chinese envoy stared at the Russian as though unsure whether he was being praised or mocked. For a moment his elegant face was dusky with blood. The other diplomats gathered close, making ready to defuse the situation. Politeness was ever a necessity in such a group.

Then the envoy from the Teutonic States said, "Is that not the prince arriving now?"

"Where?" Michael demanded in a tight-strung voice. "Where is he?"

Sir Anthony's hand shot out to seize Michael's wrist. He squeezed it unsparingly.

In a low tone he said, "You will cause no difficulties, young sir. Remember that you are English. Your breeding must rule your passions."

Michael, glaring toward Little Father as the prince approached the city gate, sullenly pulled his arm free of Sir Anthony's grasp and amazed himself by uttering a strange low growling sound, like that of a cat announcing a challenge. Unfamiliar hormones flooded the channels of his body. He could feel the individual bones of his cheeks and forehead moving apart from one another, he was aware of the tensing and coiling of muscles great and small. He wondered if he was losing his mind. Then the moment passed and he let out his breath in a long dismal exhalation.

Little Father wore flowing green pantaloons, a striped robe wide enough to cover his arms, and an intricately deployed white turban with brilliant feathers of some exotic sort jutting from it. An entourage of eight or ten men surrounded him, carrying iron-shafted lances. The prince strode forward so briskly that his bodyguard was hard pressed to keep up with him.

Michael, watching Selima out of the corner of his eye, murmured to Sir Anthony, "I'm terribly sorry, sir. But if he so much as glances at her you'll have to restrain me."

"If you so much as flicker a nostril I'll have you billeted in our Siberian consulate for the rest of your career," Sir Anthony replied, barely moving his lips as he spoke.

But Little Father had no time to flirt with Selima now. He barely acknowledged the presence of the ambassadors at all. A stiff formal nod, and then he moved on, into the midst of the group of caravan leaders. They clustered about him like a convocation of eagles. Among those sun-crisped swarthy upright chieftains the prince seemed soft, frail, overly citified, a dabbler confronting serious men.

Some ritual of greeting seemed to be going on. Little Father touched his forehead, extended his open palm, closed his hand with a snap, presented his palm again with a flourish. The desert men responded with equally stylized maneuvers.

When Little Father spoke, it was in Songhay, a sharp outpouring of liquid incomprehensibilities.

"What was that? What was that?" asked the ambassadors of one another. Turkish was the international language of diplomacy, even in Africa; the native tongues of the dark continent were mysteries to outsiders.

Sir Anthony, though, said softly, "He's angry. He says the city's closed on account of the Emir's illness and the caravan was supposed to have waited at Kabara for further instructions. They seem surprised. Someone must have missed a signal."

"You speak Songhay, sir?" Michael asked.

"I was posted in Mali for seven years," Sir Anthony muttered. "It was before you were born, boy."

"So I was right," cried Manco Roca. "The caravan should never have been allowed to enter the city at all. Incompetence! Incompetence!"

"Is he telling them to leave?" Ismet Akif wanted to know.

"I can't tell. They're all talking at once. I think they're saying that their camels need fodder. And he's telling them that there's no merchandise for them to buy, that the goods from upriver were held back because of the Emir's illness."

"What an awful jumble," Selima said.

It was the first thing she had said all morning. Michael, who had been trying to pay no attention to her, looked toward her now in agitation. She was dressed chastely enough, in a red blouse and flaring black skirt, but in his inflamed mind she stood revealed suddenly nude, with the marks of Little Father's caresses flaring like stigmata on her breasts and thighs. Michael sucked in his breath and held himself stiffly erect, trembling like a drawn bowstring. A sound midway between a sigh and a groan escaped him. Sir Anthony kicked his ankle sharply.

Some sort of negotiation appeared to be going on. Little Father gesticulated rapidly, grinned, did the open-close-open gesture with his hand again, tapped his chest and his forehead and his left elbow. The apparent leader of the traders matched him, gesture for gesture. Postures began to change. The tensions were easing. Evidently the caravan would be admitted to the city.

Little Father was smiling, after a fashion. His forehead glistened with sweat; he seemed to have come through a difficult moment well, but he looked tired.

The trumpets sounded again. The camel-drovers regained the attention of their indifferent beasts and nudged them forward.

There was new commotion from the other side of the plaza.

"What's this, now?" Prince Itzcoatl said.

A runner clad only in a loincloth appeared, coming from the direction of the city center, clutching a scroll. He was moving fast, loping in a strange lurching way. In the stupefying heat he seemed to be in peril of imminent collapse. But he staggered up to Little Father and put the scroll in his hand.

Little Father unrolled it quickly and scanned it. He nodded somberly and turned to his vizier, who stood just to his left. They spoke briefly in low whispers. Sir Anthony, straining, was unable to make out a word.

A single chopping gesture from Little Father was enough to halt the resumption of the caravan's advance into the city. The prince beckoned the leaders of the traders to his side and conferred with them a moment or two, this time without ceremonial gesticulations. The desert men exchanged glances with one another. Then they barked rough commands. The whole vast caravan began to reverse itself.

Little Father's motorcar was waiting a hundred paces away. He went to it now, and it headed cityward, emitting belching bursts of black smoke and loud intermittent thunderclaps of inadequate combustion.

The prince's entourage, left behind in the suddenness, milled about aimlessly. The vizier, making shooing gestures, ordered them in some annoyance to follow their master on foot toward town. He himself held his place, watching the departure of the caravaneers.

"Ali Pasha!" Sir Anthony called. "Can you tell us what's happened? Is there bad news?"

The vizier turned. He seemed radiant with self-importance.

"The Emir has taken a turn for the worse. They think he'll be with Allah within the hour."

"But he was supposed to be recovering," Michael protested.

Indifferently, Ali Pasha said, "That was earlier. This is now." The vizier seemed not to be deeply moved by the news. If anything his smugness seemed to have been enhanced by it. Perhaps it was something he had been very eager to hear. "The caravan must camp outside the city walls until after the funeral. There is nothing more to be seen here today. You should all go back to your residences."

The ambassadors began to look around for their drivers.

Michael, who had come out here with Sir Anthony in the embassy motorcar, was disconcerted to discover that the envoy had already vanished, slipping away in the uproar without waiting for him. Well, it wasn't an impossible walk back to town. He had walked five times as far in his night of no sleep.

"Michael?"

Selima was calling to him. He looked toward her, appalled.

"Walk with me," she said. "I have a parasol. You can't let yourself get any more sun on your face."

"That's very kind of you," he said mechanically, while lunatic jealousy and anger roiled him within. Searing contemptuous epithets came to his lips and died there, unspoken. To him she was ineluctably soiled by the presumed embraces of that night of shame. How could she have done it? The prince had wiggled his finger at her, and she had run to him without a moment's hesitation. Once more unwanted images surged through his mind: Selima and the prince entwined on a leopard-skin rug; the prince mounting Selima in some unthinkable bestial African position of love; Selima, giggling girlishly, instructing the prince afterward in the no doubt equally depraved sexual customs of the land of the Sultan. Michael understood that he was being foolish; that Selima was free to do as she pleased in this loathsome land; that he himself had never staked any claim on her attention more significant than a few callow lovesick stares, so why should she have felt any compunctions about amusing herself with the prince if the prince offered amusement? "Very kind," he said. She handed the parasol up to him and he took it from her with a rigid nerveless hand. They began to walk side by side in the direction of town, close together under the narrow, precisely defined shadow of the parasol beneath the unsparing eye of the noonday sun.

She said, "Poor Michael. I've upset you terribly, haven't I?"

"Upset me? How have you possibly upset me?"

"You know."

"No. No, really."

His legs were leaden. The sun was hammering the top of his brain through the parasol, through his wide-brimmed topee, through his skull itself. He could not imagine how he would find the strength to walk all the way back to town with her.

"I've been very mischievous," she said.

"Have you?"

He wished he were a million miles away.

"By visiting the prince in his palace that night."

"Please, Selima."

"I saw you, you know. Early in the morning, when I was leaving. You ducked out of sight, but not quite fast enough."

"Selima—"

"I couldn't help myself. Going there, I mean. I wanted to see what his palace looked like. I wanted to get to know him a little better. He's very nice, you know. No, nice isn't quite the word. He's shrewd, and part of being shrewd is knowing how to seem nice. I don't really think he's nice at all. He's quite sophisticated—quite subtle."

She was flaying him, inch by inch. Another word out of her and he'd drop the parasol and run.

"The thing is, Michael, he enjoys pretending to be some sort of a primitive, a barbarian, a jungle prince. But it's only a pretense. And why shouldn't it be? These are ancient kingdoms here in Africa. This isn't any jungle land with tigers sleeping behind every palm tree. They've got laws and culture, they've got courts, they have a university. And they've had centuries to develop a real aristocracy. They're just as complicated and cunning as we are. Maybe more so. I was glad to get to know the man behind the facade, a little. He was fascinating, in his way, but—" She smiled brightly. "But I have to tell you, Michael: he's not my type at all."

That startled him, and awakened sudden new hope.

Perhaps he never actually touched her, Michael told himself. Perhaps they had simply talked all night. Played little sly verbal games of one-upmanship, teasing each other, vying with each other to be sly and cruel and playful. Showing each other how complicated and cunning they could really be. Demonstrating the virtues of hundreds of years of aristocratic inbreeding. Perhaps they were too well-bred to think of doing anything so commonplace as—as—

"What *is* your type, then?" he asked, willy-nilly.

"I prefer men who are a little shy. Men who can sometimes be foolish, even." There was unanticipated softness in her voice, conveying a sincerity that Michael prayed was real. "I hate the kind who are always calculating, calculating, calculating. There's something very appealing to me about English men, I have to tell you, precisely because they *don't* seem so dark and devious inside—not that I've met very many of them before this trip, you understand, but—oh, Michael, Michael, you're terribly angry with me, I know, but you shouldn't be! What happened between me and the prince was nothing. Nothing! And now that he'll be preoccupied with the funeral, perhaps there'll be a chance for you and me to get to know each other a little better—to slip off, for a day, let's say, while all the others are busy with the pomp and circumstance."

She gave him a melting look. He thought for one astounded moment that she actually might mean what she was telling him.

"They're going to assassinate him," he suddenly heard his own voice saying, "right at the funeral."

"What?"

"It's all set up." The words came rolling from him spontaneously, unstoppably, like the flow of a river.

"His stepmother, the old king's young wife—she's going to slip him a cup of poisoned wine, or something, during one of the funeral rituals. What she wants is to make her stupid brother king in the prince's place, and rule the country as the power behind the throne.

Selima made a little gasping sound and stepped away from him, out from under the shelter of the parasol. She stood staring at him as though he had been transformed in the last moment or two into a hippopotamus, or a rock, or a tree.

It took her a little while to find her voice.

"Are you serious? How do you know?"

"Sir Anthony told me."

"Sir Anthony?"

"He's behind it. He and the Russian and Prince Itzcoatl. Once the prince is out of the way, they're going to invite the King of Mali to step in and take over."

Her gaze grew very hard. Her silence was inscrutable, painfully so.

Then, totally regaining her composure with what must have been an extraordinary act of inner discipline, she said, "I think this is all very unlikely."

She might have been responding to a statement that snow would soon begin falling in the streets of Timbuctoo.

"You think so?"

"Why should Sir Anthony support this assassination? England has nothing to gain from destabilizing West Africa. England is a minor power still struggling to establish its plausibility in the world as an independent state. Why should it risk angering a powerful African empire like Songhay by meddling in its internal affairs?"

Michael let the slight to his country pass unchallenged, possibly because it seemed less like a slight to him than a statement of the mere reality. He searched instead for some reason of state that would make what he had asserted seem sensible.

After a moment he said, "Mali and Songhay together would be far more powerful than either one alone. If England plays an instrumental role in delivering the throne of Songhay up to Mali, England will surely be given a preferential role by the Mansa of Mali in future West African trade."

Selima nodded. "Perhaps."

"And the Russians—you know how they feel about the Ottoman Empire. Your people are closely allied with Songhay and don't get along well with Mali. A coup d'etat here would virtually eliminate Turkey as a commercial force in West Africa."

"Very likely."

She was so cool, so terribly calm.

"As for the Aztec role in this—" Michael shook his head. "God knows. But the Mexicans are always scheming around in things. Maybe they see some way of hurting Peru. There's a lot of sea trade, you know, between Mali and Peru—it's an amazingly short hop across the ocean from West Africa to Peru's eastern provinces—and the Mexicans may believe they could divert some of that trade to themselves by winning the Mansa's favor by helping him gain possession of—"

He faltered to a halt. Something was happening. Her expression was starting to change. Her façade of detached skepticism was visibly collapsing, slowly but irreversibly, like a brick wall undermined by a great earthquake.

"Yes. Yes, I see. There are substantial reasons for

such a scheme. And so they will kill the prince,'' Selima said.

''Have him killed, rather.''

''It's the same thing! The very same thing!''

Her eyes began to glisten. She drew even further back from him and turned her head away, and he realized that she was trying to conceal tears from him. But she couldn't hide the sobs that racked her.

He suspected that she was one who cried very rarely, if at all. Seeing her weep now in this uncontrollable way plunged him into an abyss of dejection.

She was making no attempt to hide her love of the prince from him. That was the only explanation for these tears.

''Selima—please, Selima—''

He felt useless.

He realized, also, that he had destroyed himself.

He had committed this monstrous breach of security, he saw now, purely in the hope of insinuating himself into her confidence, to bind her to him in a union that proceeded from shared possession of an immense secret. He had taken her words at face value when she had told him that the prince was nothing to her.

That had been a serious error. He had thought he was making a declaration of love; but all he had done was to reveal a state secret to England's ancient enemy.

He waited, feeling huge and clumsy and impossibly naive.

Then, abruptly, her sobbing stopped and she looked toward him, a little puffy-eyed now, but otherwise as inscrutable as before.

''I'm not going to say anything about this to anyone.''

''What?''

''Not to him, not to my father, not to anyone.''

He was mystified. As usual.

"But—Selima—"

"I told you. The prince is nothing to me. And this is only a crazy rumor. How do I know it's true? How do *you* know it's true?"

"Sir Anthony—"

"Sir Anthony! Sir Anthony! For all I know, he's floated this whole thing simply to ensnare my father in some enormous embarrassment. I tell my father there's going to be an assassination and my father tells the prince, as he'd feel obliged to do. And then the prince arrests and expels the ambassadors of England and Russia and Mexico? But where's the proof? There isn't any. It's all a Turkish invention, they say. A scandal. My father is sent home in disgrace. His career is shattered. Songhay breaks off diplomatic relations with the Empire. No, no, don't you see, I can't say a thing."

"But the prince—"

"His stepmother hates him. If he's idiotic enough to let her hand him a cup of something without having it tested, he deserves to be poisoned. What is that to me? He's only a savage. Hold the parasol closer, Michael, and let's get back to town. Oh, this heat! This unending heat! Do you think it'll ever rain here?" Her face now showed no sign of tears at all. Wearily Michael lowered the parasol. Selima utterly baffled him. She was an exhausting person. His head was aching. For a shilling he'd be glad to resign his post and take up sheep farming somewhere in the north of England. It was getting very obvious to him and probably to everyone else that he had no serious future in the diplomatic corps.

Little Father, emerging from the tunnel that led from the Emir's palace to his own, found Ali Pasha waiting in the little colonnaded gallery known as the Promenade of Askia Mohammed. The prince was surprised to see a string charm of braided black, red, and yellow cords dangling around the vizier's neck. Ali Pasha had never been one for wearing grigri before; but no doubt the imminent death of the Emir was unsettling everyone, even a piece of tough leather like Ali Pasha.

The vizier offered a grand salaam. "Your royal father, may Allah embrace him, sir—"

"My royal father is still breathing, thank you. It looks now as if he'll last until morning." Little Father glanced around, a little wildly, peering into the courtyard of his palace. "Somehow we've left too much for the last minute. The Lady Serene Glory is arranging for the washing of the body. It's too late to do anything about that, but we can supply the graveclothes, at least. Get the very finest white silks; the royal burial shroud should be something out of the *Thousand and One Nights*; and I want rubies in the turban. Actual rubies, no damned imitations. And after that I want you to set up the procession to the Great Mosque—I'll be one of the pallbearers, of course, and we'll ask the Mansa of Mali to be another—he's arrived by now, hasn't he?—and let's have the King of Benin as the third one, and for the fourth, well, either the Asante of Ghana or the Grand Fon of Dahomey, whichever one shows up here first. The important thing is that all four of the pallbearers should be kings, because Serene Glory wants to push her brother forward to be one, and I can't allow that. She won't be able to argue precedence for him if the pallbearers are all kings, when all he is is a provincial cadi. Behind the bier we'll have the overseas ambassadors marching five abreast—put the Turk and the Russian in the front row, the Maori too, and the Aztec and the Inca on the outside edges to keep them as far apart as we can, and the order of importance after that is up to you, only be sure that little countries like England and the Teutonic States don't wind up too close to the major powers, and that the various vassal nations like China and Korea and Ind are in the back. Now, as far as the decorations on the barge that'll be taking my father downriver to the burial place at Gao—"

"Little Father," the Vizier said, as the prince paused for breath, "the Turkish woman is waiting upstairs."

Little Father gave him a startled look.

"I don't remember asking her to come here."

"She didn't say you had. But she asked for an urgent audience, and I thought—" Ali Pasha favored Little Father with an obscenely knowing smile. "It seemed reasonable to admit her."

"She knows that my father is dying, and that I'm tremendously busy?"

"I told her what was taking place, Majesty," said Ali Pasha unctuously.

"Don't call me *Majesty* yet!"

"A thousand pardons, Little Father. But she is aware of the nature of the crisis, no question of that. Nevertheless, she insisted on—"

"Oh, damn. Damn! But I suppose I can give her two or three minutes. Stop smiling like that, damn you! I'll feed you to the lions if you don't! What do you think I am, a mountain of lechery? This is a busy moment. When I say two or three minutes, two or three minutes is what I mean."

Selima was pacing about on the porch where she and Little Father had spent their night of love. No filmy robes today, no seductively visible breasts bobbing about beneath, this time. She was dressed simply, in European clothes. She seemed all business.

"The Emir is in his last hours," Little Father said. "The whole funeral has to be arranged very quickly."

"I won't take up much of your time, then." Her tone was cool. There was a distinct edge on it. Perhaps he had been too brusque with her. That night on the porch *had* been a wonderful one, after all. She said, "I just have one question. Is there some sort of ritual at a royal funeral where you're given a cup of wine to drink?"

"You know that the Koran doesn't permit the drinking of—"

"Yes, yes, I know that. A cup of *something*, then."

Little Father studied her carefully. "This is anthropological research? The sort of thing the golden-haired woman from England came here to do? Why does this matter to you, Selima?"

"Never mind that. It matters."

He sighed. She *seemed* so gentle and retiring, until she opened her mouth.

"There's a cup ceremony, yes. It isn't wine or anything else alcoholic. It's an aromatic potion, brewed from various spices and honeys and such, very disagreeably sweet, my father once told me. Drinking it symbolizes the passage of royal power from one generation to the next."

"And who is supposed to hand you the cup?"

"May I ask why at this particularly hectic time you need to know these details?"

"Please," she said.

There was an odd urgency in her voice.

"The former queen, the mother of the heir of the throne, is the one who hands the new Emir the cup."

"But your mother is dead. Therefore your stepmother Serene Glory will hand it to you."

"That's correct." Little Father glanced at his watch. "Selima, you don't seem to understand. I need to finish working out the funeral arrangements and then get back to my father's bedside before he dies. If you don't mind—"

"There's going to be poison in the cup."

"This is no time for romantic fantasies."

"This isn't a fantasy. She's going to slip you a cup of poison, and you won't be able to tell that the poison is there because what you drink is so heavily spiced anyway. And when you keel over in the mosque her brother's going to leap forward in the moment of general shock and tell everyone that he's in charge."

The day had been one long disorderly swirl. But suddenly now the world stood still, as though there had been an unscheduled eclipse of the sun. For a moment he had difficulty simply seeing her.

"What are you saying, Selima?"

"Do you want me to repeat it all, or is that just something you're saying as a manner of speaking because you're so astonished?"

He could see and think again. He examined her closely. She was unreadable, as she usually was. Now that the first shock of her bland statement was past, this all was starting to seem to him like fantastic nonsense; and yet, and yet, it certainly wasn't beyond Serene Glory's capabilities to have hatched such a scheme.

How, though, could the Turkish girl possibly know anything about it? How did she even know about the ritual of the cup?

"If we were in bed together right now," he said, "and you were in my arms and right on the edge of the big moment, and I stopped moving and asked you right then and there what proof you had of this story, I'd probably believe whatever you told me. I think people tend to be honest at such moments. Even you would speak the truth. But we have no time for that now. The kingship will change hands in a few hours, and I'm exceedingly busy. I need you to cast away all of your fondness for manipulative amusements and give me straight answers."

Her dark eyes flared. "I should simply have let them poison you."

"Do you mean that?"

"What you just said was insufferable."

"If I was too blunt, I ask you to forgive me. I'm under great strain today and if what you've told me is any sort of joke, I don't need it. If this isn't a joke, you damned well can't withhold any of the details."

"I've given you the details."

"Not all. Who'd you hear all this from?"

She sighed and placed one wrist across the other. "Michael. The tall Englishman."

"That adolescent?"

"He's a little on the innocent side, especially for a diplomat, yes. But I don't think he's as big a fool as he's been letting himself appear lately. He heard it from Sir Anthony."

"So this is an English plot?"

"English and Russian and Mexican."

"All three." Little Father digested that. "What's the purpose of assassinating me?"

"To make Serene Glory's brother Emir of Songhay."

"And serve as their puppet, I suppose?"

Selima shook her head. "Serene Glory and her brother are only the ignorant instruments of their real plan. They'll simply be brushed aside when the time comes. What the plotters are really intending to do, in the confusion following your death, is ask the Mansa of Mali to seize control of Songhay. They'll put the support of their countries behind him."

"Ah," Little Father said. And after a moment, again, "Ah."

"Mali-Songhay would favor the Czar instead of the Sultan. So the Russians like the idea. What injures the Sultan is good for the English. So they're in on it. As for the Aztecs—"

Little Father shrugged and gestured to her to stop. Already he could taste the poison in his gut, burning through his flesh. Already he could see the green-clad troops of Mali parading in the streets of Timbuctoo and Gao, where kings of Mali had been hailed as supreme monarchs once before, hundreds of years ago.

"Look at me," he said. "You swear that you're practicing no deception, Selima?"

"I swear it by—by the things we said to each other the night we lay together."

He considered that. Had she fallen in love with him in the midst of all her game-playing? So it might seem. Could he trust what she was saying, therefore? He believed he could. Indeed the oath she had just proposed might have more plausibility than any sort of oath she might have sworn on the Koran.

"Come here," he said.

She approached him. Little Father swept her up against him, holding her tightly, and ran his hands down her back to her buttocks. She pressed her hips forward. He covered her mouth with his and jammed down hard, not a subtle kiss but one that would put to rest forever, if that were needed, the bit of fake anthropology he had given to her earlier, about the supposed distaste of Songhayans for the act of kissing. After a time he released her. Her eyes were a little glazed, her breasts were rising and falling swiftly.

He said, "I'm grateful for what you've told me. I'll take the appropriate steps, and thank you."

"I had to let you know. I was going just to sit back and let whatever happened happen. But then I saw I couldn't conceal such a thing from you."

"Of course not, Selima."

Her look was a soft and eager one. She was ready to run off to the bedchamber with him, or so it seemed. But not now, not on this day of all days. That would be a singularly bad idea.

"On the other hand," he said, "if it turns out that there's no truth to any of this, that it's all some private amusement of your own or some intricate deception being practiced on me by the Sultan for who knows what unfathomable reason, you can be quite certain that I'll avenge myself in a remarkably vindictive way once the excitements of the funeral and the coronation are over."

The softness vanished at once. The hatred that came into her eyes was extraordinary.

"You black bastard," she said.

"Only partly black. There is much Moorish blood in the veins of the nobility of Songhay." He met her seething gaze with tranquility. "In the old days we believed in absorbing those who attempt to conquer us. These days we still do, something that the Mansa of Mali ought to keep in mind. He's got a fine harem, I understand."

"Did you *have* to throw cold water on me like that? Everything I told you was the truth."

"I hope and believe it is. I think there was love between us that night on the porch, and I wouldn't like to think that you'd betray someone you love. The question, I suppose, is whether the Englishman was telling *you* the truth. Which still remains to be seen." He took her hand and kissed it lightly, in the European manner. "As I said before, I'm very grateful, Selima. And hope to continue to be. If I may, now—"

She gave him one final glare and took her leave of him. Little Father walked quickly to the edge of the porch, spun about, walked quickly back. For an instant or two he stood in the doorway like his own statue. But his mind was in motion, and moving very swiftly.

He peered down the stairs to the courtyard below.

"Ali Pasha!"

The vizier came running.

"What the woman wanted to tell me," Little Father said, "is that there is a plot against my life."

The look that appeared on the vizier's face was one of total shock and indignation.

"You believe her?"

"Unfortunately I think I do."

Ali Pasha began to quiver with wrath. His broad glossy cheeks grew congested, his eyes bulged. Little Father thought the man was in danger of exploding.

"Who are the plotters, Little Father? I'll have them rounded up within the hour."

"The Russian ambassador, apparently. The Aztec one. And the little Englishman, Sir Anthony."

"To the lions with them! They'll be in the pit before night comes!"

Little Father managed an approximation of a smile.

"Surely you recall the concept of diplomatic immunity, Ali Pasha?"

"But—a conspiracy against Your Majesty's life—!"

"Not yet 'my majesty,' Ali Pasha."

"Your pardon." Ali Pasha struggled with confusion. "You must take steps to protect yourself, Little Father. Did she tell you what the plan is supposed to be?"

Little Father nodded. "When Serene Glory hands me the coronation cup at the funeral service, there will be poison in the drink."

"Poison!"

"Yes. I fall down dead. Serene Glory turns to her miserable brother and offers him the crown on the spot. But no, the three ambassadors have other ideas. They'll ask Mansa Suleiyman to proclaim himself king, in the name of the general safety. In that moment Songhay will come under the rule of Mali."

"Never! To the lions with Mansa Suleiyman too, Majesty!"

"No one goes to the lions, Ali Pasha. And stop calling me *Majesty*. We'll deal with this in a calm and civilized way, is that understood?"

"I am completely at your command, sir. As always."

Little Father nodded. He felt his strength rising, moment by moment. His mind was wondrously clear. He asked himself if that was what it felt like to be a king. Though he had spent so much time being a prince, he had in fact given too little thought to what the actual sensations and processes of being a king might be, he realized now. His royal father had held the kingdom entirely in his own hands throughout all his long reign. But something must be changing now.

He went unhurriedly to the edge of the porch, and stared out into the distance. To his surprise, there was a dark orange cloud on the horizon, sharply defined against the sky.

"Look there, Ali Pasha. The rains are coming!"

"The first cloud, yes. There it is!" And he began to finger the woven charm that hung about his neck.

It was always startling when the annual change came, after so many months of unbroken hot dry weather. Even after a lifetime of watching the shift occur, no one in Songhay was unmoved by the approach of the first cloud, for it was a powerful omen of transition and culmination, removing a great element of uncertainty and fear from the minds of the citizens; for until the change finally arrived, there was always the chance that it might never come, that this time the summer would last forever and the world would burn to a parched crisp.

Little Father said, "I should go to my father without any further delay. Certainly this means that his hour has come."

"Yes. Yes."

The orange cloud was sweeping toward the city with amazing rapidity. In another few minutes all Timbuctoo would be enveloped in blackness as a whirling veil of fine sand whipped down over it. Little Father felt the air grow moist. There would be a brief spell of intolerable humidity, now, so heavy that breathing itself would be a vast effort. And then, abruptly, the temperature would drop, the chill rain would descend, rivers would run in the sandy streets, the marketplace would become a lake.

He raced indoors, with Ali Pasha following along helter-skelter behind him.

"The plotters, sir—" the vizier gasped.

Little Father smiled. "I'll invite Serene Glory to share the cup with me. We'll see what she does then. Just be ready to act when I give the orders."

There was darkness at every window. The sandstorm was at hand. Trillions of tiny particles beat insistently at every surface, setting up a steady drumming that grew and grew and grew in intensity. The air had turned sticky, almost viscous: it was hard work to force oneself forward through it.

Gasping for breath, Little Father moved as quickly as he was able down the subterranean passageway that linked his palace with the much greater one that shortly would be his.

The ministers and functionaries of the royal court were wailing and weeping. The Grand Vizier of the realm, waiting formally at the head of the Stairs of Allah, glared at Little Father as though he were the Angel of Death himself.

"There is not much more time, Little Father."

"So I understand."

He rushed out onto his father's porch. There had been no opportunity to bring the Emir indoors. The old man lay amidst his dazzling blankets with his eyes open and one hand upraised. He was in the correct position in which a Moslem should pass from this world to the next, his head to the south, his face turned toward the east. The sky was black with sand, and it came cascading down with unremitting force. The three saintly marabouts who had attended Big Father throughout his final illness stood above him, shielding the Emir from the shower of tiny abrasive particles with an improvised canopy, an outstretched bolt of satin.

"Father! Father!"

The Emir tried to sit up. He looked a thousand years old. His eyes glittered like lightning bolts, and he said something, three or four congested syllables. Little Father was unable to understand a thing. The old man was already speaking the language of the dead.

There was a clap of thunder. The Emir fell back against his pillows.

The sky opened and the first rain of the year came down in implacable torrents, in such abundance as had not been seen in a thousand years.

In the three days since the old Emir's death Little Father had lived through this scene three thousand times in his imagination. But now it was actually occurring. They were in the Great Mosque; the mourners, great and simple, were clustered elbow to elbow; the corpse of Big Father, embalmed so that it could endure the slow journey downriver to the royal burial grounds, lay in splendor atop its magnificent bier. Any ordinary citizen of Songhay would have gone from his deathbed to his grave in two hours, or less; but kings were exempt from the ordinary customs.

They were done at last with the chanting of the prayer for the dead. Now they were doing the prayer for the welfare of the kingdom. Little Father held his body rigid, barely troubling to breathe. He saw before him the grand nobles of the realm, the kings of the adjacent countries, the envoys of the overseas lands, all staring, all maintaining a mien of the deepest solemnity, even those who could not comprehend a word of what was being said.

And here was Serene Glory, now, coming forth bearing the cup that would make him Emir of Songhay, Great Imam, master of the nation, successor to all the great lords who had led the empire in grandeur for a thousand years.

She looked magnificent, truly queenly, more beautiful in her simple funeral robe and unadorned hair than she could ever have looked in all her finery. The cup, a stark bowl of lustrous chalcedony, so translucent that the dark liquor that would make him king was plainly visible through its thin walls, was resting lightly on her upturned palms.

He searched her for a sign of tremor and saw none. She was utterly calm. He felt a disturbing moment of doubt.

She handed him the cup, and spoke the words of succession, clearly, unhesitatingly, omitting not the smallest syllable. She was in full control of herself.

When he lifted the cup to his lips, though, he heard the sharp unmistakable sound of her suddenly indrawn breath, and all hesitation went from him.

"Mother," he said.

The unexpected word reverberated through the white-washed alcoves of the great Mosque. They must all be looking at him in bewilderment.

"Mother, in this solemn moment of the passing of the kingship, I beg you share my ascension with me. Drink with me, Mother. Drink. Drink."

He held the untouched cup out toward the woman who had just handed it to him.

Her eyes were bright with horror.

"Drink with me, Mother," he said again.

"No—no—"

She backed a step or two away from him, making sounds like gravel in her throat.

"Mother—lady, dear lady—"

He held the cup out, insistently. He moved closer to her. She seemed frozen. The truth was emblazoned on her face. Rage rose like a fountain in him, and for an instant he thought he was going to hurl the drink in her face; but then he regained his poise. Her hand was pressed against her lips in terror. She moved back, back, back.

And then she was running toward the door of the mosque; and abruptly the Grand Duke Alexander Petrovich, his face erupting with red blotches of panic, was running also, and also Prince Itzcoatl of Mexico.

"No! Fools!" a voice cried out, and the echoes hammered at the ancient walls.

Little Father looked toward the foreign ambassadors. Sir Anthony stood out as though in a spotlight, his cheeks blazing, his eyes popping, his fingers exploring his lips as though he could not believe they had actually uttered that outcry.

There was complete confusion in the mosque. Everyone was rushing about, everyone was bellowing. But Little Father was quite calm. Carefully he set the cup down, untouched, at his feet. Ali Pasha came to his side at once.

"Round them up quickly," he told the vizier. "The three ambassadors are persona non grata. They're to leave Songhay by the next riverboat. Escort Mansa Suleiyman back to the Embassy of Mali and put armed guards around the building—for purely protective purposes, of course. And also the embassies of Ghana, Dahomey, Benin, and the rest, for good measure—and as window dressing."

"It will be done, Majesty."

"Very good." He indicated the chalcedony cup. "As for this stuff, give it to a dog to drink, and let's see what happens."

Ali Pasha nodded and touched his forehead.

"And the Lady Serene Glory, and her brother?"

"Take them into custody. If the dog dies, throw them both to the lions."

"Your Majesty—"

"To the lions, Ali Pasha."

"But you said—"

"To the lions, Ali Pasha."

"I hear and obey, Majesty."

"You'd better." Little Father grinned. He was Little Father no longer, he realized. "I like the way you say it: *Majesty*. You put just the right amount of awe into it."

"Yes, Majesty. Is there anything else, Majesty?"

"I want an escort too, to take me to my palace. Say, fifty men. No, make it a hundred. Just in case there are any surprises waiting for us outside."

"To your old palace, Majesty?"

The question caught him unprepared. "No," he said after a moment's reflection. "Of course not. To my new palace. To the palace of the Emir."

Selima came hesitantly forward into the throne room, which was one of the largest, most forbidding rooms she had ever entered. Not even the Sultan's treasure-house at the Topkapi Palace had any chamber to match this one for sheer dismal mustiness, for clutter, or for the eerie hodgepodge of its contents. She found the new Emir standing beneath a stuffed giraffe, examining an ivory globe twice the size of a man's head that was mounted on an intricately carved spiral pedestal.

"You sent for me, Your Highness?"

"Yes. Yes, I did. It's all calm outside there, now, I take it?"

"Very calm. *Very* calm."

"Good. And the weather's still cool?"

"Quite cool, Your Majesty."

"But not raining again yet?"

"No, not raining."

"Good." Idly he fondled the globe. "The whole world is here, do you know that? Right under my hand. Here's Africa, here's Europe, here's Russia. This is the Empire, here." He brushed his hand across the globe from Istanbul to Madrid. "There's still plenty of it, eh?" He spun the ivory sphere easily on its pedestal. "And this, the New World. Such emptiness there. The Incas down here in the southern continent, the Aztecs here in the middle, and a lot of nothing up here in the north. I once asked my father, do you know, if I could pay a visit to those empty lands. So cool there, I hear. So green, and almost empty. Just the red-skinned people, and not very many of them. Are they really red, do you think? I've never seen one." He looked closely at her. "Have you ever thought of leaving Turkey, I wonder, and taking up a new life for yourself in those wild lands across the ocean?"

"Never, Your Majesty."

She was trembling a little.

"You should think of it. We all should. Our countries are all too old. The land is tired. The air is tired. The rivers move slowly. We should go somewhere where things are fresh." She made no reply. After a moment's silence he said, "Do you love that tall gawky pink-faced Englishman, Selima?"

"Love?"

"Love, yes. Do you have any kind of fondness for him? Do you care for him at all? If love is too strong a word for you, would you say at least that you enjoy his company, that you see a certain charm in him, that—well, surely you understand what I'm saying."

She seemed flustered. "I'm not sure that I do."

"It appears to me that you feel attracted to him. God

knows he feels attracted to you. He can't go back to England, you realize. He's compromised himself fifty different ways. Even after we patch up this conspiracy thing, and we certainly will, one way or another, the fact still remains that he's guilty of treason. He has to go somewhere. He can't stay here—the heat will kill him fast, if his own foolishness doesn't. Are you starting to get my drift, Selima?"

Her eyes rose to meet his. Some of her old self-assurance was returning to them now.

"I think I am. And I think that I like it."

"Very good," he said. "I'll give him to you, then. For a toy, if you like." He clapped his hands. A functionary poked his head into the room.

"Send in the Englishman."

Michael entered. He walked with the precarious stride of someone who has been decapitated but thinks there might be some chance of keeping his head on his shoulders if only he moves carefully enough. The only traces of sunburn that remained now were great peeling patches on his cheeks and forehead.

He looked toward the new Emir and murmured a barely audible courtly greeting. He seemed to have trouble looking in Selima's direction.

"Sir?" Michael asked finally.

The Emir smiled warmly. "Has Sir Anthony left yet?"

"This morning, sir. I didn't speak with him."

"No. No, I imagine you wouldn't care to. It's a mess, isn't it, Michael? You can't really go home."

"I understand that, sir."

"But obviously you can't stay here. This is no climate for the likes of you."

"I suppose not, sir."

The Emir nodded. He reached about behind him and lifted a book from a stand. "During my years as prince I had plenty of leisure to read. This is one of my favorites. Do you happen to know which book it is?"

"No, sir."

"The collected plays of one of your great English writers, as a matter of fact. The greatest, so I'm told. Shakespeare's his name. You know his work, do you?"

Michael blinked. "Of course, sir. Everyone knows—"

"Good. And you know his play *Alexius and Khurrem*, naturally?"

"Yes, sir."

The Emir turned to Selima. "And do you?"

"Well—"

"It's quite relevant to the case, I assure you. It takes place in Istanbul, not long after the Ottoman Conquest. Khurrem is a beautiful young woman from one of the high Turkish families. Alexius is an exiled Byzantine prince who has slipped back into the capital to try to rescue some of his family's treasures from the grasp of the detested conqueror. He disguises himself as a Turk and meets Khurrem at a banquet, and of course they fall in love. It's an impossible romance—a Turk and a Greek." He opened the book. "Let me read a little. It's amazing that an Englishman could write such eloquent Turkish poetry, isn't it?

"From forth the fatal loins of these two foes
A pair of star-cross'd lovers take their life;
Whose misadventur'd piteous overthrows
Do with their death bury their parents' strife—"

The Emir glanced up. " 'Star-cross'd lovers.' That's what you are, you know." He laughed. "It all ends terribly for poor Khurrem and Alexius, but that's because they were such hasty children. With better planning they could have slipped away to the countryside and lived to a ripe old age, but Shakespeare tangles them up in a scheme of sleeping potions and crossed messages and they both die at the end, even though well-intentioned friends were trying to help them. But of course that's drama for you. It's a lovely play. I hope to be able to see it performed someday."

He put the book aside. They both were staring at him.

To Michael he said, "I've arranged for you to defect to Turkey. Ismet Akif will give you a writ of political asylum. What happens between you and Selima is of course entirely up to you and Selima, but in the name of Allah I implore you not to make as much of a shambles of it as Khurrem and Alexius did. Istanbul's not such a bad place to live, you know. No, don't look at me like that! If she can put up with a ninny like you, you can manage to get over your prejudices against Turks. You asked for all this, you know. You didn't *have* to fall in love with her."

"Sir, I—I—"

Michael's voice trailed away.

The Emir said, "Take him out of here, will you, Selima?"

"Come," she said. "We need to talk, I think."

"I—I—"

The Emir gestured impatiently. Selima's hand was on Michael's wrist, now. She tugged, and he followed. The Emir looked after them until they had gone down the stairs.

Then he clapped his hands.

"Ali Pasha!"

The vizier appeared so quickly that there could be no doubt he had been lurking just beyond the ornate doorway.

"Majesty?"

"We have to clear this place out a little," the Emir said. "This crocodile—this absurd giraffe—find an appropriate charity and donate them, fast. And these hippo skulls, too. And this, and this, and this—"

"At once, Majesty. A clean sweep."

"A clean sweep, yes."

A cool wind was blowing through the palace now, after the rains. He felt young, strong, vigorous. Life was just beginning, finally. Later in the day he would visit the lions at their pit.

At the Sign of the Rose

By John Brunner

Prologue: For Reasons of State

THE MOST LUXURIOUS TRAIN EVER TO TRAVEL THAT wonder of the modern world, the Eurasian Railway, rumbled onward through the first hot spell of summer. In its specially built observation car, as far as might be from the noise and stench of the locomotive, Vladimir IX, Czar of All the Russias, Khan of most of Asia including China and Korea, and "honorable protector" of a certain troublesome cluster of islands off the eastern shore of the continent, sat beside the Maori ambassador, wishing for the latest of uncountably many times that those distant people would abandon the habit of tattooing themselves. It made it impossible to guess what they were thinking.

Which, no doubt, was why they did it.

A vision invaded his mind: Admiral Cheng-ho's sailors on their tragic final voyage when, half-starving and delirious with scurvy, they found their storm-battered junks, alist with their sails in tatters and their powder soaked so that their guns were useless, surrounded by Maori war-canoes. Many of them had jumped overside crying out that they were being attacked by devils—and could they be blamed, given those insane blue patterns the strangers wore not only on their faces but all over their bodies?

At least this one had the decency to cover himself like a civilized person. But judging by the way the tattoos ran down his neck and under his collar . . .

The Czar repressed a pang of nausea and reverted to his constant preoccupation, forcing himself to reason despite the oppressive atmosphere. It was the sort of day when superstitious people claimed to hear the Gate of Worlds grinding on its hinges. The air was still, yet it dragged almost as though it were becoming solid, hampering bodily movement, making even thought sluggish. . . .

He, however, had no time for such foolish notions. He was a practical man. And right now he was faced with an extremely practical, extremely intractable problem.

He had absolutely no way of judging whether or not he was making the right impression on his guest. And he must! All his counselors were agreed on that. Indeed, the lowliest peasant might recognize the value of a non-aggression pact with the Land of the Long White Cloud. That meant-to-be puppet the Mikado, according to intelligence reports, was showing signs of impermissible ambition. Apparently he dreamed of making his people an independent maritime power through forging a secret foreign alliance: perhaps with Mexico, perhaps with Peru, but most likely with the Maoris.

Whichever way, it would eventually lead to war. And

if anybody knew how fragile was the eastern part of the vast empire ruled from Moscow, it was the Czar. Hostilities in that region could shatter his realm to fragments, and in a generation it would have gone the way of the Sublime Porte. A war in the west, on the other hand, would be a different matter—even useful . . .

Was the ambassador properly awed by this wonderful engineering achievement, this iron road which had cost so much effort, so much money, and a full decade of time? Not to mention hundreds, perhaps thousands, of lives. . . . But there were always more serfs, and theirs had been a necessary sacrifice. Within recent memory the journey from Shanghai to Moscow had taken a year, for one was forced to overwinter en route. Now, in fine weather, it was a matter of ten days, and even in snowtime under a month.

It was of course no use expecting Maoris to be impressed by the locomotives themselves. Their chance contact with Cheng-ho's gunners had led them to understand the principle of heat expansion as though by instinct. The whole world knew of their capital Rotorua, where the houses were warmed in winter, and the factories driven the whole year round, by natural steam erupting from the ground. Thanks to the ships that resulted from combining the junk with the canoe and the catamaran, plus the all-important acquisition of the compass, which kept them on course when the sky was too overcast to navigate by their traditional star maps, they had dominated trade across a fifth of the globe for centuries. There were Maori settlements on every coast of Great West Island—which from the Old World point of view lay far to the south, but Maoris had circumnavigated it before any European set foot there. That had been achieved with oars and sail. When steampower was added theirs turned into a formidable fleet indeed. And some of their latest cannon, rumor said, could hurl a shot six versts!

The Czar bit back an oath. This damnable trip, no matter how essential it might be for reasons of state both internal and external, was interfering with so many other plans! To insure against the risk of losing its eastern lands, his empire must expand in Europe. The decline of Turkish power and constant bickering among the Teutonic States meant that great chunks of Poland and Slovakia were ripe for the picking. He had nourished independence movements there—and in many other countries—with plentiful finance and occasionally weapons. Now the moment was at hand. There would be pro-Russian uprisings the moment his army crossed the border. But the task must be complete before next winter, and time was wasting.

Still, he comforted himself, when it happened the Maori ambassador would see for himself how foolish it would be to cement a secret alliance with a client state like Japan. . . .

His mind having strayed to the delicious aroma being generated by his Chinese cooks in the adjacent galley, he grew suddenly aware that the ambassador's interpreter was addressing him, and donned a polite expression. The train was slowing, no doubt for a bridge, of which there were many on this hilly and river-beset stretch of what had once been the Silk Road. Close by, a track-maintenance gang—to judge by their appearance, mostly Tartars—had broken off from their work of stacking timber sleepers and shovelling ballast for the roadbed, and were dutifully waving and cheering. Their overseers' knouts were hidden from the travelers' view, as per orders.

"Yes, the bridges are impressive, are they not?" the Czar said when he had grasped the import of what had been said. "We owe them to the remarkable skill of Chinese engineers in the use of that equally remarkable plant, bamboo. I don't know whether it's found in your country. They tell me it's a relative of ordinary grass, but some of its more than two hundred species have amazing structural properties. Being elastic and non-brittle, they can bear greater loads than iron girders. We've been over several trestles built of the stuff already, but that was during the night. This is the first we are to cross by day. Would you care to take a look?"

Rising, he moved to the left of the car's two nacelles. They extended slightly beyond its main body and offered a limited forward view through panes of glass, ajar for ventilation. Vomiting smoke and steam, the engine was dragging its train across the bridge at barely walking pace. The trestles flexed, but held. Which was as well. Among gray boulders far below a torrent roiled.

The interpreter translated his master's comment.

"It is a great achievement to have created a railway from the eastern edge of the continent to the borders of the Sultanate. The Incas build splendid roads, and so do the Aztecs, but even they could not match this iron track. The idea has been mooted of constructing something similar across Great West Island, but that project lies far in the future, since most of the interior is still known only to its aboriginal inhabitants."

The Czar could scarcely conceal his jubilation, and some of his attendants signally failed to. He quelled their reaction with a scowl unseen by the ambassador.

"No doubt, then," he said in an affectedly casual tone, "Your Excellency will wish to view it all the way to our *present* western frontier, rather than turn aside to

Moscow. There would be little point anyhow, since I myself have—ah—business to attend to before I return to my capital."

His attendants understood instantly. The invasion was to go ahead. Shortly yet another prize would be wrested from the Turks and Teutons. They exchanged smiles as the observation car reached the bridge.

Which swayed, then lurched.

The ambassador blurted something incomprehensible, but did his best to remain impassive. So did the Czar. So did their respective retinues—but not for long.

The bridge tilted, and the observation car with it. The Czar lost his balance and fell sidelong to the floor of the nacelle, shouting. Horrified, the engine-driver pushed his regulator wide open, hoping against hope to drag the tail of the train clear of the bridge before—

Too late.

The trestles bowed and snapped. The observation car tore loose and tumbled to the river and the rocks. There, thanks to the galley stoves, it caught on fire.

The Czar was dead. The whole world held its breath, and the Russian Empire shut its frontiers, not to reopen them for half a year.

And rebellion broke out like plague all over China.

One: The Rose and Its Buds

HAVING TRAVERSED ALMOST EXACTLY ONE HUNDRED degrees of longitude, a train that had begun its journey at Hangchow on the eastern shore of Asia groaned to a halt before the walls of Kraków in the heart of Europe. It was the first to be let out of Russia since the spring, and it was six months late.

Powdery snow was drifting from the afternoon sky, but despite the bitter cold and gathering dark, a crowd had assembled which outnumbered its remaining passengers. Many of the others had had their passports sequestered and must wait still longer, while those in a position to do so had returned home, infuriated and ultimately exhausted by their virtual captivity, and in some cases bankrupted by the loss of perishable goods.

Oh, officially they'd been "guests of the Czar," fed after a fashion, allowed medical attention and otherwise provided for. But it was sheer misery to be caught up in the slow-grinding mill of Russian bureaucracy. The police had continued their investigations and interrogations long after the rest of the world had concluded that if the old Czar's death had indeed been due to sabotage, it made sense to seek the culprits not in the west but in the east, among disaffected minorities like the Georgians or Uzbeks—even the Mongols, despite the fact that after centuries of state intermarriage, Vladimir IX had been cousin to most of them several times over.

Moreover: what if the Chinese weren't simply seizing an unlooked-for opportunity to throw off their ancient alien yoke? And how about Japan, whose incumbent Mikado seemed determined to kick over the traces of the troika? (Propaganda from Moscow often invoked the image of that traditional Russian conveyance, in summer a carriage, in winter a sleigh, drawn by horses three abreast, implying that they were Russia-cum-Mongolia, China-cum-Korea, and Japan. Cynics pointed out that in the real-life case two of the horses had their heads twisted too far to the side to count; only the middle one actually did any pulling.)

Perhaps, though, that wasn't what tipped the balance. Perhaps it had merely dawned on the Muscovite courtiers—or their wives and housekeepers!—how much trade was being lost because the frontiers were closed, and what a boring winter it was apt to be unless foreign goods were allowed to enter normally. Why, one was still wearing last year's fashions, serving last year's dishes to one's guests!

The international situation was so tense that those who had a choice preferred not to run the risk of being trapped in a foreign—worse, a hostile—country should a war indeed break out. Some claimed that was unlikely, since the new Czar had had to order his armies eastward to contain the crisis in China. Others countered that it was therefore all the more probable: was it not traditional to unite a divided nation by invoking patriotism against an outside enemy?

That, of course, led to endless disputes about whether a Chinese, still less a Japanese, should owe allegiance to a Russian-speaking half-breed thousands of versts away in Moscow, even though he called himself a Khan. Ought Italians to obey him rather than their overlords the Turks, simply because he also bore the title *Czar* that had been *Caesar*?

Such arguments could drag on forever. But they had been a welcome means of passing time while the train was stranded at the frontier . . . so long, naturally, as no one suspected of being a Czarist spy was in earshot.

Now, though, the train had reached its destination, and its weary passengers were free to go about their business—or what of it was left after such long delay.

A few imported steam carriages, hissing and fuming, waited in hopes of wealthy customers, the sort who could rent an entire train-car for themselves and their families or retinue, instead of subletting part at a profit as did most who engaged them: those, in sum, who might be expected to require luxury transportation during their stay. But the machines' owners were due for a disappointment. The richest travelers had been the first to turn back, and indeed the police had released them the soonest. Money, one suspected, must have talked. . . .

For those not so well off but nonetheless prosperous, cabs drawn by mules or horses were for hire. Large-wheeled wagons stood in a line for those who had bulky goods to unload, but they were obliged to wait while black-uniformed customs officers moved in pairs among the throng, making sure that all necessary documentation had been completed at the border post where the Nida and the Wisla met. Some of them had dogs trained to sniff out undeclared substances easily concealed, such as tobacco, opium or coca.

Meantime dolmushes filled quickly. As soon as every seat was occupied their traditionally foul-mouthed drivers swung them about, using whips as well as tongues to clear the way. For those too poor to ride the short distance to the city there remained porters with greasy fur caps on their heads, wooden frames on their backs and wooden clogs on their feet, offering to bear loads as heavy as themselves for the price of a meal or a drink.

A little apart from the rest was parked one most unusual conveyance. Dark green, with red roses painted on either side, it was capable of seating eight, all facing forward, and built to such a high standard that even its driver was protected from the elements. Its engine and boiler, at the front, afforded him grateful warmth, while both chimney and spent-steam pipes discharged at the rear after heating the passenger compartment. Many were the envious glances cast towards it—but of them the portly personage leaning out of its left-side window took no notice. Immensely caped and gloved, he was issuing instructions to a group of teenage boys clad in the same dark green and wearing rose-red turbans.

"You're certain you know who to look for?" he pressed, in a voice that for a man of his bulk was curiously high-pitched. A chorus of affirmatives resounded.

"Very well! Off with you! But if you screw up—"

Before he could finish they had darted away. They had heard the threat in full, and because he was what he was they were prepared to accept it at face value.

Sliding the window shut, the portly man settled back in his seat and composed himself to wait.

Most of his life had been spent waiting.

Despite the apparent confusion the crowd dispersed swiftly. Not only had the train lost many of its original passengers, until chiefly those remained for whom time was more affordable than money, seasoned travelers who knew how to drive a hard bargain with a wagoner or porter; in addition, the livestock which would normally also have had to be disembarked had been sold for what it would fetch—or killed and eaten. A promising and expensive strain of carrier pigeons had lately been sacrificed to the pot.

Soon there were only half a dozen new arrivals left, apart from merchants arguing at the pitch of their lungs with the customs inspectors. Five who had never been to Kraków before stood in an uncertain cluster, like friends—which they were not.

They had been too slow, and too unfamiliar with local customs, to obtain seats in a dolmush. Now they were trying as best they could to select among the wheedling porters those least likely to make off with their belongings, occasionally glancing at the sixth—whom during the interminable trip they had come to know as Djinghiz—as though in hope that he might offer to assist.

But he was paying absolutely no attention.

* * *

He was filthy. For months he had had to make do with what he wore and the contents of the bag at his feet. He itched. His black hair was foul with grease and the all-pervading smoke of the wood-burning locomotive; his mustache retained traces of the soup that had been the main sustenance accorded by the Russians during their period of waiting; his quilted jacket too memorialized a good few meals—though few good ones; and as for his breeches, they could have stood up without his help.

Ah, but what a relief it was to have escaped the omnipresence of the trigger-happy Czarist guards who now and then shot out lighted windows on the train for target practice! He had no special love for the Teutons, but at least their soldiery was better disciplined.

Djinghiz felt his heart leap as he gazed at the familiar walls, the familiar summit of the Wawel Hill beside the river, crowned with a complex of buildings part fortress, part mosque, part palace, some of whose masonry dated back to the legendary days of the Roman Empire. Kraków might not be the greatest city in the world; it might no longer even be the greatest city of his own people, the majority of whom now lived in the region where he had spent the past five years; but here was where he had been born, and he was home at last. He had left as a boy; now he was a man. And had a man's achievements to his credit! Despite his youth, had his actions not already moved the Gate of Worlds? And more than once, at that, when most people had to be content with—

A tap on his arm distracted him. He glanced down to find a bright-eyed but nervous-looking boy bowing low and asking, "Is it the effendi's wish to find lodging for the night? If so, my master can provide it."

Djinghiz looked him over. His red turban was of silk, as was his green coat, while his breeches and boots were of brown leather.

Hah! Ismail must have done well for himself since I've been away!

Aloud he said, "Does your costume represent a rose?"

"The effendi sees and hears all!"

"And is your master called Ismail?"

"Why, you enjoy his acquaintance already!"

"Not half as much," Djinghiz said with a grimace, "as I hope to enjoy it in future."

"Forgive me, effendi. I failed to hear correctly . . ." The boy's large dark eyes scanned his face anxiously.

"Never mind. Just lead me to him. And carry my bag! My shoulders are grooved from its strap."

The boy caught up the bag with an ingratiating smile and took off at half a run.

Arriving at the green steam carriage, aware that the need for discretion remained, Djinghiz murmured as he climbed inside:

"Were your eyes, then, never off me, Ismail effendi?"

"Once," said the high voice. "While you were actually at work. Concerning that we'll doubtless speak anon. Meantime, my rachets are about their work. What do you want?"

"A drink, a bath, clean clothes, a meal, a bed."

"All those will be provided, and soon. A woman too, if you are in the mood."

"What would you know of such matters—" Djinghiz

caught himself. "Ah, that was unworthy. It was exhaustion talking. But how soon is soon? Has your net caught all the fish you're trawling? You did get my message?"

"Yes. You found me five, or rather four and a possible, much the number I was expecting." With a spyglass the portly man was scanning the zone between here and the train-halt. "Don't worry. Already two—no, three—more of my rosebuds are converging, and by nightfall we should have all of the furthest-traveled under one roof."

"The same roof?" Djinghiz forced out around a yawn. The air in the vehicle was so hot, he felt he might doze off.

"When we get there, you'll see. It won't be what you recall. But though it's made of fine Murano glass, it's still a roof. . . . Ah! Here comes my second rosebud. Inform me about his companion"—proffering the spyglass.

"You recall me to duty at once? I don't deserve a single evening's rest after all I've achieved?" Under the mockery of Djinghiz's words rang real bitterness.

Ismail laid a plump warm hand on his. He said, and his tone seemed to thrum through the contact, "You'll have your drink, your bath, your meal, your bed. And what is more you'll have amazing stories to remember, too."

"I'd rather have"—resentfully—"that woman. It's been long . . . Ah, maybe tomorrow. My weariness is marrow-deep. Your pardon again. You want to know about that man, the tawny-brown one—no, I don't need the spyglass to be sure. He's a Lankhan, name of Ratanayaka. Says he's a follower of some prince called Gautama who lived six hundred years before the Crucifixion and twelve hundred before the Hegira. He renounced his riches and the pleasures of the flesh and attained perfect enlightenment by meditating under a tree."

"And what tempts his disciple to Kraków?"

"Ratanayaka doesn't seem to care much for work. In his country, he says, holy men are given free food and lodging. With the decline of Turkish power the influence of Islam is fading, and not many people around here want to become Christian because it means identifying with Russia, right? I suspect he hopes to make rich converts to his creed, then live off their backs until he can get home."

"You've grown cynical since you left, young fellow!"

"I was born cynical," Djinghiz grunted. "And before you ask why he's taking such a roundabout route: he started his trip as a sort of ship's chaplain aboard a Lankhan freighter, but what he calls his karma—that's his fate due to the way he behaved in his previous lives—decreed that he should prove to be a bad sailor. He spent half his time throwing up. Ashore in China, he found some co-believers whose version of the scriptures was corrupt, so for the good of their souls, and his finances, he went from town to town preaching the word. Winding up far from the sea, he decided to go home as much as possible by land."

Ismail nodded. "I see. With no hope of taking a direct route, the passes between Russia and Ind being barred by the Gurkhas."

At mention of the fierce cruel warriors who ruled the mountains from Afghanistan to Burma, Djinghiz snorted. "I can't blame him for that! I wouldn't give much for my chances around there, and I'm a fighting type. Ratanayaka is forbidden by his faith to carry arms . . . Want me to tell you about the others before your rosebuds lure them here?''

''Everything you can, please.''

''Since you've taken an interest in them, I imagine you already know more than I do! But all right. The tall one on the right, even darker, is an Ethiopian, name of Feisal. Says he's a Romologist—you know, one of these people who are obsessed with Ancient Rome, like to dig around in ruins and publish descriptions of what they find.''

Ismail said musingly, ''I can well understand why he went to Russia. He spent a long time in cathedral libraries studying texts carried thither by Catholics when their last pope had to flee from Avignon. But why did he spend even longer in the Far East? The Romans never reached China, let alone Japan.''

''I wondered about that myself, but he came up with a colorable explanation.''

''That being?''

''For centuries the Turks have sold Roman relics to the highest bidder, and they've wound up all over the planet. There are even some in Rotorua. Feisal is extremely proud of the fact that, because of his scholarship, he was allowed access to the Mikado's collection in Edo.''

''Hmm!'' Ismail plied the spyglass again. ''Yes, someone who feels he's been cheated out of an empire would no doubt be interested in the greatest empire that the world has ever seen. So that is, as you put it, colorable. . . . Hello! It looks as though a couple of birds are fleeing my net!''

''Are you fishing or wildfowling?'' Djinghiz countered, pulling a face. Ismail ignored the gibe.

"I assume that's Slava, is it? With a child in tow?"

"Just as I thought. You know so much you don't need to wear me out with questions—"

"You've met them face to face, and I haven't," the fat man cut in. "Tell me about Slava, and hurry. The others are heading this way."

"His passport says he's a Balt from Riga," Djinghiz sighed. "By profession a dealer in amber. I'll lay he hasn't seen his homeland—or practiced his trade—in years. He's a full-time gambler, presumably a shark. I wouldn't know; I was never fool enough to play against him. He won Hideki at mah-jongg. We ran across a Japanese troupe of strolling players whose tour had been canceled because of the Czar's death. I guess they hoped to win enough to get home. Slava put paid to that idea. When they had nothing left he said he'd swap half his winnings for this kid they were training as an actress, and they agreed. I've no idea what became of them afterwards."

"Why did Slava want this—this Hideki?"

Djinghiz scowled. "We all assumed at first: for his own use. Some men do like their girls unripe, and at least they can't hit you with a paternity suit . . . But one night he got drunk and let the real reason slip. Seems that as well as being a gambler, he's a pimp. Said you can always pay your way by renting out a pretty child in a brothel. 'Besides, brothels are cleaner than regular hostelries. They're inspected. The bedlinen gets changed more often and there aren't so many fleas.' I quote."

Ismail's face darkened. Sliding open the window, he summoned the rosebud who had brought Djinghiz and uttered crisp orders. The boy salaamed and took to his heels.

Closing the window again, Ismail said, "Within the hour there won't be a brothel in Kraków that will admit them."

"So they'll have to come to the Sign of the Rose? Ismail effendi, if there's one thing I can't stand about you it's that smug expression you're so fond of! Want me to tell you about the last of your birds, or fish, or coneys, or whatever metaphor you're mixing this time?"

"The big Hawaiian?" Ismail's eyes were twinkling.

"Big?" Djinghiz gave a harsh laugh. "Paluka overtops me by head and shoulders, and I'm not small! Strong with it, too! Once I saw him take a gun away from a Russian guard who had annoyed him and bend its barrel like a birch-twig. *He* had some explaining to do to his officer!"

"Quickly! They're almost here! What's Paluka's excuse for coming to Kraków?"

"But surely you already know, for otherwise—"

"I said quickly!"

"He's studying engineering. Says it's intolerable that an island country like Hawaii doesn't own any ships fitted with steam engines, even auxiliary ones."

"The Maoris wouldn't approve of that, would they? Which is presumably why he didn't go to study in Rotorua. What are they planning to use for fuel? Their trees would be gone in a generation, and I don't believe they have any coal."

"He has this notion they could use sugarcane."

"Really! That's at least ingenious. It would be renewable, so . . . But his must be an expensive trip. How is he paying his way?"

"He's an amateur wrestler. Wherever he goes he arranges matches with the locals and backs himself at heavy odds. He says he did so well in Japan that they nicknamed him "The Locomotive," though he didn't care for their weird rules and the bouts that are over in an eyeblink. Next he wants to take on some Turks."

"You believe him?"

"Oh, he can wrestle, all right. Some of the Russian officers thought they had men who could beat him. During the first month or so we were stuck at the frontier they organized a string of challenges. He won every time, so they got bored and gave up. I believe he's an engineer, too. He earned a bit of spending money doing odd repairs on the stranded trains."

"And he waited patiently at the frontier for months on end, along with the rest of you?"

Shrugging, Djinghiz glanced at his companion. It was almost dark, but one could still make out facial details.

"He said he just had to put up with it. He won't have the money to get home unless he wins a few bouts in Turkey. Besides, having been raised on an island, he wants to find out what life feels like in the middle of a landmass."

There was a brief pause, during which Ismail slapped shut the spyglass.

"Well," he said musingly, "at least one of our about-to-be companions obviously has a sense of humor. Would you mind moving to the rear? It's easier than having everyone clamber over you, and I'd rather not make my rosebuds ride outside in such bitter weather."

Without waiting for an answer, he prepared to get out and greet his obviously puzzled "guests."

"Just a second!" Djinghiz snapped.

Turning back: "Yes, my friend?"

"Is there going to be a war?"

"Of course," said Ismail composedly. "In fact it's already begun.

"But it's of a most unusual kind."

Two: The Greatest Market

ISMAIL ADDRESSED THE NEWCOMERS EFFUSIVELY IN both Turkish and Russian, but it was plain that they had no idea why the rosebuds had brought them hither. Ratanayaka was the first to put their misgivings into words. His Russian was ill pronounced but comprehensible.

"Gospodin, your proposal is most generous! But if you send such a fine carriage for its clients, your hostelry must be a veritable palace, whereas you see before you an ascetic vowed to poverty, accustomed to privation. The lowliest shelter will suffice me. Moreover friends gave me the name and address of a family here, Buddhists like myself, and I need only directions to find their home."

"Is it not written in the Buddhist scriptures," Ismail murmured, "that one who accepts charity bestows virtue on its giver?"

The old hypocrite! Djinghiz said to himself. *He let*

me explain karma *to him when he must have known all along!* And, a second later: *I'm glad he's on my side!*

"Ah . . ." The mental struggle the Lankhan was having with himself was almost audible. Ismail pressed him.

"Besides: are your friends expecting you, six months late? They may not be at home—then what will you do? Better, surely, to seek them by daylight. Here it is not usual for even holy men to sleep in the open. You would run the risk of being apprehended as a beggar."

"That, certainly, would be unpleasant, and indeed a means of leading people into error. But do the temples in your country not offer sanctuary to the pious?"

"Only, I regret, to adherents of Islam. I see really no alternative, especially since it's almost sunset."

"Then for one night I accept, and thank you. I must confess"—this last in a near whisper—"it is far colder here than where I hail from."

"And you, sirs?" Ismail pursued, turning to Feisal and Paluka. The former responded first, in good Turkish.

"Unlike our companion, effendi, I am not vowed to poverty. Indeed, in a sense I am a merchant, albeit not of the kind who displays the wares he has for sale after the manner of a common market. I should easily be able to meet the fees of your establishment—that is, if you can introduce me to a trustworthy pawnbroker. I possess certain articles against which I would expect to raise an adequate sum."

Covertly eavesdropping through a partly open window, Djinghiz gave a thoughtful nod. Feisal had a bag that never left his side, not even when he slept. Presumably it contained Roman relics which he would not sell but might risk pawning until he found means to redeem the pledge.

"And I," put in Paluka, "likewise prefer not to be in anybody's debt. If your pawnbrokers act also as moneychangers, the way they do in most places, I'll go with Feisal. I still have a few coins to my name, and tomorrow maybe I can find somebody to challenge me at wrestling."

"It won't be me!" said Ismail feelingly. "Well, then, sirs, climb aboard!"

Ratanayaka mounted first and sat next to Djinghiz in the rear; Feisal came next, but when Paluka made to follow Ismail checked him with a touch on his arm.

"I think you and I had better occupy a bench for three. Let my rosebuds cram into the other seats. . . . Yarely now!"

They scrambled in, trying not to giggle, the four of them taking up less room than the two big men. A signal to the driver, and the machine moved off with a jerk.

By some ingenious system of piped warm air, the windows were kept free of mist despite the cold. Although the snow was thickening they had an excellent view of the city as they rolled towards it—slowly, because crowds were converging on the south gate before it closed at sundown. The sight made Djinghiz's heart ache. To be home again, after so long, after so many terrors . . .

But he fought the impulse to lose himself in gratified nostalgia. True to his character—Djinghiz had rarely met such a man for asking questions—Paluka was plying Ismail with demands for information. The latest thing to have caught his attention was a multilingual list of regulations concerning the use of steam vehicles on public highways.

"Forgive me, gospodin—I should rather say effendi, should I not?—but this section of the notice does not appear to be in Russian, though the letters are Cyrillic."

"Ah! That's because of our rather special situation. Everyone at this crossroads of the world grows up speaking at least two languages, usually Polish and Turkish. However, some out of principle prefer Russian, to show where their sympathies lie in the ebb and flow of great-power rivalry that washes about us like the ocean 'round an island country such as yours. A good many go so far as to write their native Polish in Cyrillic script—hence that portion of the notice. Others still, regarding the Teutons as our liberators, affect German."

"I see . . . Tell me, what exactly is your relationship to the Teutonic States?"

"Technically, Kraków is a free city. That's to say, we are governed by a council we elect ourselves, we impose our own taxes and customs duties, and so forth. But our status is precarious. The Ottomans resent the fact that they've lost control of this area, the Russians would like to see us exchange one foreign suzerainty for another, and—well, to adopt a metaphor from your pastime of wrestling, the Teutons 'hold the ring.' We permit them a token garrison, much though it tends to gall . . . Still, life is easier than under the Sultanate, even if it does mean that, to placate factionalism among the citizenry, the council has to issue its public notices in four versions!"

He concluded with a chuckle.

Djinghiz, having his own opinion about the way

Kraków had been "taken under the protection" of the Teutons, would have expressed himself more strongly, but he couldn't help admiring Ismail's tactfulness.

"And you, effendi?" Paluka went on. "You're Turkish?"

"No, Cracovian."

Paluka blinked. "From your name—"

"Ah, but that's no more of an indicator than calling a man Czar means he's a Roman Caesar! I wasn't born in Kraków, but I was brought here as a child and this is where I grew up. I've become attached to the place. Apart from anything else it has a fascinating history. To recount it in detail would take volumes, but some you can read—if you know how—on the very faces of the buildings."

They and the rest of the traffic had been forced to a halt by a brewer's dray unloading barrels in a street broad but not quite broad enough, lined either side by handsome merchants' houses ornamented with the symbols of Islam, crescents and moulded diaperwork, multicolored tiles and writhing Arabic script. Ismail went on: "To give you an example: see that house?"

He pointed at the one immediately to their left. A naphtha flare, flickering in the wind, cast dancing shadows on its richly carved façade. Behind lighted windows on the upper floors people moved in silhouette. There was an echo of music. But at street level crude wooden doors stood ajar to reveal crude and blackened wooden carts.

"Five kings once dined there, in that building! And now—well, as you see, it's a coal-seller's."

"Five kings?" echoed Ratanayaka, who for an ascetic had sometimes struck Djinghiz as excessively interested in royal affairs. Of course, the founder of his religion had been a prince . . . "Five actual kings?"

"Indeed! Or more exactly: the Emperor Charles plus the kings of Poland, Hungary, Denmark and Cyprus."

"It must have been a wonderful occasion!" exclaimed Feisal. "For—well, were not those monarchs Christians, planning to unite against the Turks?"

"You've studied the decline of Catholic Christendom?" Ismail inquired, glancing round.

Feisal spread his hands. "As a Romologist I naturally take an interest in what was for so long the state religion of the Roman Empire."

"Yes, naturally." Ismail's tone was perfectly neutral. "However, their hopes were swiftly dashed."

Paluka murmured, "Would you amplify, for the benefit of one who knows little of European history?"

"Certainly," Ismail answered. "They failed through no fault of their own, simply by the will of Allah. The King of Cyprus brought the Black Death in his retinue. Before, it hadn't reached this far. After . . . well, there was no hope of resistance."

"But Kraków survived!" Djinghiz cried, just as white-cloaked mounted police cantered up to reprimand the draymen for blocking the way. Since escaping the grip of Moslem orthodoxy, purveyors of alcoholic drink seemed to feel they could do as they liked. Sullenly, however, they shifted their dray enough for normal flow to resume.

Jerking his head around, Ismail favored Djinghiz with a frown. But the younger man was in a reckless mood. He went on doggedly, "Thanks to my people, Kraków survived!"

"Your people being—?" Paluka demanded.

"I'm a Tartar!"

Ismail's frown became a glare. Djinghiz ignored it.

"Oh, I know people think all the Tartars live in the Far East or down in the Crimea! But this was the first great Tartar city! And I don't give a gob of spittle for the people who say we had to steal it! We were driven back from it once, but we came again and found it deserted and half-ruined. Had it not been for us, today it would be as dead as Petra!"

"And then"—Ismail's words united the delicacy of a scalpel with the brutality of a club—"your cousins the Turks came along and rolled you up like one of their own carpets."

"Yes, but look at why they were so jealous of us! *Look!*"

He flung out his arm as though he could physically hurl the strangers' attention forward. They turned as one.

And froze for a long moment, not fixated but transfixed.

By flickering firelight, resin torches, and harsh naphtha flares, they saw the greatest marketplace in all the world, standing to your run-of-the-mill bazaar as an ocean port to a coveful of fishing smacks. Not even the markets of Mexico could rival it.

Over its vast paved surface, ten acres in extent, were pitched the yurts, the vardos and the pavilions of traveling merchants, including some who had arrived aboard their own train and made haste to snatch what space there was. Certain areas were reserved to certain nationalities, whose flags and banners flew defiantly, but all were subject to police who, as they stared, cuffed aside a whimpering boy under orders from his master to light a campfire in the middle of the pavement, and soaked his firewood—bought at inflated price from one of the eager peddlars who wove their way among the throng—to rub in the lesson that here fires might be lit only in appointed places. That meant on the hearths punctuating the waist-high brick-built walls to either side of the square . . . but they, of course, were already occupied, and one must wait, and pay a fee, to use them. It came even more expensive when one had to dry out one's fuel on someone else's embers. That served in effect as an instant, if informal, fine, which was why the police carried waterbuckets.

As they passed on they left behind an atmosphere compounded of resentment crossed with resignation. Djinghiz had experienced it before, but he judged that his companions hadn't: the tense uneasy truce of the serai.

Well satisfied with the impact the spectacle was having, he felt his fit of nationalistic pride recede. Later he might even apologize to Ismail. But he wasn't sorry to have boasted on his people's behalf. A vision of how Kraków might have been flared in imagination: its paving buried under grass and mould, its buildings reduced to scrub-covered hummocks, its sole inhabitants wild birds and animals, the only sound their cries and the moaning of the wind . . .

If this market had not remained theirs, then at least, six hundred years ago, it had been Tartars who kept it in being.

At the northeast corner of the square two towers of unequal height marked the city's chief mosque: originally a church, it had been adapted to Islam by grafting a dome above its main roof and converting the towers to minarets. It being the sunset hour, from the taller of them a muezzin called the faithful to prayer, or at least the rump who were left now the influence of Turkey had receded. Automatically their driver braked his vehicle to a halt, allowing them to drink in the unparalleled vision of the market.

The fading of echoes broke the spell. Scarcely had they died before cheerful music resounded, twanging bouzoukis, wailing shawms, clashing cymbals. Relaxing, those in the carriage painted with roses looked at one another as though they had never met before.

Unused to acting so totally on impulse, Djinghiz shivered. It was as though he had been taken over by a power outside himself. As a firm rationalist, who had rejected Islam on political grounds—Tartars had always resented being forced to identify with the Turks, even though as Ismail had observed they were cousins—he had equally dismissed the pagan beliefs which some Tartars were trying to revive as a symbol of independence.

Indeed, over to his right, illuminated by one of the authorized fires around which a group of laughing men were roasting chunks of meat on skewers (the scent, fragrant with herbs, awoke hunger deeper than his belly, deep as his soul) stood several wooden idols, copied from those dug up by archaeologists, such as nowadays were reappearing even within Imperial Russia in flagrant defiance of Moscow and its Christian bishops. Could they, noted subconsciously from the corner of his eye, have triggered his outburst?

"Djinghiz," Ismail murmured, "are you trying to

make your face imitate one of those hideous carvings?''

What?

It was as though the portly man had read his mind. He jolted to full alertness, appalled that his secret thoughts should be shared with these strangers.

But they hadn't been. The truth dawned. Ismail had addressed him not in Turkish, not in Russian, not in Polish, but in Tartar such as he had learned at his mother's knee, and no one else in earshot could have understood.

Fortunately they were too polite to probe.

Grinning to disguise embarrassment, Djinghiz composed himself for the remainder of their ride.

Three: Roses in a Time of Snow

TWO BLOCKS NORTH OF THE MARKET, ON THE LEFT-hand corner of an intersection, the silhouette of a rose in wrought iron shone above a doorway, illuminated from behind by a lamp that glowed without flickering despite the ever-keener wind that now was brooming snow along the street. Paluka said, sounding impressed, ''Is that light electrical?''

''Hmm?'' Ismail was preparing to descend as a tall commissionaire strode towards the carriage. ''Oh—no, it's only gas, but the brightness is enhanced by a special mantle. It's a Teuton invention, I believe. I'm afraid I don't know much about such matters.''

The door admitted icy air. With bows and flourishes the commissionaire—an ex-soldier, no doubt, blind in one eye and sporting a blunt scimitar—greeted his master, ushered him and his companions inside, shouted at the rosebuds to make haste with their belongings.

In the entrance hall the rose design was omnipresent, but especially in the pattern of six splendid carpets that hung from ceiling to floor. Against their green and crimson backdrop adult staff hastened to take the new arrivals' outdoor clothes, and their passports for police inspection, while more rosebuds darted to help their comrades with the luggage. Two of them, Djinghiz noticed with surprise, were not boys but girls, although identically dressed. That was new since his last visit.

Near the entrance a middle-aged African couple wearing incongruous fur coats and hats over sweeping Malian robes exchanged puzzled glances, clearly wondering what such a disreputable-seeming person as Djinghiz was doing in this select establishment—not that his companions looked much more presentable. But before they could comment aloud the commissionaire announced the arrival of a coach bound for a popular music-hall, and they departed into a flurry of snow.

Letting events pass him by, Djinghiz stood aside while rooms were allotted. As at a vast distance he heard Paluka inquire, after thanking Ismail, "Effendi, have I correctly deduced that you are in fact the proprietor?"

Behind the spoken question another was implied, and it was obvious from the way Feisal and Ratanayaka glanced round that they too hoped to hear it answered. Ismail waved a casual, as it were dismissive, hand.

"In view of certain services I was able to render in my youth, its former owner was kind enough to bequeath this house to me upon his departure for, one hopes, a happier world. But I take no responsibility for its day-to-day operation. I leave that to its admirable staff." He bestowed a broad smile on those within earshot.

As Djinghiz knew, Ismail was doing himself less than justice. He had slaved to rescue the Sign of the Rose, the oldest hostelry in town, when old Darko was drinking it into bankruptcy because he was so angry at the recall to Istanbul of the last Bey of Kraków. (A betrayal, he'd kept saying—a rank betrayal!)

But the portly man had sensed what underlay the uttered words, and after a brief pause added, "You might say I can afford to regard it as a hobby. The comings and goings here are a source of endless fascination, and now and then I indulge myself by ensuring that particularly interesting visitors patronize my establishment rather than one of my rivals'. We have, as you know, lacked trains from Russia this half year, so when I learned yours carried passengers from exotic locales—Ethiopia, Lankha, Hawaii—I decided it was high time I again spent an evening listening to travelers' tales. That is, if you have no objection."

They exchanged glances, still visibly at a loss what to make of this extraordinary innkeeper. At last Paluka gave a shrug.

"I have none, effendi. And I trust my companions will not, either. But for you we could be printing the snow in search of where to lay our heads."

"So it's settled!" Ismail exclaimed, rubbing his hands. "I propose we meet for dinner in an hour—no, it's still early, so let's make it two. If any of you are accustomed to the hammam, we have our own on the premises"—Djinghiz couldn't disguise his excited reaction, and knew Ismail had spotted it from the cock of one eyebrow—"but there are also facilities for bathing on each floor. Until then—Yes, gospodin Ratanayaka?"

The Lankhan said diffidently, "Your invitation is

generous, but my faith forbids me to partake of animal food."

"Rest assured my cooks can meet your requirements. We never yet sent a guest away hungry."

A barely seen signal jolted the rosebuds into action. Seizing the visitors' bags, they set off up the staircase that faced the reception desk. As Djinghiz prepared to follow, Ismail laid a hand on his arm.

"This way," he murmured, as another rosebud—one of the girls—opened a door to the left of the stairs. Djinghiz braced himself by reflex, for last time he was here it had given on to an open yard, so he expected a chilly blast.

Instead: warmth, delicious smells, the clatter of metal dishes, even the song of a bulbul in a cage.

And roses! Scores of them, trained on the walls!

Advancing slowly, glancing from side to side and then upward, Djinghiz said, "Now I understand what you meant about the roof."

The courtyard had been glassed in. Some snow had settled, but one could still see lights in the upper stories of the surrounding buildings. Below, benches and tables were set out; in one corner a small dais waited to receive musicians or other entertainers, while down the left side cooks were at work over firepits sunk in a stone counter under ventilation hoods. One was having trouble lighting the charcoal that would roast, on a vertical spindle driven by clockwork, the ingeniously assembled concoction of lamb known as doner kebab. Cursing, he borrowed a spoonful of glowing embers from the oven where the pita bread was to be baked, and that solved his problem. Satisfied, he dipped a branch of rosemary in oil to baste the meat.

"What do you think?" Ismail inquired, walking at Djinghiz's side the length of the former courtyard.

"You've made not one fortune since I went away, but two."

"A lucky chance enabled me to purchase the houses on the other side of the yard, and the investment has proved, as I hoped, quite profitable. . . . Do you want to patronize our hammam? The rosebud will unpack for you and have your laundry done, and bring fresh garments in your size."

"It sounds," Djinghiz said sincerely, "more and more like a foretaste of Paradise. Especially if someone will fetch me a drink."

"Don't tell me, let me guess. You've been in the East. Did you develop a taste for koumiss?"

"Fermented mare's milk? Traditional it may be, but—no! Do you have any rice wine? That can be drunk at hammam temperature."

"We stock it for Japanese visitors. This way."

Stretched out infinitely at his ease while a muscular masseur squeezed and pounded months of stiffness from his body, Djinghiz said, "I could purr like a cat!"

"In here, you may purr as much as you like," Ismail said from an adjacent bench, naked save for a towel. The temperature of the hammam was near boiling point. "Tibor—" Nodding at the masseur, he set two fingers to his lips and pinched.

Ah. Deaf and/or dumb, thought Djinghiz. Ismail had acquired a reputation for good works because he was prepared to hire disabled people. Many were the lame and hunchbacked who had found their first employment in his kitchens—if only peeling vegetables or washing dishes—and some education with it; many were the grateful spies, in consequence, who kept him apprised of what went on throughout the city.

After all, Ismail too was handicapped.

Though not in his wits. He added after a moment, "As to purring, though: I wish you could have bridled your tongue until you arrived here where it's safe to talk freely. Our market is, I grant you, one of the most remarkable sights in the world. *But.*"

"I don't know what came over me," the younger man said sheepishly.

"I know only too well!"—in a tone of sharp reproof. "You're proud of what you've achieved and eager to spread the news! But where do you want to wind up? Before a firing squad? Down an alley with a dagger in your back?"

"Worse thing have been done to my people!"

"Worse things have been done to my person. And here I am."

The words hung in the air like steam. Eventually Ismail judged that the point had sunk home, and spoke again.

"What of your fellow-travelers' reaction to my offer of hospitality? Amusing, was it not?"

Relieved at the change of subject, because he was still too young to contemplate a rational discussion of his own demise, Djinghiz said, "You could practically hear Paluka's mind working, couldn't you?"

"You mean when he was deciding whether to ask how I knew about the 'interesting passengers'?"

"Mm-hm." Djinghiz reached for the sake jug and refilled his thimble-size cup.

"In your view, what's the question most likely to be on their minds at the moment?"

The younger man pondered, sipping.

"I think you've convinced them you're a genuine eccentric. If not, I'm sure the rosebuds will finish the job. I assume you've primed them with amusing stories about previous visitors?"

"Of course. Most of them by the way true, albeit a trifle embellished." Ismail chuckled, and the rolls of fat around his belly shook in rhythm.

"In that case . . . Hmm! This hadn't struck me until now, but the tiredness is being beaten out of my mind as well as my body." Rolling over, signaling to Tibor, he indicated that his right thigh needed more attention.

In a musing tone he continued, "I suspect they may be wondering what makes me such an interesting traveler."

"Ah, you're Kraków-born. We're old friends. I knew your parents, didn't I?"

"On any given day at least a handful of expatriate Cracovians must by the law of averages be visiting their natal city. Over the course of a year the total must be hundreds at least. Why should you pick on Djinghiz—on me—out of that many? I'm not from an 'exotic locale'!"

"As I said: an old friend. Although . . ." Ismail rubbed his multiple chins, looking rueful. "You have a point, I confess. I'll bear it in mind. Now!" He briskened. "Do I get to hear how you accomplished your mission? Or is it a professional secret?"

"You might put it like that."

Djinghiz grinned to himself, fully expecting that Ismail would proceed to wheedling and cajoling, and fully intending to explain in due course, for he was consumed with the urge to brag about his ingenuity to the one person in the world in whom he could safely confide. Moreover, he was anxious to know what Ismail had meant about the war "of a most unusual kind," and assumed this exchange would lead to an explanation.

However—

"Do you intend to pursue that profession full-time?"

The question was so remote from what he had anticipated that Djinghiz sat up, brushing Tibor aside. Although he had yet to rub down his client, Ismail signaled the masseur to depart. Throwing a towel at Djinghiz, he said, "I take it you would rather not answer with anyone else in earshot. Very sensible. There's always the risk that even somebody profoundly deaf may learn to lip-read."

"I'd rather not answer at all!"—indignantly. "What a thing to say!"

"Then what do you plan to do with the rest of your life, now you've accomplished what since childhood has been your most burning ambition?"

And, while Djinghiz was still mentally reeling from the shock of that even more unexpected question, Ismail heaved himself up, wobbling like a badly strutted dirigible.

"Slava and his—ah—companion should be succumbing to the blandishments of my rosebuds about now. I want to be clad and present when they get here."

"Wait!" Djinghiz implored. "*I* want to know what you meant when you said a war already—"

"My dear boy!" Ismail fluttered his eyelashes in a way that in his youth had monstrously impressed his numerous suitors. "I sit here like a spider in a web, receiving news in telegraphic form, crudely abridged. You, on the other hand, were on the spot. You were the one who moved the Gate of Worlds."

"I did, didn't I?" said Djinghiz huskily. The awesome fact of what he'd accomplished, the amazing fact that he was here to speak of it, came close to overwhelming him anew, and shivers racked his spine.

And I was so looking forward to describing what I did!

Yet he was able, a heartbeat later, to regain his usual insouciance.

"But it was you, Ismail, who oiled the hinges!"

"For that, I will take credit. . . . Go get dressed! It might amuse you to witness what I have in mind for Slava.

"Bear in mind, though, that—like the war—his fate may manifest in a peculiar form."

Four: Thorns

In the lobby the business typical of a well-reputed hostelry on the first cold evening of the winter continued as normal. Prospective clients arrived; some were accorded lodging, others were advised to apply elsewhere. Servants entered, shaking snow from caps and cloaks, to inquire whether their employers might dine here tonight; some were granted reservations, others wishing to bring too large a party were politely turned away. Ensconced on a canopied divan swung from a frame, mistakable for customers awaiting friends, Djinghiz and Ismail watched the passing show. It still lacked forty minutes of the time the latter had set for dinner with his "guests."

Just as Djinghiz had concluded that the place must by now be full save one room reserved for Slava and Hideki (and while she, poor brat, well deserved a comfortable bed by herself, in his view her owner deserved to freeze in the gutter!), something happened to disabuse him. A young couple entered, the boy with his arm around the girl, both in snow-soaked black, each carrying a carpetbag, his yellow and hers blue. Her face was covered with a yashmak, but her large eloquent eyes darted from her companion to Djinghiz; to Ismail; to the clerks at reception, the rosebuds, two other clients asking directions to a concert hall . . .

Summoning his courage, the boy approached the desk and under his breath murmured a half-audible request.

Ismail signaled one of the girl rosebuds. She bent her ear to his lips, nodded, ran to reception where the young people's passports were being inspected, asked two rapid questions and returned.

Ismail pondered a second, then signaled affirmation.

All this went unseen by the couple. But instantly their carpetbags were being carried up the stairway. Seeming unable to believe their luck, they rushed after, almost colliding with a Teuton family descending en masse.

Djinghiz said sourly, "Turkish runaways?"

"Mm-hm." Ismail's face was expressionless. "Both from rich families; both doomed to arranged marriages in order to increase their parents' wealth . . . but not, of course, with each other. And both students of the University of Istanbul. Which is, one must admit, performing sterling service in the cause of freedom."

"You knew all that—?"

"Just by looking at them?" Ismail chuckled. "Hardly! Turkish passports are difficult to forge, and it's hideously expensive to buy one in a false name. I'm assuming they presented their real ones, in which case—"

"In which case you'll have a hold over their families!" Djinghiz snapped.

Ismail regarded him coolly. "You have reason to hate Russians. I have reason to hate the Ottomans. Puppy-love doesn't last. I doubt theirs will survive this escapade, don't you? But if in two or ten years' time some pot-bellied Stamboulian learns his daughter has been shamed by bedding with the son of his most hated rival—"

He broke off.

"More of that another time," he murmured. "Here come the stray fish, or, if you'd rather, birds."

Djinghiz's heart pounded. What snare had this unpredictable yet ultimately honorable man contrived for loathsome Slava? He rose and turned, trembling with anticipation.

And found himself once more confounded.

Just as when he himself had arrived, along with his chance companions, other guests were in the lobby: to wit the Teuton family, consisting of one elderly couple, another in their forties—daughter and husband, or son and wife—and four teenage children, variously inquiring about entertainment, transportation, and, inevitably, what bargains could be found in the great market after the arrival of the first train from Asia in six months.

They glanced around; they checked; they stared in disbelief as the tall one-eyed commissionaire escorted the newcomers toward the reception desk. Arrogant, dirty, hand on the hilt of a knife that he wore conspicuously at his belt, all his other visible belongings in a greasy black bag slung across his back, here indeed came Slava. And, beside him, poor Hideki, who seemed to possess nothing bar what she stood up in. When Djinghiz first set eyes on her she had worn a richly embroidered kimono of dark blue silk with dragons writhing up the back. Her sash, her obi, had been of brilliant crimson. Now—if she retained them—they were hidden under a coat of coarse brown stuff sodden with wet. For want of headgear her elegant coiffure, held in place with six bejeweled pins, was collapsing around her shoulders, while her tiny delicate feet, once silken-slippered, were crammed into clumsy felt boots that left smeared wet patches at every step.

Under huge dark eyes pale cheeks glistened with melting snowflakes . . . or were they not more likely to be tears?

Djinghiz would have jumped to his feet and called out the Balt despite his ready knife, but for the plump restraining hand that closed on his wrist and held him still for long enough to realize—

Oh, if I believed in a god I would beg forgiveness! Will the day ever dawn when I learn to trust another's judgment?

—that the commissionaire was not escorting Slava.

At which point he had to struggle to stop himself from laughing.

Making certain that what they did was registered by all present, those of the staff—and particularly the rose-buds—who were not immediately occupied with other customers closed on Hideki, bowing. Slava slipped the strap of his bag off his shoulder, obviously expecting that it would be taken from him. Instead, he was ignored, even by—no, especially by!—Ismail, hauling himself out of his chair.

He spoke in a language Djinghiz had scarcely heard.

Can it be—? It must be! Japanese!

For the thin pale face lighted up as though one of the

newfangled Teuton gas lights had been ignited behind it, and two little hands clutched at Ismail's sleeve, while a hoarse shrill voice replied.

And was answered.

And two rosebuds converged, making clucking noises like a mother hen over a wet chick, as Ismail issued crisp instructions. His honor was to be taken to the reserved room, bathed, given fresh raiment (Djinghiz noted in passing the deliberate archaism of his speech, but afterwards was unsure which of the many languages they both understood had been in use at what moment) and brought to join the rest of the company at dinner, in—now—half an hour.

The rosebuds complied.

And Slava was still standing there, his mouth agape like a new-caught carp.

He said, muddling Russian and Turkish and maybe a good few other vocabularies into a barely comprehensible stew:

"What about me? Don't I get any sort of a look-in?"

Ismail, donning a sleepy smile, turned to him.

"Ah, yes. Well, it would be better if you were clean, at least . . ."

And snapped his fingers. One of the porters behind the reception desk, a burly youth who doubtless had been a rosebud a few years ago, indicated to Slava that he was to follow, but made no attempt to relieve him of his bag.

For a moment Djinghiz thought the Balt might lose his temper at this sort of treatment . . . but he was too cold and weary. Shoulders slumping, he let himself be led toward the part of the hostelry where servants and coachmen were lodged.

After him, Ismail called: "If you wish to join Hideki

and my other guests at dinner, you may! But be quick! And by then be clean!''

And turned to Djinghiz. Puzzled, the younger man whispered: ''You said, did you not: *his* honor?''

''Ah. Just as I thought. You're not as observant as you like to pretend.''

''But I spent six months trapped with them at the—''

Ismail glared. ''And never bothered to look twice at Hideki!''

''Why should I have paid attention to that bastard's underage whore?''

''Because in Japanese *Hideki* is not a girl's name. It's a boy's.''

Ismail let the words rankle for a long reproving moment. Then, uttering a harsh laugh, he clapped Djinghiz on the shoulder.

''You're forgiven. You've had other things on your mind than visiting the theater. But if you'd bothered to watch a performance by the Kabuki troupe Hideki worked for, you'd have noticed that in that tradition all the female roles are played by boys. Or men. Some of them continue until my age.''

''Are they—?'' Djinghiz had to swallow hard.

''Are they treated as I was? Not so far as I know. Dialogue is relatively unimportant in Kabuki. But they are, I understand, not infrequently—ah—used by their seniors. . . . You have something else on your mind. What?''

''Why 'his honor'? Just to annoy Slava?''

''That,'' Ismail said in his most sanctimonious and infuriating tone, ''you will have to wait till after dinner to find out. Speaking of dinner, I must check on how it's coming along. Fancy a peep behind the scenes?''

"Not particularly," Djinghiz sighed. "But it might save me from running after Slava and beating him to pulp."

"How inelegant," Ismail murmured. "One of these days you'll realize violence is never desirable and very seldom unavoidable. . . . This way!"

Dinner was to be taken in a private room on the second floor, overlooking through large half-curtained windows the main restaurant in what had been the courtyard, where early clients were already being served.

Up here waiters were arranging cutlery, dishes of ice containing jugs of wine and fruit juice, and bowls of—naturally—roses on an oblong table spread first with a thick Bokhara rug, then with a white lace cloth. To sit on, there were firm fat cushions covered in a fabric that matched the rug. A hoist set in the wall permitted full dishes to be raised from the kitchen below and empty ones returned. A hookah waited on a low wooden stand, rose petals floating in its glass belly.

Nodding approval, Ismail walked around the room to the far corner, where between the curtains he glanced down towards the dais where his musicians were assembling—Gypsies, by the look of them. Pushing the window open, he attracted their leader's attention with a whistle and a wave. Recognizing him with a start, the man ordered the band to pick up their instruments, and they launched into a lively air. Judging its volume with a cock of his head, Ismail adjusted the window to admit enough of the music to be pleasant, not so much as to interfere with conversation, and summoned one of the waiters to close the curtains.

"Well, it's time," he said at length. "We might as well sit down. Take the place at the east end, facing me . . . I wonder which of the guests will show up first."

Five: The Meaning of the Symbol

A FEW MOMENTS LATER DJINGHIZ REALIZED WHAT HE should have known already, and would, had not half his mind still been preoccupied with the mystery of the war that "had already begun": Ismail actually had no need to speculate in what order his guests would arrive, for he had given orders and—as ever—they were being obeyed.

In the interim, waiting for the door to open, he found himself wondering for the latest of uncountable times what sort of person Ismail was. If he had been forced to sum up his impression in a single sentence, he would have said, "I think of him as an actor."

For, long as they had known each other, he could never be sure whether he was seeing the real Ismail, or some mask that he was adopting because it suited his current purpose.

Of course, he too had been obliged to play roles often

enough, to disguise if not himself, then his origins and his intentions . . . especially the latter. But doing so was not at all to his taste. That was why he had been disappointed when Ismail denied him the chance to boast of his achievement; it would have been a compensation. Yet he could not be angry about that. He trusted the older man. Had to. Had always had to—or at least since his teens. And so far he had never been let down.

Ismail compared himself to a spider at the center of its web. That makes the guests tonight his prey, to be sucked dry of information like flies of their vital juices. But where does that leave me? What am I to him?

Am I perhaps the son he could never have?

The insight sparked at the edge of his mind in the same instant as the door opened and a deferential rosebud ushered in the first three of their dinner companions: Feisal, Paluka, and—coming third with ostentatious humility—Ratanayaka, whom Ismail placed at Djinghiz's left, with Paluka facing him. Feisal he seated at his own left. Djinghiz felt a stir of puzzlement. Given what he knew of Slava's nature, it was entirely likely that he would overindulge in the wine and become quarrelsome, yet by the way the table was laid it looked as though he would now be seated at Ismail's right (why in the world?), with Hideki between the two other men. Was this for protection, in case Slava vented his ill temper on him? He was capable of it, Djinghiz felt sure. Therefore it made better sense to put him next to Paluka, who could hold him down with one finger.

Surely Ismail wasn't intending to seat him between Ratanayaka, an avowed pacifist, and himself, who expressed such contempt for violence . . . ?

No. He wasn't. For here came Hideki, transformed,

accompanied by the girl rosebud who had taken him in charge and wearing, save the turban, identical garb. Djinghiz repressed an oath. In this attire it was impossible to mistake the sex of the young Japanese despite his still long hair. The shape of the throat alone, with its newly prominent Adam's apple—!

Whereas his companion was developing in totally different areas.

There was no time to waste, though, on reproaching himself for his blindness. Immediately on spotting Ismail, Hideki had dropped to his knees and was approaching him in what ought to have been a clumsy, even ridiculous manner, rather like scuttling very slowly, and making obeisance every few seconds. Yet, because it was done with all the dignity of the theatrical tradition in which he had been trained, it was curiously impressive, indeed moving. No one could have mistaken the action for other than what it was: an expression of respect and gratitude.

Far better acquainted with the customs of Japan than anybody had a right to be who had never visited those strange and far-off islands, Ismail waited until the boy was within arm's reach and making a final bow so deep his forehead rested on the carpeted floor. Then, with surprising agility for so heavy a man, he rose to his feet in a single smooth motion, with a gesture invited Hideki also to stand, and in his turn performed a sweeping bow, as though before a sultan or a czar.

A grunt of annoyance sounded from behind Djinghiz. He glanced over his shoulder. There in the doorway, rendered presentable by the ministrations of Ismail's staff—and, incidentally, deprived of his dagger—was Slava with a face like thunder. To him Ismail accorded no more than a nod acknowledging his presence, and a waiter ushered him to the place between Feisal and Paluka while Ismail himself fussed over Hideki and made sure he was comfortable.

It was clear that the other three were even more mystified than he was by these odd goings-on. Well, in due time they would no doubt all discover what their purpose was . . .

"Pray do not consider our seating arrangements tonight in the context of precedence," Ismail murmured, resuming his own place. "It is for convenience. Ratanayaka effendi is as you know a vegetarian, and in Japan little use is made of meat, although much fish is eaten; therefore it seems sensible to place these two together where they can share appropriate dishes."

As though that were more than just the beginning of an explanation, the others relaxed. Ismail clapped his hands and a waiter hastened to pour wine and water, while two others brought in the first course, serving the Orientals first. They were given beans cooked in a sauce fragrant with herbs, mushrooms with cream, baby turnips glazed with sugar or possibly honey, a grilled carp sprinkled with almonds, and sweet peppers stuffed with rice and raisins. Also, of course, baskets of pita bread, almost too hot to touch, were placed along the table. For the meat-eaters came slices of succulent doner kebab, broiled lamb cutlets, quinces stuffed with minced lamb in honey sauce, and a chicken boiled with lemons and almonds after the Circassian style, appearing intact but already jointed in the kitchen so one needed only fingers to divide it.

Ratanayaka, surveying the spread, heaved a loud sigh. "Gospodin Ismail," he said before touching the food placed before him, "your charity is indeed a great work.

I must express my thanks for such a meal as I have not enjoyed in many months.''

Hideki also uttered something, in Japanese—presumably the same kind of compliment. Ismail, though he smiled, waved it aside and raised his winecup, waiting for the others to do the same. They imitated him, even Slava, though it was obvious he would rather have grabbed at the food straight away.

''To a memorable evening,'' the host proposed, and they all dutifully drank, even Ratanayaka, although after one sip he set his wine aside and continued only with water.

''And now—'' Ismail ceremoniously offered bread to Hideki, and the waiters did the same to the others. Released from the bonds of politeness, Slava seized the nearest leg of the chicken and, disdaining cutlery, stripped it to the bare bone within seconds, then snatched a lamb cutlet and a piece of bread and gobbled as though trying to choke himself.

Seeming offended by the behavior of their chance companion, Feisal and Paluka ate with greater neatness and reserve, but displayed just as much appetite—as did Djinghiz when he finally managed to put aside for the time being the mystery of Hideki.

Before tackling the sherbets that followed, delicate concoctions of fruit pulp whipped with artificial snow, and the red apples and Georgian or possibly Persian peaches of so pale a yellow they were almost white that succeeded them, all of them had recourse at least once to the closet of ease in the far corner of the room. Warmth and wine and the seductive music from below combined to generate a mood of relaxation. Even Slava forgot the grievances he had been nursing. Indeed he was the first to transform the stilted conversation which accompanied the meal into a free and easy mode such as might obtain among real friends. Unable to contain a monstrous burp, he made a laughing apology and took it as his cue to recount what he said was a Nordic folktale, extremely coarse but indubitably very funny. Even Paluka looked more kindly on him after that—even Djinghiz, to his own surprise.

Most astonishing of all, even Hideki relaxed. Ismail had to translate the punch-line, and the young Japanese then proceeded to enact it, in dumb show, the way a Kabuki actor would have illustrated the story without the need for words. If anything, it was funnier than the original.

Yet, so far, nothing of importance had been said. The host's avowed intention of hearing travelers' tales was unfulfilled.

Abruptly Djinghiz realized they were alone. The waiters had vanished. The table had been cleared save for their goblets, dishes of fruit and loukoumi, the roses, and the hookah, which was uttering aromatic smoke through its several mouthpieces. Feisal, Paluka even Ratanayaka were partaking along with Ismail, though Hideki declined as did he himself, it not being a habit he had learned to enjoy. It felt as though it must be very late, yet it could not be, for they had started their meal comparatively early. Besides, the music from below was continuing, and one might guess that now it was accompanying a belly dancer, for it was frequently punctuated by applause and the sound of breaking crockery. But the sound seemed peculiarly far away, muffled as though by deep snow.

A gust of wind whistled under the eaves, and Ratanayaka—who had contributed little to the talk so far—

said suddenly, "I wonder if the kiteway worked this year."

The others turned inquiringly to him. Seeming embarrassed to find himself the center of attention, he went on, "Perhaps it means nothing to you: the kiteway?"

Certainly it meant nothing to Djinghiz. He looked at Ismail, who was glancing politely from one to other of the company, and read from his plump face that he knew what was meant.

Typical!

"Ah, it would have been a great achievement," Ratanayaka sighed. "You are perhaps aware that in my part of the world—that is, more exactly, further north on the subcontinent of Ind—there are two main seasons known by a name that means 'steady wind': *monsoon*. For part of the year it blows east to west, for the other part the opposite direction."

"Ah, we have indeed heard of that," said Feisal. "But I never thought of Ind as a land of kites. China, now, and in particular Japan—"

"But these were to be kites of a different and special kind," Ratanayaka interrupted. "There was a man at the court of the King of the Mahrut, who conceived a plan for moving goods and even people over land instead of sending them around by sea. His idea was to build a sort of track, not exactly a railway but with wagons running on a bed of carved stone, to be towed by kites—huge strings of them, up to a dozen maybe—during one season in one direction, during the other, the opposite."

It occurred to Djinghiz that for someone so abstemious Ratanayaka sounded remarkably like a man whose tongue had been loosened by liquor. Had there been something in the food, in the hookah, in the very air of the room? There were all sorts of perfumes that could mask it—

But at this point Ismail put in a word.

"Ah, I believe one has heard of this project. Was the name of its inventor Babu Ram Dass?"

"It was indeed!" Ratanayaka exclaimed, and gave his host a look eloquent of respect for his peculiar knowledge.

"I am most interested! Pray continue!" Ismail took a sip of wine. "If I dare say so, I doubt you Lankhans were in favor. Would it not have reduced the reliance of your northern neighbors on the ships that earn so much for your island people?"

"Think you that I have much love for seafaring?" Pulling a face, Ratanayaka launched into a description of his miserable experiences aboard ship, when, he said, no matter what he ate he was obliged to renew acquaintance with it, and there always seemed to be something in what came up again that he could not possibly have ingested . . .

By the time he finished he had them almost weeping with laughter. Slava, his former anger quite forgotten, slapped the table with an open palm and declared that he would like to see Hideki imitate that in dumb show, adding in an almost shamefaced tone that if he'd realized how clever a student of the profession he was separating from his fellow actors, he'd have settled for keeping his mah-jongg winnings intact.

Well, I suppose that's as near as a fellow of his stamp will ever come to apologizing . . .

But Ismail was guiding the conversation back to the main subject, the kiteway, and Ratanayaka, wiping his cheeks, was saying:

"Yes, you were right, of course. The Lankhans were less than enthusiastic. But there was no need to worry."

"Why?"

A shrug. "The monsoon failed for the first time in living memory. The king was so angry, he ordered Babu Ram Dass crushed to death beneath the wheels of one of his useless wagons."

There was a sudden chilly silence. As though regretting what he had said (Djinghiz wondered why, because everyone knew how cruel the Kings of Mahrut were), Ratanayaka reached blindly for one of the cups before him and drank a healthy swig, not caring that it held wine rather than water.

Sensing more clearly than the others the nature of his reaction, Ismail reached across the table to the nearest bowlful of roses. Selecting a particularly handsome bloom, bright red at its petal tips, almost white at its heart, he contemplated it musingly.

The music from below died away, as though he had given an unheard order, then resumed, but far more softly.

At length he said, not raising his eyes from the flower, "The sign of this house is the rose. There is an ancient tradition attached to it. I wonder whether it's a symbol you're acquainted with."

Having indulged in more wine than was commensurate with adherence to the laws of the Prophet—which allowed none at all—Feisal hiccuped.

"Sounds like my field of study! If, as I take it, you mean a certain Roman custom?"

"I do indeed!" Ismail beamed avuncularly.

"We're not on land that Romans ever ruled!"

"What difference does that make? Were your beliefs

less strongly held while in Shinto Japan or Christian Russia? Are Ratanayaka effendi's, here where Islam was so long dominant and still preponderates? Is Djinghiz's contempt for all religions affected by his current location?''

Having thus contrived to arrange for three people to answer him at once, he sat back smugly and waited for one clear voice to emerge from the confusion. Even as he spoke up in reply, Djinghiz found himself envying more than ever this fat old man's ability to manipulate those around him. Whereupon a strange thought crossed his mind:

Maybe I ought to study with him, find out whether such a trick is teachable. I could see it being very useful . . .

Then the clear voices emerged: not one, but two. The first was Hideki's.

''Gospodin Ismail, it is true that the official religion of Japan is Shinto. More important, though, in the daily life of my people, is the Buddhism I share with the holy man at my right.''

Ismail bowed acknowledgment of the correction, but went on waiting. His eyes, half-hidden by the suety rolls of fat that were his eyelids, were—Djinghiz could tell—focused on Paluka . . .

Who duly spoke up, having said very little during dinner because his mouth was otherwise occupied. Djinghiz had heard tales about the vast quantities of food that Japanese wrestlers could put away; what he regarded as a meal, it was reported, they would dismiss as a mere snack. For the first time he had seen proof of the fact, albeit in the person of not a Japanese but a Hawaiian. Without appearing in the least discourteous, let alone greedy, Paluka had engulfed enough for three ordinary men.

And, contentedly reposing on his digestion, was saying:

"Earlier on I mentioned that I am ill acquainted with European history. Be so kind as to enlighten me concerning this Roman custom."

"Why!" Ismail returned. "In any house, or any room, where a rose was placed above the door, those within might reveal their inmost hearts, free from fear of retribution. No matter what they said, it must remain in confidence, and punishment awaited those who broke the seal."

He glanced at Ratanayaka.

"Some of their punishments, by the way, were worse than what the King of Mahrut inflicted on your bold inventor."

Renewed silence. At last Paluka gave a harsh laugh.

"I'll speak my mind anywhere! It's not the custom of my people to dissimulate or lie! Openness is all!"

"You've never used a feint in wrestling?" said Ismail, feigning, himself, wry innocence. Paluka blinked.

"Ah . . . Well, I regard that as a different matter!"

"Yes, I'm sure you do." Ismail tossed the rose into the air. How it was done, not even Djinghiz could tell, who had seen the portly man perform similar tricks in the past, but it darted upward to the ceiling and remained there. In the same instant, the last vestige of sound from outside died away, except the recurrent growling of the wind.

"Now!" Ismail said with unexpected briskness. "If you are persons of honor, and I'm sure you are, it's time to pay for your dinner."

"I said I would take travelers' tales in trade. We have heard from our Lankhan friend, and—in a sense—from Hideki also, although he used no words in the telling. Who will be next?"

Six: Ramblers

BRIEFLY DJINGHIZ WONDERED WHETHER—INDEED hoped that—this was the moment Ismail had appointed for him to brag of his deeds. He tensed as words rose to his lips, yet instinctively he bit them back, fearing with half his mind that even under the sign of the rose it was too risky. And his reaction proved to be the right one, even though none of the others ventured to speak up.

Instead, having waited a long moment, Ismail resumed in a musing tone.

"Perhaps you mistrust my promise of secrecy. It's no wonder, if you never before encountered the symbol of the rose. Besides, you no doubt still regard me as a stranger. Let me speak a while of myself, therefore. I shall do my utmost"—inclining his head towards Paluka—"to live up to your ideal of openness."

Leaning back, drawing now and then on the hookah,

his eyes focusing on some point far away in time as well as space, he began in his high yet resonant voice to recount a story Djinghiz already knew, that of his journey from Istanbul to Kraków and the reasons behind it.

Listening as attentively as the others, as though he too were hearing it for the first time, he felt a shiver crawl down his spine at the emotionless tone of the words, the apparent absence of resentment, the bald detachment he displayed, as though these terrible events had happened to someone else, a virtual stranger.

He told how his father, whose only son he was, had run afoul of powerful rivals at the Sublime Porte; how they had schemed and plotted to bring about his downfall, and succeeded, so that in the end the Sultan ordered the bowstring put about his neck, and for fear he might become a later focus of rebellion sent the boy to this city which at the time had still been an outlying corner of the Ottoman Empire. Later, when word was sent that he had entered puberty, it was decreed that he must be shorn of his nascent manhood so greatly did the Sultan still fear his years-dead courtier, for no reason save a pack of cunning lies.

The Sultan died; his successor withdrew his armies from Poland; the boy contrived to remain in Kraków, living under the protection of wealthy old men with a taste for pretty youths. When he could no longer attract such patrons he fell in with Darko, who then owned this hostelry, and—as Djinghiz had already reminded himself—not only restored it to its former glory but made it one of the most famous in the world . . . among, at least, the monied and discerning. That part of his narrative, however, he summed up in a couple of sentences, concluding with, "And here I am, as you see me."

Yet that was not the ending. As though the recital of his life story had provoked deeper reflections, he went on in so low a voice it was scarcely audible.

"There is, I often suspect, more than a grain of truth in that teaching to which our friends on my right adhere: the notion that there are inexorable trends and patterns in events."

Djinghiz almost blurted a contradiction. Had he not, himself, and recently, so acted as to break the pattern—to move the Gate of Worlds so that history adopted a new course? But perhaps that was not the point Ismail was driving at. He forced himself to be patient, and his guess was confirmed.

"Some, too, would of course maintain that whatever we puny human beings set out to accomplish, we can never overrule the will of Allah." Ismail's gaze, Djinghiz noticed, was fixed without seeming to be fixed on Feisal—whose lips, most curiously, did not move in response to mention of the Deity. Even those less than obsessively devout were conditioned from childhood to append some such phrase as "may his name be exalted." Djinghiz himself had taken years to conquer the habit.

Suddenly, however, as though recollecting himself, the Ethiopian reacted. What he uttered was a soundless whisper, but it seemed to satisfy Ismail, who continued.

"They would say—would they not?—that despite our boldest efforts the course of events laid down by the All-Knowing, who is infinitely patient, will sooner or later resume. Who save he can know the purpose of the world? For example . . ."

Their attention was riveted on him now; they were following every word as though listening to a great mullah. Infuriatingly, he took a slow deliberate pull on the hookah before completing his remark.

"For example: you will recall my mentioning on the way here that four kings and an emperor once dined in Kraków, at a house which is now a coal-merchant's shop. What might have been the outcome had their plans not been aborted by the Black Death, Allah alone knows. Conceivably the time was not ripe. Conceivably it's ripe now, after centuries. What say you all?"

Djinghiz was expecting Feisal to speak up, in an effort to cover his gaffe of a moment ago. Instead, Slava—who had indulged more freely in the wine than the rest—gave a snort as though trying to laugh but failing.

"What I say is that we live once and have to make the best of our single chance! According to the tales of my people, not even the old gods could escape their doom. If they failed in wisdom, failed in virtue, failed in the pursuit of righteousness, their time too would end, and there would have to be a new creation. Perhaps it happened; who can say? But in my part of the world there have been few signs of divinity of late."

"Was it in search of them that you left home?" Ismail prompted.

Slava sighed. "In a way, I suppose," he muttered. "In my youth I wandered from the Baltic to the Bosporus, looking for something to believe in, something that might lend me hope. I never found it. In the end I came to trust nothing but the swiftness of my blade and the blind laws of chance."

"Which you have never been averse from—shall we say?—helping a little."

Slava's face contorted with sudden rage. His hand fell

to his side. Not finding his knife, he controlled himself. In a thick voice he said, "Were I not a guest under your roof, and disarmed, I'd make you pay for that, innkeeper! Yours was a touching story, I must grant, but you have no conception what it's like for a landless man trying to survive in this harsh world!"

"You were, I take it, once the lord of an estate?"

"Yes, that I was!" Slava slapped the table so hard he made the goblets ring. "Or should have been, but that my false brother and my accursed wife conspired to rob and disinherit me! All they left me was one ship, that might as well have borne me to the sunset on a pyre!"

"Your passport," Ismail murmured, "calls you a Balt and an amber merchant. But you're a Norseman, nobly born."

His eyes were suddenly wide open, and so piercing they seemed to cast beams of brilliant light. Before that stare all hope of lying melted. Sullen, not understanding how he could have been exposed, Slava let his shoulders slump.

"Ah, for me it's always Fimbulwinter. There is no more warmth or sunshine in my life . . . Yes! You see before you him who once was Erik, Jarl of Odinshavn, whose ships plied the northern reaches of the Ocean Sea, to the fishing grounds of Dogger and Vinland itself! I took revenge for what was stolen from me, but it wasn't sweet."

"In other words," Ismail said, somewhat less softly than before, "the blood-oath has been sworn against you, and the wergild has never been paid."

"Oh, I've tried. Don't think I haven't tried!" Slava-Erik drained his wine savagely, and Ismail refilled the goblet with impassive face. "That was what I wanted most and what I failed in worst. To think I've been reduced to gambling—not always honestly; you're right; I was driven to it after my sole remaining ship was wrecked—and worse still hiring out my young companions in stews! I who was a landed jarl! I disgust myself! And most recently of all, when I thought I had the chance to recoup my fortunes and my honor at a single blow, I was cheated yet again!"

"This time, by whom?"

"I do not know. But this I swear: should ever I find out, I'll make it my last act on earth to slay him instead!"

Instead? Instead of whom?

But before Djinghiz could voice the question, Ismail had said with abrupt sternness, "Even if he were under this roof now?"

"Nothing would stop me! Not the knowledge that I'd die a heartbeat later!"

"Wrong—I would stop you," rumbled Paluka. His right hand had closed on Slava's shoulder with the speed of a striking snake, and was pressing so hard it forced a grunt of pain from the smaller man. "Good manners do not permit one to behave so on premises where he is a guest. Besides, you said you have found vengeance far from sweet."

He released Slava warily. Rubbing his shoulder, the latter subsided unwillingly and took refuge in more wine.

"That was courteous of you, effendi," Ismail murmured. "Especially since you yourself, I imagine, have reason to hold a grudge or two."

Paluka looked him straight in the eyes. They were back to their normal half-closed state between their suety lids. After a moment he said, "I don't know what on earth you mean."

"Why"—and another intolerable pause while Ismail drew again on the hookah—"it cannot be easy for you to live as a man without a history."

For an instant Djinghiz feared the huge Hawaiian was going to scramble to his feet and fling the table bodily at Ismail. But his training as a wrestler must have stood him in good stead; a wrestler who loses his temper risks losing the bout.

Calming himself with such effort that the veins on his neck stood out like cords, he said, "You will explain. Do not do it in such a way as to tempt me to infringe the code of hospitality."

"If I have done so," Ismail said, bowing his chin to his ample chest, "forgive me, but I have only complied with the police regulations—though the matter will go no further."

"My passport?"

"Yes, your passport."

"I see. Well, it passed muster in Russia, but here . . . I suppose you have extra reason to be careful about strangers."

The others were patently bewildered. Hideki started to ask a question, but thought better of it.

Eventually Paluka heaved a mountainous sigh. "Ah, you have the sharpest eyes I ever ran across. Sharp as our navigators' in the days before we had the compass."

Insight flashed lightning bright in Djinghiz's mind.

Of course! He's not Hawaiian at all! He's—!

"But I thought you were all tattooed!" he exclaimed.

Paluka turned a burning gaze on him. "So usually we are. Do you know what purpose the tattooing serves?"

Djinghiz shook his head dumbly.

"Your fat friend does." Turning his head: "Will you enlighten him?"

Ismail's face showed pity. He said, "If what I have been told is accurate, it's not mere decoration. It's a statement of identity, which includes a record of one's lineage. Your case is a strange one, possibly unique. You were not deprived of it. You were denied it. There must be a reason."

"It is not one I'm ashamed of!"

"On the contrary. I suspect it is the sign of a very brave man."

Breathing heavily, Paluka relaxed. After a pause he took up his goblet and raised it in the gesture of a toast. Ismail copied him. Eyes locked, they drank together.

And then, just as everyone else was eagerly awaiting an explanation of this mysterious exchange, the host turned to Feisal.

"Your turn, I think, effendi. Have you nothing to tell us of the wonders of Edo? Few foreigners in history have gained access to the Imperial Palace, let alone the private apartments of the Mikado. Did you not see great marvels?"

"Why, yes!" Feisal exclaimed proudly, and launched into a lengthy description, salted with frequent references to his own remarkable scholarship. Hideki, eyes wide, hung on every word, hungry for news of his distant homeland.

But the others kept casting puzzled glances at Paluka, thinking so clearly it could be read on their faces:

A Maori without tattoos? Incredible!

Finally Feisal attained his peroration, and the loudness of his voice drew their attention back. He was declaring, "You might say I succeeded beyond the dreams of those who came in search of Prester John!"

Blank looks. But, as ever, Ismail got the point.

"Those Europeans, you mean, who believed in a priest-king in Ethiopia where rivers flowed with rubies and where the sand was gold dust? Ah, yes. Unlike you, they were disappointed. 'Prester John' turned out to be entirely mythical, and the letter—was it not sent to the Pope of Rome?—extolling his fabulous realm proved a forgery."

"Entirely mythical?" Feisal bridled. "Exaggerated, I grant, but there was indeed a great Christian kingdom in my country, and in time—"

He broke off, as though dismayed to hear his own words.

"In time it will be restored?" Ismail prompted.

I can't believe it! He's unmasking another pretender! Djinghiz clenched his fists in excitement.

"In time, I meant to say," Feisal forced out, "now the power of the Turks is waning, we can look forward to a new epoch of independence and prosperity."

"I see." Feisal glanced down at the hookah mouth-piece as though seeking inspiration. "Well, I'm sure we were all fascinated by your experiences in Edo. Now, Djinghiz!"

The young man tensed.

"What about telling us how you killed the Czar?"

Seven: The Wreath

THE SILENCE NOW WAS ABSOLUTE. WHILE FEISAL WAS talking the music had ceased, for the last diners were departing; afterwards there had been clanging sounds from the kitchen as resonant metal pans were washed and put away, but that too had ended and the air of the room was utterly still save for the echo of that amazing question.

It was like listening to the fall of snow.

Blinking, the others had all looked at Ismail as though suspecting a joke. When they realized he had spoken literally, they turned to Djinghiz. Their eyes seemed as dark and round as the gun muzzles of a firing squad.

So this was to be the audience for his moment of glory—this chance-met group of deceivers and impostors. Yes, all of them, for was not an actor a professional impostor, especially a boy trained to imitate women?

He had known all along that his achievement could never be shouted from the rooftops, or not in his lifetime at any rate. Even his own people must be kept from such a deadly secret, or someone might be tempted to vaunt the news abroad, thereby bringing swift and dreadful retribution. Everybody knew how brutally the great empires could treat a rebellious subject nation. In both Russia and the Ottoman lands there had once been proud peoples whose names were now no more than footnotes to history. In the New World too, according to what he had heard. Another folk had occupied the site of Mexico City, grandest metropolis on Earth, and had been—erased . . .

Yet he did at least have an audience, an audience of more than one. He didn't have to confide in Ismail alone. Suddenly he felt a vast wave of gratitude to the elderly eunuch. Pausing only to utter silently what, had he been religious, would have been a prayer concerning the security of the rose, he donned a sleepy smile.

"Rope of the same kind used to lash the bamboo trestles, with a loop partway across the bridge. A hook to snag the loop mounted under the observation car, so that the harder the engine pulled the faster it tore the bridge apart. The fire destroyed the evidence apart from the hook, but it was an ordinary coupling hook, worn and rusty although still sound, and during the construction of the bridge a load of spare parts had been spilled into the gorge."

"And how did you make good your escape?"—gratingly, from Slava.

"By not being there when it happened. Of course I'd have liked to witness the outcome, but it was safer not to. By then I was aboard a train on a branch line, cars from which were later included in the one we all arrived on today. I didn't ask how it was arranged. I can only say that we Tartars have been great wanderers throughout our history, and there are even, so I'm told, oceanic routes where nowadays we aren't unknown . . .

"Of course"—Djinghiz hesitated, swallowing, for this was the point he had least looked forward to admitting, but honesty compelled it—"they interrogated the maintenance gang. Tortured some of them, I guess. But they had no responsibility for the trestles, only the ballast and the permanent way. So in the end they were let go."

"Now most people suspect the Chinese?" Feisal offered.

"Apparently . . . Well, there you have it." Djinghiz sat back, waiting for Slava to attack him.

And indeed murder shone for an instant in the Norseman's face.

But it isn't mine.

Djinghiz knew it—how, he could not tell—even before Paluka's hand rose to hover warningly again over his neighbor's shoulder . . . in an absentminded sort of fashion, as though his concentration was on something else. It was as though a spell had been cast, transforming not just them but the whole world between one moment and the next. Sick with disappointment, the young man realized:

Ismail didn't merely "oil the hinges" of the Gate of Worlds. With me as his tool, he moved it. Now he's doing it again, right here in this room! How? How?

And, almost before the question had framed itself:

Now wouldn't that be something? Wouldn't it be a real achievement to possess powers like his?

Insofar as anything in this mirror-maze of a world can be called "real" . . .

Ismail was nodding at him. As if he could read his very thoughts, he wore the betraying look of smugness Djinghiz had this afternoon complained of.

The spider in the middle of the web . . . But this is no mere cobweb that he's spun. It's stronger than the rope I used to kill the Czar, stronger than the hawsers that can moor an ocean liner, stronger than anything.

How much of it is in our world, how much—elsewhere?

But that was far too frightening to contemplate.

"Thank you, Jarl Erik," Ismail was saying. "I knew the people at my table would be liars, but I also knew they'd not be fools."

"Am I not a fool?" Slava returned bitterly. "So simple—so effective!"

"But, for you, unreachable." Ismail tossed aside the hookah mouthpiece and leaned back, hands folded on his paunch. "You'd have had to be, as Djinghiz is, a Tartar, able to go among the remnants of his people in the eastern lands to which the Turks first, then the Russians, drove them, where now they follow humble occupations, farming and laboring, who once rode on the path of conquest even to the gates of Europe. You'd have had to pass for a dull-witted railroad worker resigned to the blows of his overseer's knout. I think your pride would have forced you to kill anyone who treated you that way—Yes, Djinghiz?"

The young man ventured, "Do I understand aright? Slava, or Erik, or whatever your name is: did you too plan to kill the Czar?"

Everyone except Ismail tensed noticeably. The

Norseman hesitated, but at length gave an almost imperceptible nod.

"You heard me say I had the chance to redeem my fortunes—earn enough, perhaps, to go home and pay the wergild for my wife and my brother. But I was forestalled. Now I know it was by you."

"Why then have you not kept your word to kill me?"

"Because now I understand why you did it. I'd become a hired assassin—lower, maybe, than a professional gambler, lower even than a child-prostitute's pimp. I thought I had the necessary motivation. But I dawdled. I missed two chances, maybe three. You, though!"

He threw back his head, and for the first time Djinghiz saw in his face some hint of the nobility he laid claim to.

"You did it! Simply and effectively! Not for your own sake, not for the sake of someone who would pay you well, but for your people. Am I right?"

Djinghiz's heart swelled so with pride that he could not utter a word in reply. Ismail spoke up on his behalf.

"You are. There sits the last pure-blood descendant of the last of the Tartar Khans. By right of inheritance, he should be his people's prince; by right of deeds, for he prevented Czar Vladimir from overrunning Kraków as he planned, he is this city's savior; but he may never enjoy more fame than here, than now."

I am of the pure blood? The bastard never said!

While Djinghiz was still recovering from that new shock, he felt a touch on his right arm. He glanced round to find Paluka regarding him with a wry expression.

"You performed a service for me also," he grunted.

"I? How? Why in the world should a Maori want to kill the Czar?"

"Not him, but—Oh, ask the fount of wisdom opposite! He knows more about us than we do ourselves!" To vent his repressed annoyance Paluka seized his wine goblet; finding it empty, he crushed it with his bare hand.

Truly this was not a man to cross. Djinghiz appealed, mutely and anxiously, to Ismail.

"If not the Czar," the eunuch murmured, "who?"

"The—the Maori ambassador?"

"Yes!" Paluka rasped.

"Because—uh, excuse me, but—because he forbade you to wear the honorable tattoos that . . . ?" Djinghiz's voice failed him as he realized, not for the first time, how little he knew of the world beyond his own city and his own Tartar people. Paluka was gently shaking his great head.

"No, that was the decision of my own family, and I respect their reasons. They foresaw, having some such gifts as Ismail"—he omitted any honorific, implying that he had recognized his host as one of his own kind—"that a powerful man would arise intent on conquest, and he would admire the kind of warfare practiced by Asians and Europeans: not a cleanly battle hand to hand, but using weapons to kill from far away, even to batter cities down with all their citizens. Our—not mine, but my country's—late ambassador was traveling with the Czar to spy out his empire's weaknesses. He was plotting to split Japan from Russia—China too, if he could. We Maoris were then to inherit the leavings."

His voice rose to a pitch of intensity. "But are we sharks, that swallow anything the currents drift their way? Are we carrion-eating birds that peck at floating carcasses? Or are we honest warriors and sailors? We don't need to burn down cities to prove our bravery, any more than we need compasses to prove our skill in navigation! We have our history . . . that is, most of us do''—with a rueful glance at his arm. ''It should suffice.''

''Luckily it had been ordained that a number of us should be sent abroad as children, to be raised with skin unblemished, in order to preempt any such scheme. When the time arrived . . .'' He gave a mountainous shrug. ''Well, I won't go into details of what was planned for the ambassador in the course of his grand tour. Like Slava, I was well and truly beaten to it.''

''You've left something out,'' Ismail interjected.

Paluka blinked. ''I thought I was being frank—''

''So far as you went. What you omitted was any reference to the family whose tattoos you would normally be wearing. Am I not right in guessing that yours is the premier family in all the Land of the Long White Cloud, descendants of the navigator who first steered your folk across the trackless sea?''

For a long moment Paluka sat impassive. At last he bent his head.

''So I have been told. But I do not like to brag about what I personally take no credit for.''

This is becoming more amazing by the moment! Three great nobles at this table—why, Ismail's dinner bids fair to rival the famous one of centuries ago, even though we lack the trappings of state! Is he now going to conjure up an emperor as well?

Or is he the emperor? He wields such power . . . ! Or even Hideki, whom he referred to as ''his honor''!

Indeed, Ismail's tally of surprises was far from at an end. He turned now, politely, to Ratanayaka.

"You spoke much, effendi—" he began. The other cut him short.

"I should have said this earlier. *Effendi* denotes a superior rank. You should not address me that way."

"Then how ought I to address you? Should I say . . . *Shri*?"

If it had been possible for someone of his complexion to turn pale, Ratanayaka would have done so. He sat rock still, save for his mouth, which trembled betrayingly.

"You're no Lankhan," Ismail said eventually, a trace of contempt in his voice. "Nor even a Buddhist. You're a Mahrut spy and potentially, like Slava, a paid assassin."

The man's composure shattered. Almost babbling, he blurted, "Don't call me so! I'm—"

He bit his lip so hard a trace of blood oozed down.

"You don't want to be thought of in those terms?" Ismail's tone was dangerously soft. "In that case you must tell the truth. We are still under the sign of the rose. By the way, has it occurred to you that you are ingesting animal food?"

He had automatically licked away some of the blood.

The pretended Lankhan slumped where he sat. Staring at the table, he muttered, "I think you're a deva. You're not human, anyway. No ordinary human could know so much of what is hidden."

"At least you think I'm a kindly spirit. Good. Well?"

No reply. Ismail waited, then leaned forwards and said fiercely, "Do you want us to laugh at you the way you laughed at Babu Ram Dass, crushed beneath the wheels of his useless kite-carts?"

"How did you—?"

But he had betrayed himself too completely this time. Broken, he buried his face in his hands. Through muffled sobs they heard agonized words.

"How could you possibly have known my title? No one has called me *Shri* since I began my training! Not on orders from the King, but of my own volition!"

"Who was your father?" Ismail snapped.

The brown hands were lowered. From a tear-smeared face: "Not a deva! A veritable rakshasa!"

"Your father was a rakshasa?" Ismail purred.

"No! I meant . . . *you're* a rakshasa, perverting my words even as I speak them! My father was a great and good man, who sought to breach the barrier between Ind and the rest of Asia, to undermine Gurkha rule—"

"By stirring up rebellion among the Chinese. The consequent civil unrest was supposed to tempt the Gurkhas into a war of conquest they were bound to lose simply because the Chinese are more numerous than any other people, then open up trade routes that would make your country independent of the seaborne commerce, operated by the Lankhans, on which they have depended until now for contact with the rest of the modern world. Have I read your story aright—*Shri*?"

"If I'm any judge," said Feisal bluffly, "you have. See how he weeps and cringes!"

"And why aren't you doing the same?"

"What?"

"You heard me! How are you going to pay your score for lodging?"

Feisal looked and sounded confused. "You said you'd introduce me to a pawnbroker tomorrow! I possess certain valuable relics which—"

"You mean the Roman stuff they palmed off on you

in Edo? Save your breath. The Japanese items are all right, but the Roman ones are modern imitations.''

Feisal's eyes bulbed. He muttered, ''But they came from the Mikado's private—''

''Private factory! Ah, people like you have no business getting involved in the machinations of the real world, let alone the worlds beyond the real.''

Djinghiz's nape tingled. Once, only once before, had he heard Ismail refer directly to the worlds transcending this one. That had been when he spoke of the mission Djinghiz alone was fitted to accomplish . . . !

So what does this presage? Yet another shifting of the Gate of Worlds?

''The Mikado isn't much good at it either, if that's any comfort. The rich collectors he's relying on for foreign funds are far too canny to be taken in. So what price your scholarship now?''

Feisal was gaping like a new-hooked fish. He choked out, ''You claim you can recognize forgeries that I accept as genuine?''

''Ah, you don't know what genuine means—nor how to fake even a simple identity for yourself!''

''What?''

Was there pity in Ismail's eyes? Djinghiz thought so, and found himself admiring him the more therefor.

''To start with, you're not a Moslem. If you were, you'd never have taken so long to react when I mentioned Allah. You're a Christian, aren't you?''

''You didn't learn that from my passport!''—with a flare of defiance.

''No, it's among the best I ever ran across. Your people undoubtedly have talents. It's just your ill luck to have stagnated for so long in a backwater of history . . .

You are a Christian. I know that for certain now. What's your real name?''

At last, in a sullen tone: ''Menlik.'' With a glance at the ceiling.

''Don't worry. I honor the rose. No one save us has heard you say that and they'll repeat it at their peril . . . Menlik! Is that not a royal name in Ethiopia?''

''Yes! And I bear it by right!'' He straightened his back. ''It has been my people who preserved the tradition of the meek and loving Jesus amidst the onslaughts of the Turks and other Moslems who by their behavior, their cruelty, might as well have been pagans, or worse!''

''The Christian Russians don't have a much better record, do they? But by alliance with an extremist faction among them—the sort of people who regarded the late Czar as overcautious even though, had he lived, his armies would have occupied Kraków months ago!—you hoped to 'liberate' your country. I see. Did it not trouble you to buy their support with phony Roman relics?''

Feisal-Menlik's face crumpled like wet paper. He whispered, ''But I honestly believed they were genuine!''

''I don't suppose many of your dupes still do,'' Ismail said curtly. ''The idea of enlisting Japanese help to buy the support of the people the Japanese are trying to break loose from! Heaven help us all, if this is the caliber of talent the forces of freedom have at their disposal! Well, I suppose I'm turning into a senile fool. I dared to think this might be an echo of the dinner of five kings, for nobles overt or unacknowledged have come to join me. Now, well, all I can say is: *look* at you! Just *look*!''

A stir of understanding burgeoned at the back of

Djinghiz's mind, though he read on all the other faces renewed incomprehension.

I think I finally had a glimmer of what the old devil is up to. I don't believe it. I don't want to!

But he isn't finished yet . . .

Eight: While the Petals Fade

ABRUPTLY IT DAWNED—WHAT ISMAIL WAS AWAITING from the man who alone among this company had truly moved the Gate of Worlds, albeit as his instrument.

But he said his eyes were off me while I was actually at work . . .

Djinghiz's mouth was parched, his belly taut, and all the weariness that massage had removed was flooding back. It must be late, it must be very late—past midnight, maybe, but there was no clock in view.

Nonetheless:

"Ismail effendi?"

"Yes?" The face looked as tired as he felt, the eyes had lost their brilliance and sparkle, the voice was dull as last week's wine. But that was acting.

"I think—I don't know why or how, but I feel it—I think you're right. It's just that you've omitted someone from your list. You sent a message asking to meet 'those who had traveled furthest'—right?''

Ismail allowed himself to perk up. ''Go on!''

''Earlier you put on a show. It was designed—was it not?—to shame one among us who has made amends.'' *My mouth is so dry I can barely shape the words, yet I daren't break the spell I seem to be creating, with a gulp of wine!* ''It may nonetheless have possessed some—some validity. I can't find a better word.''

Now their entire attention was focused on him, but in a different way from when he described how he had killed the Czar. They were hoping for enlightenment amid the empty cups and jugs, the forlorn scraps left on the dishes that had held loukoumi, fruit and other delicacies, the sour stale vapors from the hookah in whose bowl the rose petals which had earlier been red were dying to brown even as the coals below had died to gray.

He said: ''Hideki . . . ?''

And waited. It felt as though eternity dragged by.

Then, at last, with the marvelous grace he who had pretended to be she had so long been schooled in, the boy rose to his feet and bowed to Djinghiz.

''You are right,'' he said in Russian better pronounced and better accented than he had ever previously heard from him. ''I too was assigned to kill the Czar. Our troupe was to be presented at the Moscow court, where—so I'm told—there has lately been a fad for Japanese culture. There is a particular play that offered an opportunity . . . But you spared me from having his death on my conscience. May your karma bear the burden lightly.''

Ismail had totally recovered his spirits. He said explosively, "Of course! I'm a fool! Feisal—Menlik—whatever your name is! In your case it would have been poison, wouldn't it?"

"What?" The Ethiopian started.

"You aren't just carrying fake Roman relics! You also have some jade and soapstone—what do they call them?—feeling-pieces!"

"Netsuke," Hideki supplied.

"Right!" Ismail banged fist into palm. "They're genuine enough, and really valuable! And just before you sold the one you were sure would pass through the Czar's own hands, you were going to coat it with something deadly but slow acting . . . I can tell that I'm right."

Menlik's face was stiff as an Egyptian statue, save his lips. He whispered, "God and Jesus forgive me, but—yes."

"I don't understand why, but—Ah, of course I do! Leave it for the moment! Shri Ratanayaka or whatever you are really called: what were your means to have been? They say certain persons in Ind are adept in the use of silken scarves. Does the goddess Kali figure in your pantheon?

"You are indeed a rakshasa!"

"I see. Expert strangulation, very quick." Ismail plucked his lower lip. "You, Slava-Erik?"

The Norseman shrugged. "They gave me a gun. I am a first-rate shot."

"Paluka?"

The Maori said nothing. He merely raised his monstrous right arm and swept it forward.

"I see. Anything heavy enough and hard enough that you could throw from close enough. Were you planning, say, to enlist in the embassy guard?"

"Yes. But no."

Ismail's forehead creased for a second, then smoothed.

"Ah. Not just a rock or a spear. You would have used—what's the term? It reminds me of a fruit . . . I have it. A grenade? Which you could have made from local materials? And if other people got caught in the blast—? I see. It didn't matter."

His normal composure, his normal dominance completely restored, he sat back and beamed around.

"Well, then! I was right after all! This is an echo of the dinner of the kings—and make what you like of the fact!"

"What does that make you?" Paluka rasped, echoing Djinghiz's thought of a moment ago. "The missing emperor?"

"My dear fellow!" Quite carried away, Ismail fluttered his eyelashes, forgetting that age had reduced them to a few isolated tufts. "You misread the situation! I was right when, purely to offend Slava, I called Hideki 'his honor.' So should I have addressed you all, for here at this table are guests superior to kings!"

Djinghiz drew a deep breath. It felt like his first for a week. He hadn't realized he had been awaiting just this resolution of the climax Ismail had built up to . . .

But how much of it did he choose to build to? A moment back he seemed disappointed, disillusioned, defeated. . . .

How much of it did he control? How much controlled him?

Us.

Me. . . .

The eunuch's tone was affable now, as though he had convinced himself completely of his all-along rightness.

"Don't you see? We have here Hideki who planned to kill the Czar on behalf of the Mikado, in hopes of prying loose Russia's grip from his country. We have also Feisal—excuse me: Menlik—who was naive enough to imagine that in the confusion following the Czar's death the Christians of Ethiopia might declare their independence from Moslem rule with purchased Russian, that is, Christian, help . . . Take advice from me, my gullible friend: never rely on confusion to yield the outcome you hope for! It's too contagious! Remember what I said about factionalism in Kraków obliging our council to issue notices in four languages? You'd more likely have wound up with a full-blown civil war!"

Menlik-Feisal husked, "You talk as though you've read this in tomorrow's news sheets!"

"In a sense," said Ismail dryly, "yes, I have . . . but so could anyone who's been following the news from China!"

And at once resumed.

"We know about Paluka now, we know about Slava—and of course we know about the last of the company, the Tartar prince who succeeded while the others were still mooning about and making fruitless plans. So there you have it."

Djinghiz grated, "We have what?"

"My dear young friend! We have, as I thought you of all people would realize, the kind of gathering that I dared to foresee."

"A bunch of pretenders, of down-and-outs, of exiled wanderers?"

"Not at all! I said: those superior to kings!"

"Because . . ." Djinghiz had to drive the words between his lips. There had been a tongue-loosening substance in the air, the food, or the wine; he was convinced of it. During his travels he had been invited to experiment with drugs, and to maintain his cover among the Eastern Tartars he had been obliged to indulge; several had dried his mouth in the same way, and more than one had done things to his sanity that he detested . . . Was the authority he respected in Ismail due to no more than a shamanic trick?

"Because," he began anew, "there is one power greater than a prince's."

"Or a king's, or even an emperor's."

"That being—?" But he knew the answer as he spoke.

"Death."

Sourly: "And what does that make you at this echo of a royal dinner? The emperor, as Paluka said?"

Unruffled, the eunuch shook his head. "No. Mine is the role of their host, Councillor Wierzynek."

"And what became of him?" Djinghiz leaned forward.

"Why! What would you expect? He succumbed to the power which, as you correctly say, is greater than any prince's."

"You mean he died of plague?"

"Indeed. As did his family and servants."

"So what follows from this meeting? As many deaths, or maybe even more?" Djinghiz's head was ringing with imagined echoes of a modern war. He had foreseen, of course, some of the consequences that must flow from Czar Vladimir's assassination: no informed person could fail to predict at least a few, and news had drifted westward—despite the Russian censorship—to announce that half China was aflame. So, therefore, must be the territory where his Tartar cousins lived. The interregnum might afford them the chance to secure their independence; so he had hoped, so he had believed. Only he could not escape the fear that such a dream might prove as vacuous as Feisal-Menlik's . . .

"No: many fewer. That is why it had to happen."

"Is this—?"

"The war I said would take a most unusual form? Of course it is."

"What's unusual about it?" Djinghiz cried. "There must be thousands dying, tens of thousands wounded, who knows how many rendered homeless, taking to the roads as refugees! That sounds to me like any ordinary war!"

"If only you could see beyond the Gate of Worlds . . ." Abruptly Ismail's tone was gray. So was his face.

"You claim you can?" Djinghiz was halfway to his feet. "Prove it! Show me!"

There was a sullen thud. Paluka's head had dropped forward on the table. Bewildered, Djinghiz glanced at the others. Hideki was leaning on his folded arms, smiling peaceably in sleep. Beside him Ratanayaka, eyes closed, was rehearsing a mantra with what seemed to be autohypnotic powers. Slava was simply and audibly in a drunken stupor; his snores confirmed it. As for Feisal-Menlik, he had produced a little book whose cover was embroidered with seed pearls and ornamented with a teardrop sapphire, from which he was reading aloud, but in a whisper, in a tongue that Djinghiz did not recognize.

"Amharic," Ismail said.

"What?"

"The language his holy book is written in. It's very old. Few people understand it."

"You're one of the exceptions?"

"I recognize it, no more than that . . . Young friend,

you seem suddenly to have turned against me. Are you disappointed that I couldn't find you a larger audience to boast to about your cleverness?"

"No, it isn't that!" Recollection of his gratitude at having more than one person listening bloomed and faded in Djinghiz's mind. "It's—"

But what he had intended to say had also faded. He licked his lips, searching for lost words.

Ismail hoisted himself to his feet and began to plod back and forth along the room. He said eventually, "Do you not believe that I can see beyond the Gate?"

"I—"

"Not always, but sometimes. With vast effort."

"I—"

"I detect that you doubt. Even with this proof before you."

"Proof?"

"Evidence, at least! Five would-be assassins of the greatest ruler in the world . . . plus the one who actually rid us of him! Who else could have called to his table those wielding a power greater than—?"

"Than any power of princes! Yes! I accept that!" *Is it really me uttering these words? Am I still affected by whatever drug dried out my mouth?* "What I can't accept—"

"Is that in spite of your valor and my scheming, our world is not a place of liberty and beauty."

"Yes!"

Ismail halted confronting him, fists on fat hips.

"Then you should see what I have seen! Can you imagine a battle line that stretches for a thousand versts, where for years neither side has gained more than a single verst yet half a million brave young men have died? A place where no trees grow and no birds sing?

Where the only music is the scream of shells in flight, concluded by the drum-thud of their burst in mud?''

''It isn't possible!'' Djinghiz whispered. ''It's like what Paluka talked about! Artillery destroying whole cities at a time!''

''It could have been! And worse to come! I swear it! Battles not confined to land, nor even to the sea, but— Oh, I can scarcely credit it myself! High in the air and deep within the oceans! And we are at risk of the same!''

''When? How?''

Ismail wiped his forehead with his sleeve; it had been glistening with sweat.

''The faction that the Maori ambassador represented is amassing funds to develop submersible warships. They have devices to extract oxygen from water so the crews can breathe. What is more, when fed with sea-water the same machines produce a noxious gas which they intend to put in shells and bombs, to kill their enemies not cleanly but by choking them. And that's not all. Shri—whoever—mocked the kite-train, but behind the dream too lay one more sinister.''

''Explain!'' Djinghiz felt his nails biting his palms.

''To overfly the Himalaya, dropping aerial bombs.''

''On Gurkha regiments?''

''Of course.''

''And break their rule, and loose the Mahruts to the north?''

''Of course . . . Despite their evil reputation the Gurkhas have remained content with their domain for centuries. The Mahruts, though—!''

''Are notoriously fretting at the confines of theirs?''

''Would you care to see them marching through our market?''

"No, I would not! I'd rather see the Turks return, than that!"

Followed a long and empty pause. At last Ismail said mildly:

"Well? Do you want the woman that I offered you? She must be getting rather tired of waiting."

Djinghiz started. "You honestly think that after all that's happened this evening I could still—?"

With malice: "As you remarked earlier, I'm in no position to know about such matters . . . But I'll dismiss her. And, I think, your fellow-travelers deserve some rest." He clapped his hands. Instantly a line of servants filed into the room, including the girl rosebud who had earlier attended Hideki, or perhaps her twin. The boy woke with no objections and allowed himself to be led away. Feisal and Ratanayaka were equally docile; their eyes had the bemused look of sleepwalkers. Slava and Paluka, however, had to be carried out. Two men sufficed for the former, but the weight of the latter demanded three.

When the door closed again, Djinghiz burst out, "I don't understand how you know about these—these other worlds!"

"Do you want to?" Ismail returned quietly.

"Of course!"

"Do you want to—enough?"

Slowly, for he was almost dropping with fatigue, the younger man contrived to grapple with the question. He ventured at length, "You mean it requires training. Some kind of apprenticeship."

"Of course."

"In that case I suppose it's too late for me to start."

"On the contrary . . . Let's sit down again." Suiting

action to word, Ismail deposited his bulk at the head of the table, motioning Djinghiz to the place where Hideki had sat.

"On the contrary," he said again. "The perfect juncture is a point in life where one doesn't know which of a myriad possible courses one should follow towards the future. It creates an ideal mind-set, open to the strange and awful visions that lie beyond the Gate of Worlds. And you don't, I'm sure, wish to turn your achievement into a career that Slava called inferior to living off immoral earnings."

"Of course not. But—"

"What?"

Djinghiz drew a deep breath. "I'm not sure I could stand having my head full all the time of the sort of imaginary horrors you've just been describing."

"Imaginary?" Ismail said stabbingly. "Far from it!"

"Yes, yes. I'm doing my best to understand . . . You mean they're just as real for the people beyond the Gate as—as this world is to you and me."

"True. But if we act aright, we at least shall not have to endure them."

"There's no end to this!"

"How can there be? Every tick of passing time creates an infinity of might-have-beens, and there they are, in some incomprehensible dimension . . . Young man, I need my sleep. Are you sure about that woman? I forgot to give orders for her to dismiss."

"No you didn't." Djinghiz grinned around a yawn.

"You dare to contradict me?" But the eunuch's eyes were twinkling.

"Nothing in your world happens by accident, not even forgetting. Does it?"

"Well, one does one's best—though in the end old

age betrays us all. I simply felt, knowing you as I do, that without some distraction you might well have bad dreams. She is, I promise, pretty and well trained . . . We live in strange days, my friend.'' He stretched his fat arms, left first, then right, and also yawned. ''It's an age the like of which Europe hasn't seen since the fall of Rome, an age when empires are dying. The rot at the heart of the Sublime Porte is manifest for all to see. So, very soon, will be the canker in the sprawling Russian fungus. Across the world new peoples and new cultures are arising.''

''Like the Maoris?''

''Oh, they will never have their chance of empire. Even as they strive to exploit the chaos that is now inevitable they will find power slipping from their grasp. What I said to Feisal—Menlik—was the truth. No, they'll be left gawping and frustrated, while the Gate flaps like a cat's trapdoor in a high wind . . . I won't live to see it, but you will. I envy you.''

He hoisted himself awkwardly to his feet.

''Sleep well, Djinghiz. I look forward to hearing your decision in the morning. And if by ill chance you suffer nightmares, bear in mind: ours may not be the best of all possible worlds, but if we strive aright we can ensure it is far from the worst.''

As he headed for the door the young man leapt up and embraced him. They hugged for a long moment. When they drew apart, Djinghiz felt a trace of moisture on his cheek, but Ismail kept his back turned as he left, so he could not see whether or not it was a tear.

Epilogue: Though Thorns Draw Blood

"YOU'VE MADE UP YOUR MIND?"

"Yes. You were right. I don't know what path to pick towards the future. So why should I not choose many?"

"Can you endure your mistakes?"

"I have so far. Why?"

"Some of the other worlds one senses may seem better, and might have been attainable had one acted differently."

"But did not another version of me reach them?"

"It is well. You've understood. Djinghiz, I'll teach you all I can. And you will move the Gate not once or twice like most of us, but countless times!"

Afterword

"At the Sign of the Rose" takes place in a universe devised by Robert Silverberg for his novel *The Gate of Worlds*, in which the Black Death killed not a quarter of the population of Europe but more like three-quarters, so that the Turks were able to conquer the Mediterranean, and Peru and Mexico were never overthrown by European invaders.

Mutatis mutandis, the setting is authentic. The oldest hotel in Kraków is indeed *pod Róża*, "at the sign of the Rose," and I have had the pleasure of staying there twice. I have also eaten a couple of times in the excellent restaurant *u Wierzynka*, "at Wierzynek's," that now occupies the house where four kings dined with an emperor—though not in the same year as in this story, nor for the same reason—and it is indeed located just south of the enormous market, ten acres in extent. As to the Tartars, their attack is commemorated every hour by a trumpeter sounding the alarm from the Marian Church. He breaks off and begins again because his long-ago predecessor was taken in the throat by an arrow before he could finish.

An Exaltation of Spiders

By Chelsea Quinn Yarbro

ONCE HE WAS ALONE SATHALE II CURSED HIS SECOND cousin, using language that would have appalled his court. It was too late for direct action: if the despised Flatlands completed their alliance with the foreigners, he and his people were lost, and that he could not endure. At least he had been warned; he was grateful for that.

It was the third messenger who had brought word of his cousin's betrayal. Two previous messengers had not been able to cross the mountains; had been caught by the men of the False Inca. They would be mourned with formal sacrifices and a day of fasting. The True Inca entered the names of all three messengers among those who would serve him in the afterlife, the Four High Priests adopted the messengers as their children, and the second telegraph office in the country was named in their honor.

"We need a diversion," said Sathale, very late that night while the lamps guttered.

"Yes," muttered his advisor, who was too exhausted to say more.

"Something convincing," Sathale said, musing. "Something that would be believed, plausible, even for our people."

His advisor, Imhuro, nodded. "Yes."

"Yes," said Sathale, his eyes gleaming.

So at his next public function, the True Inca vowed on his place in the afterlife that he would not permit his second cousin to triumph through his alliance with the False Inca of the Green Banner and these "Turks" from across the Eastern Ocean. He promised that his land would emerge from the conflict more powerful than before, with alliances across the Western Ocean with the Maoris and the Japanese. It was agreed by all the Incan nobility that Sathale II was given to grand visions; what they said privately was another matter. But no one dared to oppose the True Inca Sathale, and everyone was afraid of what the False Inca Helaoku IV was trying to do. As outrageous as Sathale's plan might be, it provided hope when hope was sorely needed.

On the morning of the Hawk Goddess in the Fifth Month, Sathale II and most of his court took the royal Incan funicular cars from the sacred city of Machu Picchu down the peaks, over the valleys and away to the sea, to the great port of Algoma, where the ships were built, and all the kites of the Spider clan.

The men of the Whale clan were drawn up in ranks to greet the True Inca, and they hailed him, calling him the Sacred Royal Messenger, and Adopted Son of the High Gods, as well as all his lesser titles. The two leaders of the ships, valorous men of the Whale clan, swore on their place in the afterlife to complete the mission given to them by the True Inca. They declared they would cross the Western Ocean to the land of the Maoris, though none but legendary heroes had gone straight across that enormous, empty ocean. Then they cursed the False Inca and the False Inca of the Green Banner, and the sacrifice of two llamas was offered to the High Gods. With the ceremonies over, the True Inca went to review the ships of his fleet, and to meet with the leaders of the Whale clan.

"How many ships do we have capable of the journey?" Sathale asked his advisors as they gathered behind closed doors. "I don't want to hear tales; tell me what we can truly do."

"Perhaps five of them are," said Ouninu, who supervised maintenance of the ships.

"No more than that?" Sathale said. "So few, and yet there are hundreds of ships here."

"They aren't designed to cross the sea, but to follow the coast. If that was your wish, we could send twenty ships."

"No: we must go straight over the ocean." Sathale addressed Ouninu directly. "So there will be no more than five?"

"At most."

"And if we use the others?" Sathale persisted.

"It is not what you would like. We can use them, of course, but the journey would be long, and we would stop often and there would be no chance to keep our mission . . . unknown. Five can cross the open waters. Five at most. Three is more realistic."

"You command one of those ships, Meliwa," said the True Inca. "You've said that the venture is desperate. How would you assess our position with regard to that of the False Inca of the eastern plains?''

''I have met those from across the Eastern Ocean,'' Meliwa said. He was the younger of the two Whale clan leaders. ''There is danger coming, that much is certain.'' He coughed and went on. ''In the times I have gone through the Teeth of the Gods, I have found more and more of those from across the Eastern Ocean in the lowlands of the False Inca. I must assume that they are there with the invitation of the False Inca.''

Ilatha of the Spider clan added, ''When I have crossed to the lands of the False Inca in my untethered kite, I have seen signs of these men as well.''

This was precisely what Sathale wanted them to say, and he added his own emphasis to their fears. ''According to my messenger,'' said Sathale, and everyone was still to hear his words, ''there are many men from Urop in the lands of . . . my second cousin.'' He felt their shock at his choice of words. ''The messenger saw men from Urop who claimed to have come to the lands of the False Inca Helaoku in order to escape the False Inca of the Green Banner.''

Dyami, Second of the Four High Priests said, ''It is a sign of their fate, that they escape one False Inca to find another.''

Sathale shook his head. ''It does not matter why they have come, only that they are there, with cannon and other weapons that we do not possess. Consider that before you dismiss them.'' He put his hand on the table, the palm flat down. ''If we don't have aid of our own, then they will press us like ever-increasing weights until we are crushed.''

Pallatu, the other leader of the Whale clan, spoke.

"I know the men from the Western Ocean. Their eyes are turned in other directions. They seek China."

"Then they will not help us," said Bemosetu, the Third High Priest. "If we can't offer what they want, they won't help us."

"But we do have certain things they want," Ilatha said. "They have nothing like our kites, either tethered or untethered, and they admit they have uses for these kites. I have spoken to some of the Maoris when we were in the lands to the north, and I have learned much: I and my five sons have taken time to learn the words, and my first daughter, Etenyi, has written down for us what we have learned."

The daughters of the Spider clan were known for their industry and education, but the accomplishments of Etenyi were regarded as unusual even among Spiders.

"Tell her that the Four High Priests wish to review the work she has done," said Pathoain, the First High Priest.

"Too great an honor," Ilatha said. The High Priests objected to the study of foreign languages. "Her writings will be copied at once and brought to you by the Royal Messenger of the Spider clan."

"Thank you," said Pathoain with formal gestures of appreciation. "If we can speak with these Maoris, perhaps we can establish the treaties we seek. At least there is a chance."

"Yes," said Sathale. There was something in his eyes, grim and cold, that the others feared to recognize.

"The True Inca is right," Pallatu said. "If we are to convince the Maoris of our worth and our sincerity, we must show that our intentions are genuine. We must be the ones to make the first journey."

"If it's possible," Bemosetu said.

"It must be possible," said Sathale.

Ilatha spoke up. "My sons and I will carry out your orders to our last breaths, and praise you to the High Gods as we die in your service."

Sathale nodded. "But first I will see what your daughter has done. It would be good for you to carry my greetings to the Maoris in their own tongue as well as in ours. And then you and your sons will undertake this mission for me."

"Whatever you command," said Ilatha without flourish.

"No matter what I may ask you to do?" pursued Sathale.

"There is nothing you could require that we would refuse: ask any of us to leap from the highest peaks without our kites and we will do it, because it is your order we follow."

Akando, the Fourth High Priest, who had been silent until now, looked directly at Ilatha. "That is a binding vow. You have accepted a great task, Ilatha. May the High Gods make it no heavier than you can bear."

Ilatha knew it was sensible to be cautious dealing with High Priests. He said formally, "If we cannot accomplish the tasks of the True Inca, then we are not deserving of the favor he shows us by giving us the task. We would not wish to live with such dishonor, and would seek to eradicate our shame, for ourselves and for all Spiders."

"May you not come to regret this," said Sathale with a trace of inner satisfaction. "I am fortunate in my subjects."

There was a moment of silence at the table.

Then Akando spoke. "What of the High Gods, True Inca? We are going beyond our mountains, beyond our clans. We decry that the False Inca has made foreign alliances, and yet we seek the same thing."

It was a question that none of the others had dared to raise. Everyone looked at Sathale.

"The High Gods know that we are not profaning them or corrupting the clans. We have given them sacrifice and will again until it is certain that we will not be conquered by my cousin Helaoku."

"What if the Maoris expect marriage as a symbol of the treaty?" asked Akando, disapproval in every line of his body. "You are True Inca. There is no reason for you to accept a Maori into your clan."

"They haven't yet spoken with us; there is no reason to suppose they will do that. In fact, we don't know if they will permit us to deal with them in any way. To anticipate such a demand is . . . premature."

"And if they do," said Bemosetu, "what will you say?"

Sathale half-rose from his chair. "I am true to the High Gods." It was no answer, but no one challenged him.

"Of course, of course," said Dyami hastily.

"No one doubts that," Pathoain said.

"Very well," said Sathale. "I'll want to know how soon the ships can be made ready for the journey. I'll want three to be ready, and while they are gone, I'll want more sea-going ships built, so that we won't be so ill-prepared a second time."

Now Ouninu spoke up at last, reluctantly. He had listened with a falling heart, knowing that much of what was asked would not be possible in the time the True Inca expected it. "We cannot carry enough fuel to cross the Western Ocean on the power of the engines. We will have to use all the sails as well."

"Very well," said Sathale. "If this is as hazardous as you suggest, order the sails to be made; all the weavers and seamsters in the Rat clan in Algoma are to be put to work on the project if that is necessary in order to have the sails ready for the departure." He glanced at Ilatha and added, "You'll have to make sails for the kites, as well, for there will need to be at least one tethered kite aloft throughout the journey."

"As you wish," Ouninu said.

Sathale rose. Immediately every other man in the room did so too. "I'll return to inspect again in twenty days. I will want to see great progress."

"The Whale clan will start to improve the ships at once," said Pallatu. "You have only to choose which three are to make the journey, and they will be given first attention."

"My orders will be announced before sundown," Sathale said.

The men made obeisance as the Inca passed out of the private chamber.

"If the False Inca gets wind of this before we are ready, who knows what will come of it?" said Dyami to Pathoain as they followed Sathale through the Great Ocean Hall.

"Then we must pray that it will not happen," said Pathoain.

Three cups of bitter beer were set out on the elaborate tray, though no one had tasted the drink. Sathale sat facing the stranger, the leader of the Tortoise clan on the low bench beside him, wide-set eyes narrowed to slits. For once Sathale looked older than his thirty-one years. "How much do you demand of me, then?"

"Double the amount you offered," said the stranger.

His accent was filled with the abrupt sounds of the north. "I am taking the greatest risk; it is fitting that I have a commensurate reward. Who knows when you might decide to throw me to the gods? Or, if these negotiations fail, my masters might tear my heart out."

"Very well. Imhuro, give him another full measure of gold." The True Inca stared at the loose feather vest the stranger wore. "Aren't you afraid that your clothes will give you away? No one wears such garments here."

"Of course not," said the stranger, who answered to Llotl, though it was not his name. "But they know I'm from the north, don't they? I don't look as you do, I don't speak as you do, so it's useless of me to try to pretend I am one of you. If I were to attempt to blend with you, I'd be recognized in a moment. This way, there is nothing to recognize. Sometimes the best disguise is no disguise. Therefore, I have no reason not to wear this vest." He held out his hand as Imhuro offered a second pouch. "That's good," he said as he weighed the pouch in his hand. "Very good."

"If you carry out your orders, I'll reward you when you return."

"If I bring word from my country, and you have the answer you want," Llotl corrected. "That is understood." He tied the pouches to his belt and rubbed his hands together. "It *is* understood, isn't it? It would be easy for you to deny me, or to order me into prison."

"Not if you bring me word from your ruler, quickly and without detection." The True Inca tapped his fingers on the arms of his chair.

Llotl gestured abruptly. "They say you are a perfect man, True Inca. If that is the case, then you can be perfect in treach— . . . statecraft." His correction was so smooth and his smile so practiced that Sathale was convinced the insult was calculated.

"You would be advised to remember it," Imhuro said. He rested his hand on the hilt of his dagger. "If you betray us, we'll know of it. And you will pay for it."

"Why would I betray you?" Llotl asked. He patted the concealed pouches of gold. "I'll leave before dawn tomorrow. I will be away from here by the end of the day. You will have word from me before the agreed date."

"We had better," said Imhuro when Sathale did not speak.

Llotl barked a single laugh and turned toward the side door.

When he was gone, Imhuro said, "He's not trustworthy."

"Who is?" Sathale asked, reaching for his cup. "Surely not I." He finished the beer in two quick swallows and reached for Llotl's untouched cup. "I'm worse than any of the others."

Imhuro shook his head. "You're trying to save us. It must be done. The Four High Priests would disagree, but what else do you expect of priests? They don't know how great the danger is from the False Inca of the Green Banner, once he sends more troops into the Flatlands." His use of the contemptuous word for the Lands of the False Inca stung Sathale.

"They are worthy foe," he snapped. "Don't speak of them that way."

"Your pardon," said Imhuro without emotion.

Sathale finished the second cup of beer and stared up at the fine lamps that glimmered around the room. "They'll be stronger than we are, Imhuro. Once the

False Inca of the Green Banner sends soldiers, they'll be much stronger than we are. I have to stop them. Nothing else is as important as that."

"What if Llotl fails you?" Imhuro suggested. "You've given him enough gold to buy passage to Russia and leave him money for land."

"He won't fail me. He's greedy, I grant you that, but his delight is in power. He'll do my bidding because he'll gain more power than money from it."

"And you are satisfied with such a tool?" Imhuro demanded.

"Of course not. What Inca is pleased with a spy?" He smiled. "But I have to employ them. It's necessary. I don't want to lose those ships, either, but we must if they are to accomplish their purposes."

Imhuro rubbed his chin. "There is no other way?"

"None that I can see." The True Inca sighed. "It will be a great loss to the Whales; at least there are only four Spiders going with the ships, and they're youngsters; that's something."

"Is there any chance they might actually reach the islands of the Maoris?"

"Of course not," the True Inca said. He gnawed at his lower lip, scarcely noticing it when it started to bleed.

Apenimon and Tulapa faced Meliwa, both of them trying valiantly to look older than seventeen.

"So you're the twin flyers we're to take across the ocean," Meliwa said. It was impossible to tell if he was pleased or angry.

"Our father has told us that we and our younger brother Iyestu are to be ready to sail with you," said Tulapa. "Iyestu has taken schooling for two years and will go up next month. We've—my twin and I—been trained for watching passes, and we all have experience with untethered kites as well as the tethered ones. I rode out a storm last summer, and all that happened is that one of the sails of the kite got ripped." He patted his chest. "I wasn't afraid."

This boast evoked a scowl from Apenimon, who had been on the ground when the tempest had closed in. "I've ridden on an untethered kite from the Teeth of the Gods to Machu Picchu. I landed twice during the journey."

"Quite a lot of experience for youngsters," said Meliwa.

"Our father enrolled us as soon as the Spider clan would permit us to go aloft," said Apenimon. "I wanted to go earlier, but there are rules."

"Our youngest brother will be taken as an apprentice for the funicular railway," added Tulapa. "He'll start in a year."

"There is a fourth brother?" Meliwa asked.

"Nigantu," said Apenimon. "He wants to be a priest. He's already filed petitions to be permitted to leave the Spider clan so that he can enter the priests' school." The two boys exchanged looks.

"You are not pleased to have one of your family become a priest?" asked Meliwa. He sat at his enormous writing table, watching Ilatha's twin sons with growing interest.

"Well, he'll have to leave the Spider clan, won't he? Then where is the pride for the rest of us? If he becomes one of the Four High Priests, he enters the Sun clan." Tulapa tried to shrug, but the movement was quick and graceless. "He is determined to do it, and that's what he will do."

"All your family seems determined," said Meliwa, getting up and coming toward the two young Spiders. "You probably know our journey has never been tried before, and that there is great risk."

"Our greatest pride is with our greatest risk," Tulapa said, his chest expanding.

It was difficult not to laugh, but Meliwa, who had sons of his own, managed to keep his expression severe. "I see. And when you're on a tethered kite and the wind is howling and you are beyond the sight of land in any direction, what then? Do you think your pride will sustain you? Or your younger brother?"

"I think the High Gods will sustain us," said Apenimon.

"And you?" Meliwa said to Tulapa.

He showed his reckless smile. "I will offer a young llama, to be sure they do."

At the border between the east and west Incan lands, a party of soldiers wholly unfamiliar to the west Incan guards attacked a trading fort, killing most of the men there and taking all women as their slaves. News spread along the border passes, bringing panic to many of them. Members of the Llama clan demanded armed escorts and double watches.

Sathale heard the news with growing fury when the kite guard was brought to him and the Four High Priests for judgment.

"You saw them coming, you say?" the Inca asked, as the slender, large-chested Spider clan guard collapsed in shame before him.

"I saw them, but there was nothing warlike. They came on horses, not with the engines that the False Inca has used before. They were strangers, men from the lands across the Eastern Ocean. They looked . . . funny, with stripes on their clothes and peculiar hats on their heads. I warned only that strangers were approaching. That was all I was supposed to do. They . . . I did not suspect they wanted . . ." His voice trailed away.

The True Inca leaned back. "They came without engines?"

"Horses, True Inca, only horses."

Pathoain said, "You have ordered already that peaceful travelers are not to be detained or mistreated. How was the guard to recognize the danger of these men?"

"How, yes, how," mused Sathale.

The guard wailed, clapping his hands over his face.

Sathale gestured to the men of the Raven clan who held him. "Release him. He will do no more harm.

"*I* would have known to give the alert," said the senior Raven officer.

"Nonsense," cut in Akando. "Suppose the foreigners had been nothing more than a peaceful party of travelers, perhaps carrying messages for the True Inca, and you, in your zeal, caused them inconvenience or trouble. You would dishonor the True Inca. Because you Ravens are soldiers, you'd like all the people of the True Inca to be as pugnacious as you are. But even you admit we are not prepared to war with the False Inca." He turned toward the guard on the floor. "You have not brought dishonor on yourself or on the Spider clan. You have done what you were sworn to do. The High Gods will not hold you accountable for the fall of the fort."

"Still," Sathale said, "we'd better tell the other Spiders on guard at the passes. If Helaoku attempts this once, he is apt to do it again. We'll suffer if we are not prepared."

Bemosetu spoke up, addressing Sathale with concern. "The Spider clan will have to put more guards aloft. We will need a patrol of untethered kites going the length of the Spine of the World, stopping to report regularly along the way." He looked at Pathoain. "If you had not refused to have a third telegraph station built, we might have a better warning system now. I still believe that we'll have to put telegraph lines to all the pass forts."

"And every time the wind blows or there's an avalanche or heavy snows, the lines will be down and we'll be more exposed than before," the First High Priest countered.

"If Chesmupa had been guided by a First Priest like you," said Bemosetu angrily, "we'd still be using runners instead of the funicular railway, and where would we be?"

"That's a different matter entirely," Pathoain said, glaring at the younger man. He indicated the Spider cringing before them. "Think what you are saying, Bemosetu."

"I won't have you squabbling," Sathale interrupted. "You are here to advise me, not gabble and peck like geese." He rose from the throne. His gold collar was brilliant in the reflected light of a thousand lamps. "I say you did no dishonor to your clan," he told the prostrate guard. "The Spiders have no reason to disown you. If there is any talk of it, you are to let me know. I order it entered in the records of the Spider clan that you obeyed your orders." He rounded on the Raven officer. "I want you to form a company of Ravens to take the fort from the men of the False Inca. Be ready to leave by first light tomorrow."

The senior Raven officer slapped his hand on the

Turkish-style pistol thrust through his belt. "On my life and my place in the afterlife," he answered.

"The Ravens are always touchy," said Akando, who had been a Raven himself before he became a priest and had given up his clan.

"With reason," said Dyami, who once had been an Eagle. "They carry the weight of the border on their shoulders."

"Stop it," said Sathale wearily. He went slowly back toward his throne, but did not sit. Instead, he looked down at the guard. "You may rise."

Very slowly the guard lifted his head. "I am not worthy, True Inca."

"If you insist," said Sathale. "But it would please me if you would stand." He waited until the Spider guard was on his feet again. "What is your name, Spider?"

"Misuthu. I am named for my grandfather."

"An honor to your grandfather, then," said Sathale, who was named for his. "And you are from my city?"

"From Sisipo," Misuthu said, naming a village above the elevation of Machu Picchu.

Sathale nodded. "I need you to instruct the other guards on what you saw, what these foreigners looked like and how they came to the fort." He signaled a scribe of the Cat clan. "Get this down."

The scribe hurried forward, bringing his writing materials with him. His calligraphy was meticulous and small, for in all the land of the True Inca there were only two paper mills, and paper was precious. He took his place beside the guard, his pen at the ready. "You may begin."

Apenimon had been aloft for most of the day, hanging high in his tethered kite. Spectacles strapped to his head enabled him to see far into the distance. On the ground at Machu Picchu, his twin chafed at his own inactivity, pacing as he watched the cable play out into the sky.

"Spider-father," Tulapa protested to Ilatha, glowering at the tether leading to Apenimon's kite, "if I ride the kites with the ships, just as Apenimon will, why can't I go aloft while he is up? On the ships we'll have to flash messages between us, so why not practice here?"

"Tomorrow," said Ilatha, "you'll be in the air and Apenimon will be on the ground. Once we know how the long hours will affect you, we can establish how you are to signal to one another." He patted Tulapa on the arm. "You'll have more than your fill of the air, Spider-son, when you have crossed the Western Ocean to the islands of the Maoris."

"Let it come soon," said Tulapa. He peered up in the sky, trying to find the spot against the clouds that was Apenimon. "When will Iyestu practice, too?"

"Tomorrow. You three will have to study the charts of the Western Ocean. The Whale clan will show them to you." Ilatha stared down the mountain, watching the squat funicular cars swaying on the heavy cables. "The True Inca has also decided that your sister is to be allowed to travel in the lead ship, since she has made a study of the language of the Maoris."

"Etenyi?" Tulapa asked. "Why . . . she's a woman!"

"The True Inca knows that," said his father, "but his wisdom must prevail no matter what custom dictates."

"I suppose so, but it's bad luck," said Tulapa, and

looked again at Apenimon's cable, hearing the metal sing. He longed to be in the sky, high above Machu Picchu, with all creation at his feet, the Spine of the World poking up at him.

"And what will that do to her in the clan? Will she still be marriageable after such a voyage?"

"That's for the Spider clan leaders to decide," said Ilatha carefully. "The Cat clan has allowed women who travel to marry."

"What do you expect of Cats?" scoffed Tulapa. "And Llama women can travel and marry as well, but what does that have to do with Spiders?"

"We will have to see," said Ilatha, keeping his own anxiety to himself.

Iyestu liked riding the funicular cars up the mountains and across the splendid valleys and gorges of the Spine of the World as much as he disliked descending in them. There were nine transfers between the coast and the capital, and he had made every one without difficulty, which filled him with a sense of accomplishment, for this was not an ordinary journey: he carried a leather case with him, and in it were copies of the precious charts of the Whale clan. It was an enormous responsibility, having these charts, for in the past they had never been permitted to leave the Whale clan, except for the use of the Four High Priests, and that had happened only three times in written memory. Never had another clan been privy to the Whale clan's knowledge. He was the first Spider to see the charts. Now he was under orders to show the charts to his brothers and his father; if anyone else saw them, he would be dishonored and would lose his place in the afterlife.

The Fourth High Priest met him as he left the funicular car. The station was very grand, but Akando was more than equal to his setting in his gold armor and white clothing. "The High Gods give you favor," he said to Iyestu.

"And speak to you for wisdom," said Iyestu, in the polite manner. "Where is my father?" he asked, for he had expected to see Ilatha instead of the High Priest.

"He and your brothers are waiting at the Secret School," said Akando, indicating one of the largest and most magnificent buildings in the city. "We have a chamber there where you may be assured of privacy." He indicated the case in Iyestu's hands. "When you delve into those charts, you do not want idle eyes seeing them."

"No," said Iyestu, holding the case more tightly. "Is there an escort?"

"That would draw attention to your mission," said Akando. "I am all the escort you will need. No one will approach us except the officers of the True Inca, and there are very few Ravens on the street, you see," he said, indicating all the people from the country who had come for market day in the west quarter of Machu Picchu.

"Ravens are not supposed to be in the market unless there's a war," said Iyestu.

"But Songbirds and Hawks and Pigs and Llamas and Cats and Rats are here in abundance," Akando said. "There's even a witch from the Crane clan, in the shop across the way. She trades with the Chinese, or so it's said. She goes north twice a year, in any case, and if she meets Chinese or others, who can say?"

"It's forbidden to trade with the Chinese!" said Iyestu indignantly.

"And with the people north of our land. So if she

does, wouldn't she be foolish to admit it?'' Akando indicated the various street-fronting shops that were open for market day. ''The Llama harness-makers are very good here. The Moon clan has shops in the next street, if you have need for metal utensils.''

''I know the market; I grew up here,'' said Iyestu quickly. ''I do want to talk with someone from the Moon clan later, though. I have a notion for making the sails of the kites more controllable; I will need to talk about the frame and cables and the new design with someone from the Moon clan, won't I?''

''Metals are the province of the Moon clan,'' Akando agreed. ''Very well. It will be arranged.''

They turned the corner and approached the enormous facade of the Secret School. The huge doors were guarded by hooded members of the noble Crane clan. They passed through into the entry hall, which was huge and echoed with an endless murmur of voices, its polished stone reflecting the light of two hundred oil lamps that burned every hour of the day and night. Priests and Crane clan members went busily through the hall, everyone in white cotton trousers and long white chemises. Iyestu's dark brown garment stood out glaringly.

Akando put his hand on Iyestu's shoulder. ''Come; this way. We'll meet your brothers in the private chamber.''

The room was on the second floor, guarded by Cranes, and inside Ilatha was waiting with Apenimon and Tulapa. He made a gesture of honor to Akando and turned to his sons. ''We are asked to examine the charts of the Whale clan, but we are not to discuss what we see with anyone but ourselves and Whales. It is a great honor to be permitted to break the bonds of clan in this way, but it is also a responsibility, for the secrets of the

Whale clan are theirs, not ours, and we have them at their sufferance and the order of the True Inca."

"Very good," said Akando with a slight smile.

At a sign from Ilatha, Iyestu opened the case he carried. He reached in and picked up four large sheets, folded several times, and carefully spread them out on the table. He unfolded the sheet marked in green.

"This shows the coast," he said. His father and brothers bent over the chart. "The Teeth of the Gods is here, down at this point, where the land narrows. There are savages there who run naked in the snow, or so it is said. You can see how the Flatlands spread out to the east, with rivers and jungles and plains. All that is the province of the False Inca. The men from Urop live here"—he indicated the mouth of a south-flowing river—"and here"—the second river was far to the north, east-flowing and huge at the mouth—"or so we have been told, and more will come. They have ships in these four ports, as well"—he pointed all four out—"and they travel on the trade roads within the country. The squads from the False Inca of the Green Banner are at the ports as well. If we set out from Algoma, we'll have to keep well to the north of the Teeth of the Gods or we risk being spotted by their kites or by their ships coming through the Teeth." He indicated the dangerous zones. "The Whales have marked the rivers in the ocean, and we'll have to learn the look of them if we are to be sure where we are once we leave the land. The Crane clan will give us maps of the stars for the night, but during the day we'll have to rely on the rivers of the ocean and small chains of islands if we are to reach the Maoris."

"Why not wait for the Maoris to come to us?" Tulapa suggested, mischief in his eyes.

"Because they have no reason to come," said Akando seriously. "They are a mighty people, commanding hundreds of islands and thousands of clans and millions of people. They think of us as backward and isolated, warring with the False Inca and clinging to ways that they say are out of step with the world. They are able to trade with the Czar of Russian and the merchants of China and Japan. What reason do they have to come all the way across the Western Ocean to get wool of the alpaca and silver and gold from our mines when they have riches enough? They have no enemies at their borders: we do."

"Only ignorant foreigners would think us backward," said Ilatha indignantly, stung by the observation. "They know nothing of us if they think we are backward."

Akando opened his hands. "Since there is no reason for them to know us better, they will continue in there misconception until we do something to alter their assumptions." He looked at the chart. "Consider: the False Inca controls three times the land the True Inca does. He trades with the people to the north, and the people from across the Eastern Ocean. His coffers are filling with gold from far away. We must do something to balance this." He coughed delicately. "We have the advantage of the mountains, for hardly anyone from the Flatlands is able to scale our peaks. And we have treasures in our mines, but that is not enough; in this time, we need allies. Since the High Gods are silent in this regard, we must fend for ourselves."

"Why not go to war with the people to the north and disrupt the trade the False Inca has with them?" Apenimon suggested. "Then we wouldn't have to look to the Maoris to befriend us."

"War is expensive," said Ilatha, before the Fourth High Priest could answer. "The lands to the north are rich, very rich. They have metals of their own. They can outfit an army three times the size of ours without inconvenience. We can't afford to fight them."

"Even a Pig could not have said it better," said Akando. "Show them the next chart, Iyestu."

The second chart was coded with an orange tag. Aside from one small section of land that included the port of Algoma, it showed nothing but the expanse of the Western Ocean with the rivers of the ocean marked like bands of muscle.

"They say we will be out of the sight of land once we pass this point," said Iyestu, his finger on an orange star. "In kites, we will be able to see land for a greater distance, especially with the spectacles. The land won't disappear as quickly, but by the time we are here"—the spot was a short distance beyond the orange star—"we won't see the mountains of our home, even in the air. Look how empty the ocean is. We'll be going three points east to one point south. Here we'll pass five islands on the south, and a little further on, a cluster of islands on the north. If the sky is clear, we'll see them well in advance. The Whales warned me that there are storms in that part of the ocean very often."

"If we lose our course in this stretch, it will be difficult to find it again," Apenimon said. "The beginning is the most dangerous."

"And the return," said Tulapa.

"Oh, no," Iyestu said. "Returning we have all of the coast to find, and mountains to guide us. Returning is easier than going." He pointed out a long chain of islands making almost a straight line going north to south. "The Maoris are at the south end of this line.

The other charts show the water around the islands we will pass."

"What is this?" Apenimon asked, pointing to a tremendous island west of the islands of the Maoris.

"Part of the Maori holding, the largest island they have. I'm told that most of it is desert, except here in the east and the south." He looked at the map carefully. "Everything from these islands west to the southlands of China are Maori holdings, no matter what the names may say."

The twins stared at the map with new attention. Finally Tulapa spoke. "Their lands are larger than the lands of the True Inca."

"Yes," said Akando.

"Unless we flattened the mountains," said Iyestu with sudden inspiration. "Then the lands of the True Inca would be much bigger."

Llotl came back late one night, five weeks after he had departed. Imhuro led him to the True Inca's private chambers, warning him to be silent as they went, for it was forbidden for any but priests, Ravens and Tortoises to walk the palace halls at this late hour.

"To guard against assassins?" Llotl suggested. "All a determined man would have to do is wear the dress of a Raven or Tortoise." He laughed silently, nastily.

"Keep quiet," Imhuro whispered. He disliked the Aztec more than he could express. Neither man spoke again until Imhuro unlocked the concealed entrance to Sathale's rooms. "Remember to show him respect," he said, following the spy through the door.

Sathale was seated behind his writing table, all trappings of his rank removed except for the massive gold bracelets on his wrists. The True Inca squinted as he read the pages in front of him, pausing now and again to rub his wide-set eyes. As Llotl nodded toward him Sathale motioned Imhuro to one of the hassocks.

"You must have something to report," Sathale said sharply. "What is it?"

The northerner scowled. "I don't like being pressed, True Inca." He dragged one of the hassocks a bit nearer the writing table and sank down on it. "I've had a long journey, and my bones are tired."

"Well?" Sathale said, after a time.

"There are a few things, yes," Llotl said. "But after so arduous a trek, my memory isn't as sharp as I'd like." He gazed up at the ceiling. "I'm not certain I can remember much."

"Imhuro, give him a pouch of gold," Sathale ordered wearily.

The Tortoise sat up abruptly, protesting, "True Inca, you can't do this."

"I fear I must," said Sathale. "He's as greedy as a neglected wife, though, isn't he?" He tossed a large key to Imhuro. "Go on. Bring him what he wants."

Sathale's words stung Llotl. "My memory has got much worse," he said belligerently. "I am no neglected wife, Sathale"—for a foreigner to use his name was a profound and deliberate insult—"I am one who works for your interest, if your interest works with mine."

"A pouch of gold will soothe you," said Sathale, no softening in his manner. "It had best improve your memory, Llotl."

Llotl shrugged, and took the pouch when Imhuro handed it to him. "You have no respect for my work, do you?" he asked, securing the pouch inside his clothing.

"I know it is necessary," said Sathale. "Now, what transpired?"

"How formal, and this meeting so secret," Llotl marveled. Then he took a different tone. "I had some trouble."

"Trouble?" Sathale repeated sharply.

"Not too bad," Llotl amended, hearing the alarm in Sathale's question. "It was not easy to be heard—not without telling the whole world what you wanted. Since the task required . . . prudence, I had to approach my master with circumspection. I needed to select my associates with care."

"How many?"

"Three, and one is dead for it. I had to be certain there would be no talk, and"—he shrugged—"it took longer that I expected."

Sathale grew more impatient. "What news do you have for me?"

"My master is . . . interested. He knows about the soldiers being sent to your second cousin, and he has had some experience of Helaoku, which makes him apprehensive: Helaoku's made treaty with the Turks, and they're giving him troops." Llotl pursed his lips. "You are not the only one who is endangered by that treaty. Our arrangement with the Turks could fail now that your second cousin is offering the promise of riches and . . . converts."

"What do you mean?" Imhuro asked.

"Helaoku has agreed to worship their Allah in exchange for troops to conquer you, and the north as well, perhaps." The mockery was gone from the Aztec's eyes. "It hasn't been announced yet, and won't be until more troops arrive in Helaoku's ports, in case the people don't like it. But it's whispered that the people will be required to worship as Helaoku does."

Sathale sat very still as the enormity of this revelation sank in. "Helaoku will turn from the High Gods to this Allah?" he asked quietly. "How?"

"He wants the troops and the trade and the place in the world more than he trusts the High Gods." Llotl looked away from Sathale. "My master is afraid what it would mean, for the Turks will support those who bow to Allah before they support their other allies."

"Ah," said Sathale. "Yes." He rose, walking toward the northerner. "And your ruler knows this?"

"He fears it."

"And he'll be willing to act with me if I call my army to fight the Turks and our Flatlands cousins?"

"Possibly. He wants to know more. If you wish to arrange matters, he asks that you send him word. I'll carry it, but there must be something more than what I remember. He won't do anything further until he has word from you directly." Llotl rubbed nervously at the wide belt he wore. "I am commanded to bring your message to him. Your message, True Inca, in your own hand."

"What sort of condition is that? How would he know my hand from any other?"

"He'll know because I'll tell him I watched as you wrote. He insists on it." Llotl held up his hand. "There is no bribe that would change my mind. If I lie to my master, he will order me killed. No gold is worth that."

"No," agreed Sathale.

"So write your message and I will carry it for you. I should warn you that he has heard of your intention to make an alliance with the Maoris, and he is troubled by that. He doesn't want to be your stopgap, and he doesn't want to be traded from the Turks to the Maoris. You can understand his thinking, can't you?'' Llotl slapped the hassock. ''He is no one's pawn. Neither he nor his country.''

''I will explain all in my note,'' Sathale promised grimly.

Imhuro made a gesture of protest. ''True Inca, think. These things are not to be written, for fear that others learn of them. Don't reveal to that northerner what your High Priests do not know.'' He glanced at Llotl. ''I don't speak against your leader.''

Llotl had regained some of his cynicism. ''I can tell him you have refused.''

Sathale stopped the dispute before it could become worse. ''No. No, he has a right to know.'' He went back to his writing table and dropped into the chair. ''I will comply; I must.''

Imhuro started to speak, but was silenced by a single glare from Sathale.

''And you,'' said Sathale, addressing Llotl directly. ''You will destroy this if you are caught. If anyone learns of what I have written, there is no place in the earth where you will be safe from my wrath. Some may think us primitive and backward, but we have great tenacity. Fail me, and you will learn that for yourself.''

''I would not dishonor my master so,'' Llotl vowed.

''Swear on your place in the afterlife, spy,'' Sathale said. His tone deceptively conversational.

''May they pull my heart from my chest and give it to vultures to eat,'' said Llotl. ''But it isn't necessary—''

''Now watch what I write,'' Sathale said.

By the end of the month, the Spider kites guarding the coast reported sighting two Japanese ships approaching from the north. Runners were dispatched all through the city to bring those crucial clan leaders to a meeting in the Great Ocean Hall, and the telegraph lines from Algoma to Machu Picchu thrummed and sang with the news.

"They are expected to arrive here by tomorrow evening," announced Ilatha, who had been answering questions about the ships for most of the day. The Spider clan was expected to inform the other clans; Ilatha had delivered nine of the reports himself. "They are keeping to the coast and not starting out into the ocean, either for Hawaii or for the islands of the Maoris."

"The Japanese trade with the people north of us," said Dyami, who had come to Algoma ahead of the other Four High Priests to prepare for the departure of ships bound for the Maori lands. "What can have changed that? The rulers to the north do not encourage their foreign traders to come here."

"For decades the Japanese have traded with the Northern countries, not with us," seconded Meliwa. "What is their reason for changing their habits and coming to us?"

"If they *are* coming to us," Ouninu said. "They may not be seeking us at all. They may wish to go through the Teeth of the Gods, to deal with the False Inca and the Flatlands."

"Then why stay near the coast?" asked Pallatu. "If they wanted to do that, they would not have made us aware they are coming."

"How do they know we know?" Dyami countered. "They have no kites to watch for them; that much we have learned from them. They call our kites a marvel."

"If they know of them at all," said Ilatha patiently,

"they know that we can see them coming. Just as we can announce storms from far off." He folded his arms and waited for the other men in the side chamber of the Great Ocean Hall. "We must assume they are certain we have seen them, and therefore expect to come into our ports."

Dyami stared down at the polished table as if divining the will of the High Gods in its whorled surface. "The departure for the lands of the Maoris will be delayed, but not for long. It is getting into the storm season and we can't send our ships into such danger. I will notify the True Inca and the Crane clan, so that a new and more auspicious time may be found. We'll want to learn what the Japanese have to say before we undertake to cross the Western Ocean." He touched his enormous pectoral, fingering the four cabochon emeralds there. "We must wait a short while."

Half a dozen royal funicular cars arrived in Algoma half a day ahead of the Japanese ships. Sathale gave orders for his pavilion to be erected at the head of the quay, with the rest of the court pavilions behind him to show respect for the foreigners.

Akando suggested that the Four High Priests be moved to the rear of the court to avoid slighting the religion of the Japanese.

Sathale smiled as he looked at his Fourth High Priest. "There are times you cannot forget you were born a Raven," he said. "Very well, I'll give that order. But you know that Pathoain won't like it."

"He'll like it even less if the Japanese don't answer questions," said Akando. He nodded toward the ocean, shading his eyes with his hands. "Those who venture on the waters have reason to trust their gods. It isn't right for those of us who stay on land to insult their trust.'' He looked back toward the True Inca. ''I would like to make another recommendation, High Sathale. When you meet with the Japanese, include the Spiders who are going to ride the kites to the lands of the Maoris, the boys as well as their father. These Japanese have recently crossed the Western Ocean, and they may have new information that will make the journey easier.''

''The Japanese cross far to the north of us. They deal with the Hawaiians, as well as . . . others. What can they add of use to our sailors?''

''Who knows? That is one of the reasons to include the Spiders. They may have questions of their own, and it would be best if they are able to ask them. It may be that they have heard things on their travels. Perhaps a volcano has erupted in Hawaii, or in Borneo. That would change the rivers of the ocean, wouldn't it? And as the guides for our ships, the Spiders would need to know of it.'' Akando bowed to the True Inca. ''The High Gods guide you, Sathale.''

Both Japanese ships carried extensive sails and both had two auxiliary paddle wheels just forward of the rudders. They were clearly merchant ships, big-bellied and brightly painted, with plain sails showing no noble mon. The captains brought five bolts of brocade silk ashore—one for the True Inca, one for each of the Four High Priests—as soon as they tied up.

Girusa, the aged leader of the Llama clan, had been summoned to serve as translator, for he spoke four languages of those to the north. Assuming the Japanese merchants knew the language of the those to the north, they could be understood. He stood at the side of the True Inca, white hair pulled back and clubbed in bands of bright ribbons. As the Japanese dropped to their knees and bowed, Girusa addressed them in a tongue that ordinarily was as forbidden to be spoken in the land of the True Inca as the name of its country was forbidden to be spoken—the language of Mexico. "Good travelers," he said, more nervous of the True Inca than of the foreigners, unaware that the True Inca understood every word, "you are welcome in this place, to every house and clan. The True Inca, Monarch of the Spine of the World and the Western Ocean, bids you greet him as his honored guests."

The captains raised their heads. *"Arigato,"* said the older. "Our thanks to you for so unexpected an honor. Humble merchants do not seek to dine at the tables of kings." He touched the bolts of silk. "This is the most insignificant gift to show our good faith."

When Girusa had translated this, Sathale rose and said, "Tell them that we have prepared rooms for them in the Great Ocean Hall. The invitation is extended to all their men as well. Their ships will be guarded by the Whale and Raven clans, so that no harm will come to them or their merchandise."

This time it took Girusa a little longer to explain, and the Japanese captains seemed to be uncertain about the hospitality being offered them.

"Say to them that they come at a propitious time," Sathale said. "Tell them that we have been advised that messengers from far away can assist us; we honor our High Gods by showing hospitality to them."

"They are willing, or so they say," Girusa reported shortly. "They do not wish to give insult to our gods."

"Fine," said Sathale. "Tell them we will dine at sundown in the Great Ocean Hall. They will be my table companions, above the Crane clan. And warn the

Rats to cook their best." With that he turned away and went back into his pavilion, signaling to his Crane guards to come with him.

It took Girusa a while to explain to the Japanese the significance of the True Inca's invitation. When at last they grasped the magnitude of the honor extended to them, they expressed amazement, though their eyes were apprehensive.

"Tell your ruler," said the older captain, "that we seek an audience with him perhaps more private that the banquet he is planning. We have news for him, if he wishes to have it." He was kept from revealing more by his younger associate, who stopped him, speaking in their own tongue, and quickly, as though Girusa might figure out their meaning if he spoke more slowly. At last the older captain addressed the Llama leader once more. "We are grateful for the guards for our ships, but we would prefer our crews remain aboard, for the engines of these vessels need careful tending."

"Upon my honor," said Girusa, and carried these messages to Sathale.

By the time the True Inca donned his gold-scaled cloak and jeweled chemise for the banquet, he had met twice with the Four High Priests and once with Meliwa and Ilatha. "Well," he told his First Wife as he put his Sun clan ring on his thumb, "I suppose I'd best practice smiling for them. Girusa says they are very polite."

His First Wife, who was from the Fox clan, reached out and took his hand. "You have your court to smile. You need not if you would prefer not to."

Sathale shook his head. "If I want to learn from them, I'll have to persuade them to speak." He laced his fingers with hers. "In Machu Picchu I could allow you to attend, but here . . ."

She sighed. "Yes. But you'll tell me later what happened."

"I will," he promised her. He pulled his hand free of hers, letting the tips of his fingers graze her cheek and brow before moving away.

Pausing in the hall, he waited for his Crane guards to fall in two steps behind him. Then, properly escorted, he went to the chamber of the First High Priest, where Pathoain was waiting with the gold crown of the True Inca.

Sathale looked sourly at the crown and touched his forehead. "Be sure someone keeps a cup of pansy-and-willow tea ready for me all evening. There's plenty of weight there."

"I have ordered it." Pathoain indicated the golden ball at the crest of the crown. "The orb of the Sun clan, True Inca."

Sathale made the traditional gesture of respect. "The False Inca wears one like this, but with jewels as well. I am told he has to practice walking with weights on his head."

The First High Priest was not amused. "He forfeited the right to the Sun clan when his grandfather left the mountains for the plains and forests he rules now. He may have conquered the Flatlands and the jungles, and count himself ruler of all between the foothills and the Eastern Ocean, but he is no longer part of the Sun clan—nor was his father before him." Pathoain went to pick up the crown, admitting as he did, "But you are right; it is heavy."

Once the crown was properly in place, Sathale clapped his hands twice. "If the Rats have done their job properly, it is time to eat."

"The Rats have been cooking all day. There is fish

and pig and sheep all prepared, as well as berries and vegetable stews and five kinds of beans.'' Pathoain went through the door ahead of Sathale, then waited while the True Inca took his place with his Crane guards behind him. ''Are you ready, True Inca?''

''Yes,'' said Sathale. ''Let's get on with it.''

Besides the lavish dishes brought in profusion to the eighty-eight men in the Great Ocean Hall, musicians from the Songbird clan and dancing acrobats from the Rabbit clan performed throughout the evening for the enjoyment of the diners. Members of the Rat and Fox clans served the meal, the Foxes limiting their service to those of the highest nobility and the two guests.

As the last dish finally arrived, Sathale turned his attention to the Japanese captains. ''I am a fortunate host to have you as my guests. It has been more than fifteen years since we entertained anyone from Japan. I am curious how this comes about, with so many years gone by.''

The younger captain, an angular man with a scraggle of moustache on his upper lip, leaned forward and lifted his cup of honeyed wine. ''It was a very unfortunate thing, and not of our doing, the breaking off of dealings with you people of Peru. We were not part of the negotiations, of course, and our opinions were not sought. The Russians were in charge of that. Had we known more of your country and your people, we would have tried to change the treaties, or limit them, so that we might have been here from the start of our trade with this part of the world.''

''Then this has changed?'' asked Dyami. ''Why is that?''

''Well, you see,'' said the older captain, more awkward than the younger, ''Russia is not as it was. There have been three czars in the last year. One was killed in . . . an accident while traveling. His rail train was destroyed when a bridge collapsed. His nephew Evgeny succeeded him, and was murdered before he had completely moved himself into the Kremlin, and the assassins were never identified, though an exhaustive search was made to learn who they were and who had paid them. His brother Illya succeeded him, and he was shot while leading his troops against the Chinese and Tartars. Now there is a new czar, Grigori V, but everyone assumes he cannot reign long: he is over fifty and has done nothing but manage his country estates and knows very little of politics. The world is changing.''

Girusa had trouble expressing some of the words and phrases, but after a few short conferences with the Japanese, he was able to render a good account of what the two captains had said.

''So the Russians have lost their hold on China, have they?'' Sathale said.''What does that do to them in the west, with the False Inca of the Green Banner and the men of Urop, I wonder?'' His voice was distant and speculative. The Japanese would be paying close attention to his tone because they could not understand his words. ''And what of the Chinese and Japanese, now that they are not under Russian rule? Will they want to reassert their rightful places in the world? How does it seem to you?''

These questions were relayed to the Japanese, who spoke together in some consternation. Finally the younger answered. ''When we left our country, there was unrest, to be sure. The people were calling on the Mikado to be rid of the Russians and to reestablish our country without Russian patronage. The Chinese have been more assertive, for they have troops at the border and are prepared to fight the Russians. In fact, there have been a number of skirmishes already. Some of the powerful lords of Canton and Shanghai have attempted to close their cities to Russians and to unite their provinces against them.'' He cleared his throat. ''We are merchants, and we do not like to be caught in the wars of nobles.''

''No,'' agreed Sathale. ''And yet, a good merchant cannot ignore the realities of the marketplace, can he?''

Again the two Japanese conferred before offering their reply. ''No,'' said the elder. ''In peace we trade silks, in war we trade dried meat and copper.'' He stared down at the wide sash he wore around his waist. ''My companion and I do not see the situation in the same way. I have been a merchant all my life; he did not come to it until he was over twenty, and has practiced the merchant's life for only twelve years. He designed ships instead of sailing them before, until the Russians put their own men into those positions, and Yukio Shigemaro''—he indicated his younger companion—''was forced to choose another trade.''

''And the Maoris—what have you heard of them? We are preparing to send a delegation to them.''

''We saw your three ships. What can I say to you? No one troubles much with the Maoris, not with a possible uprising in China,'' said Yukio Shigemaro.

''Who can say?'' added Hisoka Hyogo, the older captain. ''The Maoris are ambitious people and their islands stretch a long way. What is true for one is not always true for another, and I have not been to their islands, not even the Great West Island, for over a year, so anything I know is not current, and probably useless." He made a philosophical gesture. "In other times I might have trusted myself to guess, but now . . . no."

The Four High Priests were divided once again. It was almost dawn and the two Japanese captains had gone back to their ships; the True Inca and the Four High Priests had withdrawn to a council room for what was supposed to be a short discussion. Now the night was almost done and there was no better consensus than when they had begun.

"Until we know what has happened with the Maoris, I say that it is wise to delay," Pathoain reiterated. "What if we arrive to discover that there is a war? What can we do then?"

"And what if they are seeking new alliances? What if they are as eager for those alliances as we say we are? If we do not act quickly, we lose the opportunity to be the first to treat with them; such a position can provide us many opportunities. Once that advantage is gone, we cannot reclaim it." Akando sat back from the table, his arms folded, his face showing none of the emotion that was in his voice. "If we wish to be there at the most auspicious time, ahead of the country to the north or Hawaii, this is the best time for us to depart, before the storms come."

"And if we delay," added Dyami, "who knows what arrangements the False Inca may make? He has already opened his country to men of the False Inca of the Green Banner, and we know that recently more of the ships of the False Inca of the Green Banner have been seen in the ports of the country to the north. That bodes ill: if the False Inca were to treat with Mexico—"

Everyone at the table was shocked, for Dyami had spoken the unspeakable name. "What is the matter with you?'' Pathoain demanded, his priestly reserve vanishing. ''How can you insult the True Inca—''

''I'd rather insult him than see him risk losing his crown and country to Helaoku and his foreign allies,'' Bemosetu said. ''So far, no one has admitted that could be possible, though we all know—or we ought to know—that it could happen. We need allies now. We need access to arms and more money. If the Maoris will have us, as we had better hope they will, we ought to begin our negotiations at once, before the turmoil across the oceans reaches our shores.''

Sathale looked over at Bemosetu with interest, for the Third High Priest had been silent for most of the night. ''Go on; what makes you say this?''

Bemosetu sighed. ''No matter what happens in Russia, there will be some unrest there and in the client countries. Judging by what the Japanese said, their country is near to breaking with Russia—I know those were not their words,'' he went on, forestalling the objections of the others, ''but it was what they were telling us. If China and Japan and Korea break away from Russia, Russia will have to take action westward into Urop or risk having the men of Urop come to them. The False Inca of the Green Banner cannot allow that, not in countries that he still controls. So the False Inca of the Green Banner will have to solidify his hold on his lands or risk losing them. Not only might he have trouble with Urop, but with China as well, for Ind is caught between the False Inca of the Green Banner and the Chinese; he will need a reliable source of supplies, and since he cannot be certain of either Urop or Ind . . . He will have to deal with the False Inca or the country to the north.''

''You were a Badger, weren't you?'' Akando asked

Bemosetu, in an undervoice roughened by lack of sleep. "Badgers do no statecraft. Where did you learn all this?"

"I have read all the reports from our messengers and I have gathered information from foreigners," Bemosetu said stiffly. "Ravens are not the only ones who know about war."

Akando shook his head. "Oh, lower your bristles! In my own manner, I'm giving you a compliment." He looked at Sathale. "He's making sense, True Inca. We cannot ignore what has happened in Russia. One way or another, it will reach our shores and our mountains. If we are not ready for it, we will be overwhelmed." Then, staring directly at Pathoain: "I say what I have maintained all evening. If we are to be successful, we must authorize those ships to leave as soon as the Cranes will permit it. If it were my decision, I would tell them to put to sea by this time tomorrow."

The senior Rat clan servant interrupted the meeting by arriving with yet another urn of coffee and a tray of fruit. He offered obeisance to the five men and departed without speaking.

"That Rat looks exhausted," said Dyami, pouring another glass of coffee.

"We all look exhausted," Akando said. He rose to get more coffee for himself. "At least we've kept most of the coffee plantations in our lands. The False Inca may have the Flatlands, but we have the coffee trees."

"Do you think we might be able to export it to anyone but the False Inca of the Green Banner? His merchants buy it through the False Inca and the countries to the north, or so the records say." Sathale watched Pathoain fill his glass. "The Chinese export their tea throughout the Western Ocean."

"True enough," Dyami said, coming to get the True Inca's glass and fill it. "But coffee is a sacred drink. Would the High Gods approve if we sold it?"

"Ask the Cranes," suggested Akando. "If they decide we can, then we know the High Gods won't object." He leaned back in his chair. "If I don't sleep soon, I won't be able think clearly."

Pathoain glared at Akando. But Dyami endorsed the remark. "With the coffee I will be able to stay awake, but my mind is becoming numb and I am not prepared to listen for the voice of the High Gods. If you will give us time to rest, True Inca, what we tell you will have more merit."

Sathale smiled. "I will call you at noon and will give my decision. And I will send word to the Crane clan." He accepted his glass of coffee. "My First Wife will be pleased."

"All our First Wives will be pleased," said Dyami, as much because the amusement was welcome as because it was true.

Iyestu was the last to take formal leave of Ilatha; the others had already shared the ritual cups of beer and given the token gifts. Ilatha's First and Second Wives were permitted to come to the quay for the departure, and both marveled at the two Japanese ships that were being refitted with lines and could not depart for several weeks.

"They have been messengers of the High Gods," said Ilatha, not wholly in jest. "If we had not known—"

"The High Gods guide us," said Hataya, who was feeling embarrassed at being left behind. "Each of us."

Ilatha looked at his sons in their uniforms and could not contain his pride. "There have been no sons of this family who have brought so much honor to the Spiders as you have.'' He put his hands on the shoulders of his twins. ''You are to listen to what the Whale captains say and you are to follow their orders for the safety of the men on the ships and the honor of the True Inca.''

Apenimon looked at his brother. ''Well, Tulapa, does this seem real to you now?''

''What does that mean?'' Ilatha demanded.

''Oh, my twin has said he thought this was all a game, that we would not be going anywhere. Now it is about to happen.''

Tulapa chuckled. ''And the only one who is prepared is Iyestu, if having those two new kites can be called prepared.''

''My new kites are better and safer than yours,'' said Iyestu with some heat. ''I know. I'll stay higher and do better than the rest of you.'' His cheeks were flushed and his eyes grew bright with anger.

''Peace, peace,'' Ilatha said. ''Tulapa always needles you, Iyestu.'' He patted his third son affectionately. Then he looked at his daughter, feeling confused, for there were no rituals for the departure of girls. ''What shall I say to you, Etenyi?''

''Wish me a safe voyage, I guess.'' She stared down at her shoes, so recently supplied by the Whale clan. ''I will emulate my brothers, I promise on the High Gods and the afterlife. I will say your name every sunrise and every sunset.''

''And we will place salt with your portraits every day you are gone,'' said Hataya, looking quickly from the First to the Second Wife. ''Every day.''

''You are a good brother,'' Etenyi said. ''This takes so long.''

All the crew were waiting on the quay while the Rats

finished loading the three ships. The food had already been stowed, as had the ships' supplies and extra fuel for the small engines. Now the Rats were engaged in more delicate and complex matters: the proper stowing of the formal gifts to the leaders of the Maori clans. Every gift to be presented had been reviewed by the Four High Priests and the leaders of the Crane clan, and each assessed for its appropriateness and merit. In all, sixty-seven gifts were approved and blessed, and now were handled as if they were as precious as the person of the True Inca himself.

Iyestu recalled the many questions from the Crane clan about his new design of kite, doubting a boy could improve the traditional design. Eventually other Spiders spoke on its behalf, and three leaders of the Condor clan, who kept the forts at the high passes, defended it too. It was the Condor endorsement that made the difference. Two new kites were stowed for the voyage.

"You will leave on the evening tide," said Ilatha. He felt an odd distress. The evening tide came so soon! "The True Inca has given his order."

"Tell the Rats and the Cranes to hurry," said Tulapa, who found it hard to stand still. He wanted to be on the ocean, to ride his kite high into the air, his spectacles strapped around his head, his eyes fixed on the western horizon. All that waiting could do was take the keen edge off his preparedness. "How much longer?"

One of the Rats carrying a chest aboard tripped. There was tremendous consternation until it was established that the chest had not touched the quay or the gangplank, but had only grazed the rail of the ship. Dyami pronounced another protective spell over the chest, just in case, and the loading was resumed.

"Have they taken our things onto the ship yet?"

Etenyi asked. "Which ship will I sail on? I want to put another vial of scent in my things."

"The Whale clan only permitted you the three vials, remember?" her mother said. "If you need more, there are sure to be perfumes in the lands of the Maoris."

"You don't need perfume, Etenyi. No one will notice how you smell on the ship in any case," Apenimon said. "Everything smells of the ocean."

Etenyi drew an impatient breath. "You can say that, and it means nothing to you. But . . ." She could not find words to express her expectations and her fears.

Ilatha's First Wife put her arm around her daughter's shoulder. "Everyone says that being on the ocean is difficult at the beginning, but that you quickly accustom yourself. Your sister will be given your gift on her wedding day, if you haven't yet returned."

"Good," said Etenyi, remembering how put out her sister had been when it was suggested that her brothers and sister might not be back in time for her wedding. "I want her to have my necklaces, too, and my combs if I . . . if I don't come back." She squared her shoulders as she said that, secretly liking the sound of it.

"Etenyi," said the First Wife.

"Just tell me you'll do it," said Etenyi in a soft, tense voice.

"Whatever you want," said her mother. She looked up as the Fourth High Priest and the leader of the Rat clan for the navy approached.

"Well," said Akando, making a ritual greeting. He looked at the four youngsters who were leaving. "You have a little more time for private farewells, and then it's my task to escort you to the True Inca for the Mandate. You, Etenyi, will travel on the *Whale's Breath*. And you boys will be one to each ship, with your kites as well: Apenimon to the *Whale Road* and Tulapa to the *Black Dolphin*. Iyestu will go with his sister, being the youngest.'' He nodded to Ilatha. ''It's almost time.''

Apenimon took the pectoral of the Spider clan given him by his father. ''We're ready,'' he said for his twin, his younger brother and his sister.

Only Tulapa looked back once, and that was to wave at his mother.

One day after the departure of the expedition to the lands of the Maoris, another messenger reached the capital of the True Inca, and desperately demanded an audience with Sathale at once. The True Inca, just returned from Algoma, had not yet visited with his three wives and their children, nor sat down to a meal, but he sighed and told his Crane guards that he would receive the messenger in his private council chamber.

The messenger was ragged and weary, his eyes sunk into his head from the rigors of his travel. ''I wanted to arrive sooner,'' he said. ''If there had not been obstruction, I would have been here seven, eight days ago.''

''Obstruction?'' Sathale, indicating the messenger could sit, clapped his hands and ordered glasses of coffee and beer from his guard.

''I'm not deserving of your courtesy,'' said the messenger. ''I have not fulfilled the oath I took to you and to the Fox clan when I went down to the lands of the False Inca.''

''Through no fault of yours, or so I suppose,'' said the True Inca. ''But tell me: What happened to you?''

''Coming back, there was fever along the Mother River,'' the messenger said slowly, ''and great numbers of ants, devouring all in their path. They came one after the other, fever, then the ants when most of us were too ill to stop them."

"My Spiders in untethered kites have seen something of this," said the True Inca.

The messenger stared up at the lavishly painted ceiling showing the positions of the clans in the night sky. "It was worse than fire, worse than illness. Helaoku ordered troops into the interior to keep order and to do something about the ants if they could, but they had not yet arrived, and it was hard to find a safe path."

"How unfortunate for the people of the False Inca."

The messenger looked up as a Rat servant brought two glasses of coffee into the chamber. "I've missed coffee. This is a drink only for the noble and the rich in the lands of the False Inca."

"My merchants won't sell to the False Inca, or not directly," Sathale said, making a show of taking a lavish sip of the hot, dark liquid.

"The Turks are very fond of it—the followers of the False Inca of the Green Banner." The Fox clan messenger contemplated his hands, clean but with ragged nails and bruised knuckles. "The authorities in remote places are like men awaiting a siege. They give as little as they can to travelers, and charge prices that only those with gold can meet."

"That has been true for some time," said Sathale. His patience was starting to wear thin. "Recently I have learned that there has been trouble in Russia. The Turks are in trouble there."

"The markets of the Flatlands are filled with more rumors than flies. It is said that the leader of the Turks is going to mount an expedition into China, to extend his territory now that Russia has lost hold of it. They have said that the soldiers will be from Urop, to avoid ambition. So far from home, none of the soldiers will seek to take holdings for themselves, or so it is thought. Some of the garrison soldiers say it is to keep the soldiers from getting too friendly with the local people. One man I spoke to, from Bilbao, said that the Bey—the local officer of the False Inca of the Green Banner—was giving notice to all merchant and artisan families to ready their sons for the army.''

''Interesting. Do you think it's true?''

''I don't know. I believe some of it is true, but I can't be certain. Though I fear someone is planning war.'' The messenger finished his glass of coffee. ''I saw soldiers from the False Inca of the Green Banner who wore striped trousers and who were said to be the fiercest warriors. They disdain the steam wagons the other soldiers use and fight the traditional way on horses. Everyone regarded them with fear.''

''How many were there?'' asked the True Inca, remembering the report of the Spider guard who had seen men in striped trousers on horseback conquer a fort.

''The squad I saw was fifty, but I was told that the False Inca of the Green Banner has sent over two thousand of them to assist the False Inca, so that Helaoku will have sufficient fighters to come into the mountains.'' He stared at his empty glass so that he would not have to look at the True Inca. ''As a Fox, I am willing to do all you order me, but I do not believe it would be wise for me to return to the Flatlands now. There are those who have come to suspect me, and if I were back in the lands of the False Inca, there is a chance I would be caught before I could end my life. They have done that to three men from Urop who were looking for others from the region of Italy to aid in a rebellion against the False Inca of the Green Banner.

When they were through with them, they hung all that was left over the market square in the capital, where the Mother River joins the Eastern Ocean."

"A rebellion in the region of Italy, you say?"

"That was what they whispered in the marketplace when the men were taken. They were men of Urop, true enough, and they spoke the tongue of the region of Italy, so it is not difficult to believe." He stifled a yawn. "You pardon, True Inca."

"You're tired," said Sathale. "Yet I need a little more of your time." He clapped again and asked for more coffee. "Do you know if the False Inca of the Green Banner is trying to make common cause with the lands to the north?"

The messenger was startled. "No," he said. "I have seen merchants from the lands to the north; one of them from the far north of the lands . . . of Mexico . . . said that the merchants of Urop did not buy as much whale-oil in recent years as they had before."

"Do you know why that is?"

"The merchant from . . . the lands to the north"—he did not wish to give offense again—"said that he thought that the regions of Urop were buying their oil from China and Russia, and bringing it in by the steam rail system, but that might have been his discontent speaking."

"So it might," said Sathale, as the Rat servant returned with more coffee. He looked at the messenger closely. "Is there anything more you wish to tell me?"

The messenger drank again. "There is one thing I do not understand. I will put it in my report and I will tell you, though I cannot fathom what it means. There is a factory in the capital of the False Inca at the mouth of the Mother River where the machines are run on lightning, or so the workers there have said. No other factory uses such fuel, and no other factory works so fast or shines so brightly as this one. They say that in the lands on the other side of the Eastern Ocean this fuel is used more commonly, though most of the workers here distrust it, for if it is not properly contained, there is fire like the fire of the High Gods that blasts the life away.'' He paused. ''An officer of the False Inca said that there were such factories in the lands to the north, and that they were seeking to build more. He also said that the fuel could be used to make lamps that do not need oil to burn, and that the lamps could be placed anywhere. But what fuel can do that?''

Sathale stared at his undrunk coffee. ''Yes; what fuel can do that.''

On the high prow of the *Whales' Breath*, Etenyi could just barely see her brother Iyestu aloft in his tethered kite. The cable holding him was anchored a little aft of the central mast; it angled away into the sky, showing the direction of the wind as much as the sails did. She shaded her eyes, studying the clouds and envying Iyestu his place among them.

''Are you afraid for him?'' asked Pallatu, as he strolled up to Etenyi with the ease of one accustomed to the roll of a ship.

''No; he has been riding the kites since he was eight years old,'' she said. ''But I was wondering what it feels like, to be part of the wind that way, and to follow a ship as he is doing.''

''When the tether has been played out all the way, you won't be able to see him, you know, even if the sky is clear.''

''Yes. I noticed that while he was up yesterday.''

"He's a very capable fellow, your young brother," Pallatu said. He gazed over the ocean ahead of them. "That's nothing against the other two; they're good at what they do and they are brave Spiders. But this one"—he indicated the speck at the end of the tether—"he is more than the others. He is alert to the whispers of the High Gods, and for that, he sees beyond the limits."

"You mean Iyestu has been touched by the High Gods?" Etenyi shook her head. "Iyestu's not a priest. He's dedicated to the kites. He's a real Spider."

"Oh, yes," said Pallatu at once. "More Spider than most, I suspect. He knows the tether for what it is: a leash, something he disdains because he soars, and wishes to be free, like the birds."

"Well, he is very good with the untethered kites. He has done Condor patrol over the Spine of the World, and the Condor leaders praised him for his skills. He was one of the youngest Spiders sent on that task."

"Left alone, he can do more than that. Left alone, he could amaze us all." Pallatu regarded Etenyi with curiosity. "How is it for you, being here on the ocean when women of the Spider clan are not supposed to travel? Does it trouble you?"

"You were there when the Mandate was read, and you know how I was charged. It doesn't matter that women of the Spider clan don't travel, because of the True Inca's Mandate." She was defensive now, for as much as she knew the Mandate of the True Inca overbore all objections of clan and tradition, she could not rid herself of the sense that she had gone too far beyond the limits of Spiders ever to return to them. As she turned her head the wind whipped the ends of the ribbons confining her hair across her face.

"But think when you return: you'll have been over

the Western Ocean of the lands of the Maoris, and it won't be correct for you to speak of it among Spider women. Won't that bother you?"

"I have told my father that I will uphold the traditions of Spider women, and if that prohibits me from speaking of this voyage, then I will not bring disgrace on my clan when the True Inca has shown me such honor." She tossed her head. "Why do you ask?"

"Because I have seen women who travel, and few of them can keep what they have seen to themselves. Few men, either. They can't wait for the chance to talk of the places they have been and the things they have seen. The lands of the Maoris aren't like the Spine of the World, and the way they live there is not as we do. How will it be, to tell only the True Inca and no one else of what you saw and heard?" He indicated the steps down into the main cabin of the ship. "Ouninu can tell other Rats about what he has done on this voyage, and that is proper. Your brothers are not sworn to keep silent for fear of causing unworthy thoughts in others. You alone are forbidden to tell of your adventure." He offered her a sympathetic smile.

"Whales are used to speaking of voyages, and you would miss it. No Spider woman can feel that way." She moved away from him and stared out over the crinkled ocean. "In any case, I am asked to write it down, and so I will have the opportunity to tell it, but in a different manner than you Whales do."

"I don't intend unkindness, girl," Pallatu said. "If I were asked, I would have encouraged the True Inca to permit you to speak about all you see and learn while we are in the lands of the Maoris. If you decide that you want to discuss this lat—"

"How gracious," said Etenyi, doing her best to

sound sincere. "I think I would prefer to watch Iyestu as the tether is played out. If that doesn't hamper you or any Whales on the ship."

"Whatever you wish," said Pallatu, going away from her.

"Who's there?" Sathale looked up, moving his arm to cover the document on his writing table. Most of the lamps were out and the guards drowsed at their posts.

"Akando," said the Fourth High Priest, emerging from the shadow of the doorway.

Sathale relaxed. "It's late; I didn't know you were up."

"I've been waiting," said Akando. He closed the door and came into the room. "To talk to you."

"Oh?" Sathale gestured toward the nearest hassock. "Nothing too difficult, I hope." He looked around the room. "Imhuro is asleep, but if you want coffee, I can—"

"No coffee," said Akando, doing the unthinkable and interrupting the True Inca. "And don't wake your Tortoise." Akando paced the chamber, his lean face drawn, his wry humor vanished.

Sathale stared at Akando. "What did you say?"

"You will not want anyone to overhear what I have to say to you," Akando told him, pausing to direct his gaze directly at Sathale. "This must be between you and me, True Inca."

"What must?" Sathale asked.

Akando made an impatient gesture. "If it weren't unthinkable I would have realized it sooner. I was a Raven: I should have seen—" He rounded on Sathale, facing him squarely across the writing table. "You sent them to death. You have no intention of allying with the Maoris. The expedition was nothing more than a ploy."

Sathale remained still as these accusations were flung at him. There was no use dissembling. When Akando fell silent, his face set with baffled rage, he said simply, "You're right."

"What?" Akando stood very still.

"I sent those three ships out knowing they couldn't succeed. I've kept the Japanese here deliberately, so that they won't have to sail in storms; they can leave when the weather improves. And they can carry a man and a message for me."

Akando dropped onto the hassock. He had been prepared for lies, for excuses, for tantrums, for anything but candor. It threw him.

"Why?"

"Because of what I must do," Sathale said. "I am arranging a secret alliance with the lands to the north."

"With *Mexico*?"

"Yes."

It took a little while for Akando to speak again. "You betray . . . everything."

"Better to betray than lose," said Sathale quietly, and saw a change in Akando's expression. "We are near to being lost. There was a time when we were alone in the world. But that time is gone. If we don't enter the world, the world will devour us."

Akando stared at Sathale.

"But how does any of this save us?"

"Think like a Raven, not a High Priest. We can't let my second cousin learn what I'm doing. Therefore he must think I'm doing something else. I tried to find something that wouldn't be too costly. Three ships is no little price, but—"

''And you sent children to do your work,'' Akando said, his eyes condemning.

''I'll need all the capable Spiders I have to keep our borders safe,'' Sathale said. ''Of all our matériel, those ships are the least important, since our fight is likely to be on land, or within sight of the coast. I begrudge Helaoku my Whales the least.''

''I serve the High Gods,'' Akando said slowly. ''I am sworn to them before I am sworn to you, True Inca.''

''Indeed.''

''It is my duty to tell the other High Priests, and to reveal your treason.''

''And will you?''

Akando considered his answer. ''Not yet.''

Apenimon and Tulapa both reported seeing a dark line near the horizon, and both knew better than to suppose it was land. Pallatu listened to their reports with misgiving, and called his officers to the main cabin on the *Whale's Breath*. He ordered coffee served and asked the Rats to see that the two Spiders were given the first glasses.

''It's a storm, sure as the ocean is wet,'' said Tulapa with bravado when Pallatu asked him to report. ''My brother saw it just after dawn, and when I went up, it was still there, at the western horizon.'' He shook his head. ''A bad storm coming.''

''When Iyestu comes down, he can give us a new report,'' said Apenimon, trying to sound as if he were used to storms on the ocean.

''The ocean is silky,'' said Enonyu, captain of the *Black Dolphin*. ''The storm will be a long one.''

Pallatu nodded. ''So I fear. If we could only be sure that the storm was moving away from us, we would—''

"Well, it isn't moving away from us," said Tulapa flatly. "I've watched over the passes above Algoma, and I've seen storms blowing in before. If that line at the horizon is spreading, then the storm is coming, and the wider the line, the more severe the storm." He indicated the room beyond this cabin where the compass was kept in a sealed glass globe. "You'll need to watch as the storm nears, for it will be less accurate, or so I have been told."

"We are aware, boy," said Pallatu. He signaled to one of the Rats and asked that they bring writing material. "I want to get this down. The Spider girl can do it. Let her have the paper and pens." He gave Etenyi an approving sign. "So long as you are sent to make records, you might as well keep a record for me." Then he leaned back, pressing his huge, calloused hands together. "Well?" This was addressed to the other two captains.

"I'd pull in sail before we can be dragged off course, and I'd use the engines so we wouldn't wallow," said Ylaipa, captain of the *Whale Road*. He was the youngest of the three, an eager, stalwart man who had been staring at Etenyi throughout the meeting. "The engines, both paddlewheels going at quarter speed, should keep us moving and will keep our faces into the storm. Anything else will mean disaster."

Pallatu, who had saved four of five ships a decade before by running ahead of a storm for three days, nodded. "As long as the engines are able to function. In heavy seas, who can say what may happen?"

"Who can say in any case," remarked Enonyu. "The High Gods will decide if we will be allowed to cross the Western Ocean." He drank more of his coffee. "If we make them an offering—"

"No sacrifices!" Pallatu slammed his palm down hard on the table. "No sacrifices on this voyage, is that understood? No Rats missing overboard in the night, no food gone, no fuel unaccounted for: do I make that clear enough for both of you?"

Etenyi was staring at the Whale captains, her eyes huge. "The Four High Priests forbid . . ." she began, then could not go on.

"The Four High Priests," said Ylaipa bluntly, "are far away, and here the old traditions hold." He gave Pallatu a long, challenging look. "One Rat, Whale leader. What is that to us?"

"If a Rat is trivial to us, he is trivial to the High Gods," said Pallatu harshly, motioning for silence as the Rat servant came back with pens and paper for Etenyi. "I thank you," he said, and motioned to the Rat to leave. "We are on a voyage at the Mandate of the True Inca, and all the sacrifices that are necessary have already been made in Machu Picchu and Algoma." He went and brought the coffee urn. "Here. Have more. I will authorize a ration for the crews tonight, for we may need to have them all alert quite late." He poured out the thick, fragrant liquid. "Tell me," he went on in a lighter tone, "do Spiders stay aloft in storms?"

"No," said Apenimon at once. "We return to the ground. Lightning often travels down our tethers if we remain aloft. Two Condor forts were destroyed forty years ago because the Spiders would not come down. The lightning not only burned the kite, but it fired the forts as well." He indicated the ship. "This wouldn't fare better."

"I think we had best give the order to bring Iyestu

down,'' said Pallatu. ''And when he is, bring him to me. I want to know what he has seen.''

''The storm would not advance so far in an hour,'' said Tulapa.

''Don't believe that,'' Ylaipa said. ''Storms can rise out of perfect calm in almost no time.'' He looked up at the low, beamed ceiling. ''I hope those Japanese merchants waited a few more days. I wouldn't like to be going to Hawaii in a bad storm.'' His studied confidence convinced no one.

It was the annual meeting of the Elders of the Eighty-eight Clans, and the grandeur of the occasion was nearly as impressive as the Mid-Winter Summoning, when the Four High Priests officially pleaded to the sun to return. Sathale II, in formal state robes with a train twice as long as he was tall, strode down the center of the Triumphal Way to the Golden Temple. The gold he wore weighed as much as he did, and his crown had long since given him a fierce headache.

Behind him came the Elders, each with the three allowed retainers, and behind them, four bands of the most accomplished musicians the Moon and Songbird clans could furnish. The Four High Priests awaited the procession at the enormous door of the Golden Temple, each carrying a symbol of the sovereignty of the land of the True Inca. Behind them, the elite Crane guard stood at the ready. Subjects of the True Inca from the length of the Spine of the World watched with rejoicing and awe as the civic ritual was enacted.

The Elder of the Fox clan was the last of those to address the assembly, and he was witty and brief. He pleased the crowd by exclaiming at the number of healthy children he saw, and congratulated the parents.

Finally he warned against complacency in the face of the False Inca, and then stepped away from the dais, leaving the way open for the Four High Priests to call down the attention of the High Gods on the annual deliberations.

"I hate these things," said Sathale later as he was relieved of his cumbersome splendor in his smaller audience chamber. He looked around at the Elders of the Llama and the Condor clans. "All right, tell me: how many spies from the False Inca have been apprehended in the last year?"

"Eleven that we know of," said the Elder of the Llamas. "I have the records with me, if you wish to review them."

"Leave them, please," said Sathale. "And you?" he asked the Condor.

"There have been travelers through our forts who were more than travelers—aside from those who actually attacked the forts—but we were not permitted to detain them or ask too many questions." He was too old to disguise his opinion. "That is foolishness; all such travelers ought to be detained and questioned. The Mandate of Chesmupa does not allow it, and you have not changed the Mandate, so—"

"Nor will I, unless I am driven to do it," said Sathale in a manner that permitted no debate. "I am going to assign Foxes to your forts. The Foxes know their craft, and they will draw out the travelers better than you could with your cells and whips." He smiled. "We don't want the False Inca to think we're at war with him."

"But we are," said the Elder of the Condors.

"It hasn't been declared," Sathale reminded him. "As long as we are able to pretend that the war is a rumor, then we have some hope of keeping it within our control."

The Condor Elder was unimpressed. "And if there is a concerted attack on the Condor forts, what then? Is my clan supposed to ignore that as well?"

Sathale sighed. "We have untethered kites patrolling the length of the Spine of the World. Surely they will be able to report on the movements of troops."

"And if they cannot?" demanded the Llama. "What if we cannot keep Spiders aloft?"

"The False Inca is not able to bring troops over our mountains in winter, and that is the only time the Spiders are apt to be on the ground." Sathale stood very still as his huge, gold collar was fastened around his neck. "I will double the Spiders patrolling, if that would reassure you."

"Telegraphs and more funicular cars would reassure me," muttered the Condor Elder. "We need more telegraphs."

"Say so in the official gathering," Sathale recommended. "If others agree, we can expand the funicular stations in the next three years. We will have more cars and move them faster."

"If the cables can support more cars moving faster," said the Condor Elder in an undervoice. "How long is this going to take to complete, True Inca? Or do you know?"

"I have no confirmation," Sathale said. "Three years would be the fastest time to put the new funiculars into service, improving the existing lines and enlarging the stations and the facilities. Longer if we expand the number of stations as well."

The Llama Elder shook his head. "From what those of my clan tell me, the False Inca won't wait that long to press us. We can't expect that the people of the False Inca will ignore our preparations." He looked at the Condor Elder for support.

"There have been a lot of soldiers coming through the mountains, though they are dressed as merchants and traders and scholars. They are not your soldiers, True Inca," the Condor Elder said. "I am certain that there will be more next year." He looked around the room as if he thought someone might be listening. "What am I to tell the clan? Should I order them to report everyone who enters the lands of the True Inca?"

"We have discussed this already," said Sathale. "Bring it up later, during our formal debates, and the clans will decide."

The Llama Elder laughed. "Debate and decisions! Once it was for keeping the clans from fighting among themselves."

"And it was successful."

"I have heard," said the Llama Elder with increasing impatience, "that the Ravens are eager for war. You have Ravens around you here, and you might listen more closely to them because their voices are familiar."

"I might," said Sathale. "I might also ignore them because I hear them every day."

"The Ravens want war," the Condor Elder said.

"It may be."

"And they will insist on it."

"Which you will not?" The True Inca rounded on the Condor Elder, his face set. With meticulous care he said, "You advocate holding foreign travelers and questioning them, you tell me we need more arms and an increase of Spider patrols, you warn me that there is an invasion none of us recognize taking place, you fear the False Inca and his forces, and then you tell me that the

Ravens want war?'' He was out of the door and between his Crane guards before either the Condor or Llama Elders could speak.

It was the second day of the storm and the seas were growing higher, the force of the waves greater as the wind increased in fury, battering the three ships as they strove to keep heading into the storm. The sails were stowed belowdecks so that if masts were broken by the typhoon, the sails would not also be ruined; the paddlewheels churned at quarter speed.

Tulapa suffered the most. He tossed on his bunk, unable to eat or take more than a little water. Apenimon was brought to the *Black Dolphin* to watch over his brother.

The Rat clan attendant shook his head and went to get some of the herbal mixture that was used to treat seasickness. As he closed the door, he was muttering about certain clans having no business on the ocean, no matter what the True Inca might mandate.

As soon as the attendant was gone, Apenimon leaned down. ''How bad is it, Tulapa? What do you need? Tell me, and I'll see you have it.''

It was an effort for Tulapa to respond, and his voice was thready when he managed it. ''I need . . . dry land,'' he said. Tears seeped from his closed eyes. ''I don't know . . . if I can . . . if I can go up again.'' He reached out for Apenimon's hand. ''It's terrible.''

''Of course you can go up,'' said Apenimon. He wiped Tulapa's brow. ''You're not to say that again, do you understand me, little brother? It's the sickness talking, that's all. As soon as the storm is over, you'll be fine. All the Rats and Whales say so, and they've been on the ocean more times than we've been in the air.''

Tulapa shuddered. "In the air over the ocean . . . I can't do that." He turned his face away.

As the storm blundered about just beyond the hull, Apenimon did what he could to comfort Tulapa, singing the songs they had shared as children, and trying to recall humorous events from their past. At last the Rat returned.

"I have a tincture. It ought to help. It will make him drowsy, though." The Rat was missing a great many teeth, and his face was as wrinkled as a walnut, but there was a good expression in his eyes. "You let me tend to your brother while you have some coffee." He made a gentle shooing gesture to encourage Apenimon to leave.

The central cabin of the *Black Dolphin* was not crowded. Most of the crew not actively on watch had kept to their quarters. Apenimon found Enonyu with two of his senior officers frowning with concentration, going over their charts.

"But the compass isn't reliable, we can't see the stars, and from here there is no way to find out which of the ocean rivers is carrying us." Enonyu had a haunted look about his eyes, as if he had not slept since the typhoon struck, which was almost the truth. "You," he went on as he caught sight of Apenimon, "come here and give a look at this."

Apenimon approached the table, almost falling as the ship lurched in the water. He grabbed hold of the edge of the table and looked sheepishly at the Whales seated there. "I don't know how to do this well."

"In this weather, no one does," said Enonyu. He rubbed his eyes. "I'm issuing more coffee. Do you want any?"

"As much as I can drink," said Apenimon. "If it

can be spared. I may have to remain here through the night.''

''You mean you'll have to remain here through the storm,'' corrected the senior officer. ''We can't risk having you rowed back to the *Whale Road* in this. You'd probably be lost, and the boat with you, and who knows if you'd ever find the *Whale Road*?''

Enonyu said, ''Look over these charts and try to remember what you saw before the typhoon came. Which of these patterns could you see ahead?''

Strive as he might, Apenimon could not bring to mind the surface of the ocean the last time he had ridden his kite aloft. His mind had been on the approaching storm, on the widening dark line at the horizon. ''I don't . . . with the storm and all . . .''

''Try,'' said Enonyu. ''Try.''

A sullen Rat clan servant brought coffee mixed with honey and beer and set it out. He moved as if his joints pained him.

''Here,'' said the second officer, holding out tall glasses to the others at the table. ''We'll need this before the day is much older.''

''What about signals?'' the older officer asked. ''Anything from the *Whale Road* or the *Whales' Breath*?''

''Not since the morning watch changed. It's nearing the time to try again. I'll order the largest mirror and the brightest candle-bubble to power it.'' Enonyu glanced at Apenimon. ''Do you want to come with us?''

''We must have this alliance with the Maoris,'' Sathale said to his Four High Priests. The Conclave had been over for five days and most of the Elders had returned to the clans. At Machu Picchu the first rains of a bad storm were falling. The funicular cars hung on their cables, empty and still, until the storm was over, the ships at Algoma were pulled out into the bay and moored to prevent their breaking up against the quays and piers. Merchants carrying goods over mountain passes were detained at travelers' inns at the expense of the Clan Elders, and Spiders aloft in tethered and untethered kites had been ordered to return to earth.

"Your expedition will achieve it," Pathoain said.

"I hope it will," said Sathale. He was unable to meet Akando's eyes. "Every hour our need for it grows. But look at that!"—he gestured in the direction of the windows—"The Hawks say it is the worst storm in fourteen years. How can we be sure that the expedition has not all gone to the bottom of the ocean? The Spiders over the coast lost sight of them the day after they sailed." He started to pace. "I don't know what is best. Do we prepare another trio of ships, and find superior crews for them, and set them out as soon as the Cranes say the time is good?" He glared at Pathoain. "I don't want you to tell me that all is well. The Cranes have not given their answers to my question yet, so we know nothing yet."

Pathoain remained discreetly silent.

"Well," ventured Akando when no one else spoke, "which is more important: a second expedition to the Maoris or more funicular stations and faster cars?" No one answered. "It seems to me that if the current ships have come through the storm and can complete the voyage, it would not be wise to follow with a second. The Maoris are ocean-riding people themselves, and they will be impressed at how well the three captains have managed. But if we send a second expedition, it will seem that we had no faith in our Whales or our High

Gods, and that isn't likely to turn the Maoris to our cause, is it?''

''It is not so simple,'' Dyami grumbled.

''Of course it is,'' said Akando. ''We want the Maoris to regard us as equals, not backward clans clinging to the sides of our mountains while the False Inca makes treaties with the False Inca of the Green Banner or some other group of armed rebels from Urop.''

The True Inca selected the most beautifully upholstered chair and sat down. ''What have the Japanese said?'' he asked.

''They have said they want to go home,'' said Bemosetu. ''They have enough goods to carry to the Mikado and their own merchants, and they have agreed to stop at two ports in the countries to the north. That is a concession we ought to honor with permission to leave, True Inca.''

Sathale shook his head. ''With this storm, I would think that they'd be grateful to us for requiring them to remain. Tell them we did not want to alarm them, for the signs were not sure until yesterday. That will have the advantage of being accurate, for the Spiders at the coast did not see the storm coming until then.''

''The Maoris,'' said Dyami, ''will see the advantage in forming an alliance with us. Between us is all of the Western Ocean as far north as Hawaii. They understand how useful this can be.'' Having stated what all men in the room had convinced themselves was true, he went on, ''Let us therefore prepare another expedition, a larger one, with more gifts, and start it on its way to them, saying that the second expedition is to demonstrate to the Maoris our good faith. We will not admit our concern for the first expedition, except to say that they have great skills for riding out bad weather.''

Pathoain nodded his endorsement. "Excellent. What could be more reasonable than that?"

"Akando?" Sathale asked, regarding the Fourth High Priest quizzically. "What do you think of that?"

"I think it's a waste of time. I think that if we send a second expedition without the certainty that the first has failed we will appear desperate and conciliatory, which would compromise our negotiations with the Maoris." He could see the disapproval of the others. "But it is not my decision to make, True Inca."

"No," said Sathale, his eyes focused in the middle distance.

"That is the thinking of one who was a Raven, always looking for advantage in battle," Pathoain jeered. "What use is your advice in these matters?"

Sathale looked directly at Pathoain. "If you can do nothing better than excoriate one of your own, then perhaps it is you I should disbelieve, not Akando." He straightened in his chair. "I want no more of this bickering."

"It was not my doing," Pathoain protested.

"Truly it should not have been," said the True Inca, his inflection severe. "What of you, Akando?"

"I have no argument with the First High Priest; I only have a different opinion from his."

"Very well. What do you make of the tales that there are devastation ants in the Flatlands? If it is so, then the False Inca can't move against us until they have gone and some order is restored."

"I have seen the reports," said the Second High Priest, "both of your messengers and of the Spiders patrolling the Spine of the World. I say that these ants are servants of the High Gods sent to protect us while we prepare to meet the onslaught of our enemies."

Akando shook his head. "We're in danger. We have had three good harvests, and we have recently widened our markets for glass, so it is known that we are prospering. Helaoku is desperate; he has soldiers to feed and house and pay. He might well prefer that *our* gold does that rather than his own." He saw resistance in the eyes of the other High Priests. "I can't help it; I was born into the Raven clan, as each of you was born into a clan. I may have renounced the Ravens, but I cannot forget their instruction."

Sathale saw that another disagreement loomed. It was, he thought, going to be a long meeting.

The skies had cleared two days ago and the ocean was once again placid, but there was still no sign of the *Whale Road*. Both Apenimon and Iyestu had searched for it while aloft, but could not find anything that looked like the ship, or its wreckage.

"We have been blown south," said Pallatu at the end of the second day of continual watching when the Spiders and three officers had been rowed from the *Black Dolphin* to the *Whales' Breath*. "If they kept closer to the course than we were able to, then they might well be beyond sight even of your Spider spectacles."

"Yes," said Apenimon, a bit too eagerly, for he wanted the *Whale Road* to be found almost more than he wanted to reach the lands of the Maoris.

Pallatu broached the awkward subject. "How is your brother, Apenimon?"

The elder twin shrugged. "He was sick for five days, so he isn't quite himself yet." He did not know what to tell Pallatu, for Tulapa had sworn several times and showed no sign of relenting in his vow that he would not ride a kite over the ocean again, not for any reason, no matter who ordered it. "In a while he will be ready to ride up the tether once more."

"I hope you are correct," said Pallatu, thinking of the dire warnings he had received from Meliwa about the long voyage. "I have ordered a corrected course to be plotted on the charts." He coughed once for tact. "The storm has left us low on fuel; we didn't anticipate such a long period against such heavy seas, even at one-quarter power. We'll have to rely more on our sails for the rest of the journey, and that is not what I'd prefer to do."

"Do you mean," asked Iyestu, who had been sitting in the corner listening, "that you wouldn't mind finding an island where we could buy more fuel, assuming that we can locate one and it can provide what we seek?"

Pallatu gave a sign of approval. "If you come upon one in your watching, let me know at once. Send a bottle down the tether, if the island appears promising." He patted the charts. "I will double the deck watch to assist you."

Apenimon stared down at his hands. "That would be useful. Once we sight land, you will need to have more eyes than ours alone."

Enonyu indicated the patches on the cabin walls. "These will have to be repaired quickly. If we encounter another storm—"

"If we encounter a second storm the likes of that first one, we'll have to accept that the High Gods don't wish us to accomplish this journey no matter what the True Inca has mandated," said Pallatu, and it was only partly in jest.

"There should have been a sacrifice," said Enonyu. "The High Gods and the Gods of the Ocean don't want to be slighted." He met Pallatu's eyes coldly. "If we had made a sacrifice at the proper time, there would never have been a bad storm and the *Whale Road* would not be missing. If we don't make sacrifices, sacrifices will be taken from us." He got up and started out of the cabin. "I have lost a Rat servant overboard. The result of the storm. I know my duty, if you do not." With that he was gone.

"Don't worry," said Pallatu, after the room had been silent for a short while, "I'll see that the tethers of your kites are guarded at all times. You have nothing to fear from Enonyu."

This casual observation startled Apenimon. "Do you think . . . it isn't possible that a kite would be cut free as a *sacrifice*, is it? Is it?"

"It is very tempting, if a man wants to make a sacrifice," Pallatu said. "But I will not permit it."

Apenimon looked aghast. But Iyestu grinned. "You mean someone might actually cut me free? Let me ride the winds without a tether as I do along the Spine of the World? Think how high I could go, and how far." He clapped his hands in approval, paying no heed to the horror in his brother's eyes. "Tell Enonyu if he wants to sacrifice one of us, I won't complain if he cuts my tether, tell him, but I would be furious if he cut Apenimon's."

"There'll be no tether-cutting at all," growled Apenimon, looking quickly to Pallatu for confirmation.

"None at all," said the Whale leader.

When the storm was over, two messengers presented themselves in Machu Picchu, one a Fox, one a Raven, both of them demanding to speak to the True Inca. The Four High Priests and two Cranes worked out how this was to be accomplished without either messenger being insulted. Finally it was agreed that the one who had come the greatest distance would be the one to speak with Sathale first.

The Raven was gaunt from his travels through the country where the ants had ravaged. "Helaoku has said he will have to send troops to keep order until new crops can be brought in. I think that is the least required, for many people are starving, and they have no place to go. At the worst sites, there was nothing left at all; the ants ate up livestock as well as all the plants, so there is very little left for the survivors to eat and nothing for them to farm or raise. It is said that herds are being driven in from the south, from the grasslands, but that will take time, perhaps as long as half a year for some. Whatever is done, it must take time, and time is against them. The Jaguar people who live by the Mother River have refused to permit soldiers of the False Inca to enter their villages, and this is considered to be a bad sign. They have said it was because of foreigners on the land that the ants came, that until the foreigners are gone the ants will continue to ravage; they will not change their minds."

"How long will it take for the land to recover to the point that the people who live there will not need aid?" Sathale asked.

"Not this year and not next. In three years, perhaps; orchards, well, they will take much longer."

"And what does this mean for the False Inca?"

"He will not be able to march an army across that territory, and if he has to go around the area—which is his only alternative if he plans to attack—it will take too long. He might want to bring his navy through the Teeth of the Gods, but we would have warning and we would be prepared. Besides, there is not enough food to keep an army on the march or a navy at sea, and there will not be until next summer at the very earliest. He cannot move now." The Raven managed a terrible smile. "You have three years to increase your fortification, to establish more funicular routes, to build more telegraph stations. In three years, it would be folly to come against you if you make ready now, and he will understand that."

"Yes," said the True Inca. "I was assuming much the same thing. I am grateful to you for what you have done." He rose from his chair. "I will see that you are rewarded. Akando, who was a Raven and is now Fourth High Priest, will adopt you as his son."

When the Fox messenger arrived not long after, he appeared better fed, but just as exhausted as the Raven; he had come through the mountains in the south, where the ants had not struck, starting at the mouth of the Silver River and coming north and west across the Spine of the World. He took the seat offered him, sprawling a little, though it was incorrect to behave this way in the presence of the True Inca. His upper arm was bandaged.

"Were you injured?" Sathale asked.

"Nothing to matter," said the Fox messenger. "I was foolish enough to get caught in a rockslide just above Titicaca. It'll heal in a few days. The Cranes helped me." He narrowed his eyes. "My hurts are not important. I bring you news that may be."

"Do you?"

The Fox messenger nodded. "The city at the mouth of the Silver River has been one of the major centers of foreigners in the lands of the False Inca. It has a telegraph and four ship-building companies, which is what the foreigners find most valuable there."

"Yes," said Sathale.

"There's been talk for some little time about a rebellion brewing in the lands of the False Inca of the Green Banner, and the foreigners in the city on the Silver River have been more outspoken than those in other places, especially those at the mouth of the Mother River. I have learned many things about the False Inca of the Green Banner. His western territories have been in disorder for a few years, if what we have learned is true—it is certainly consistent. In the last month there is another factor to consider: the False Inca of the Green Banner has summoned home all troops in the lands of the False Inca. He has sent ships to bring them back. A few have already left Helaoku's ports and more ships are arriving from over the Eastern Ocean. It was stressed to the foreign soldiers that they are needed urgently on their own soil." He grinned. "I saw four ships leave, bound for the Mediterranean, that sea they say is the center of the world. They are expected in a place called Antioch as fast as they can get there."

"Antioch. I think I know where that is," the True Inca said. "If that's where they're going, then the False Inca of the Green Banner needs their help."

"Whatever the case may be," said the Fox messenger, "they are not in the lands of Helaoku, and it is at a time when the False Inca needs aid."

"Yes," Sathale said. "Taking the foreign troops home is a new development. And it may be that the rebellions you have heard of are at the heart of it, but . . ." He looked away toward the window. "Where is the rebellion? Is it in Urop? If it is, why are the soldiers being carried to Antioch when they might better be sent directly to the rebellious territories, territories that are closer to the eastern shores here than to Antioch? Is the rebellion in the east, as the two Japanese captains told us, or is it in the west, as the rumors have suggested?''

''Or is there more than one rebellion,'' suggested the Fox messenger. ''There could be more than one, could there not?''

''The High Gods take pity on the False Inca of the Green Banner if that is so, for there will be no retreat for him, and no hiding place.'' Sathale turned and regarded the Fox messenger, a glint of humor in his eyes. ''Or might he try the lands to the north? Do you think they would make the False Inca of the Green Banner welcome in Mexico?'' To the messenger's puzzled astonishment, the True Inca started to chuckle.

They made landfall at last, at a cluster of islands that were regarded as part of the Maori outposts, peopled by their cousins the Morioris. In the city of Waitangi they were received with cautious grace by the headman and his council. Both the people of the True Inca and the cousins of the Maoris were unsure of how to proceed.

''We do not know this True Inca of the Spine of the World,'' said the headman, after Etenyi had struggled through an introduction. ''We have sometimes seen ships like yours and encountered others dressed as you are. We know the ones who trail ropes into the sky as they cross the oceans.'' He glanced at the two ships. ''There was a storm, very bad.''

''We know this,'' said Pallatu through Etenyi. ''We went through it, and one of our ships was separated from us. We have not found it again.''

There was a great deal of murmuring and headshaking among the council of the headman, and one very old fellow, so lavishly tattoed that he appeared to be blue all over, slapped a length of wood against a large wooden bell.

"Are they all like that, marked all over?" Etenyi said softly to Pallatu, "or are these marked because they are important people?"

"A little of both," Pallatu said, faintly amused. "I've seen Maoris before and it has been explained to me that the tattoos are the history of the man and his clan together." He placed his open palm against his chest, over the clan embroidery on his linen shirt. "I am relieved that the Whale Elder never decided that we needed such records made on our skins."

The leader of the Morioris carried on at some length, and though Etenyi did not catch all the words, she understood enough of them to be able to say, "He indicates we are welcome. He wants you to anchor in the bay; he is afraid the old lava flows will damage the ships. He is worried about pirates, not about two foreign ships unless we serve as guides for pirates. He will place armed guards on boats in the harbor, and they will protect your ships."

"Not what I had in mind, but thank him," said Pallatu. "Tell him that my men will stand guard on the ships, too. And I will order the men to make sure that the guns are in working order."

"Do you want me to say—" Etenyi began, only to be cut off.

"You're not stupid, girl. Don't provoke me by pretense, will you?" Pallatu lifted the cup of fruit wine he had been given, nodding to the headman of the Morioris. "Tell him that the High Gods will look on his hospitality with favor. And then find out if we can purchase fuel from him.''

''As you wish,'' said Etenyi.

Of the last few messengers to reach Machu Picchu before the False Inca closed the borders, the one from the Mantis clan was the strangest, and not because he was doing something so un-Mantis-like as spying for the True Inca. He presented himself in the private council chambers of the Inca's Palace, his clothes in disarray, his clan bracelet gone.

''You have had a difficult trek, Wothimdyu,'' Sathale said, when the Mantis messenger had got halfway through the ritualistic phrases of greeting the True Inca.

''A little,'' said Wothimdyu, startled at the break in the neat progression of manners and function.

''Then let's not waste time. What do you want to tell me?''

Wothimdyu needed a little time to organize his thoughts. He said finally, ''I wanted to reach the pass before the False Inca ordered the borders closed. There were rumors of such closure for almost a month. The people in the lands of the False Inca have heard about the ants on the northern rivers, and they have seen that the foreigners are leaving.''

''Which means that we will start to find refugees from the lands of the False Inca before much longer,'' said Sathale with philosophical resolve. ''So: he cannot continue without the soldiers from the False Inca of the Green Banner, or from another foreign leader.'' Inwardly he was aware of burgeoning hope, as he had been for almost a month. Half a year ago he was all but certain he would fall to the army of his distant cousin; now he was beginning to wonder if the reverse might be possible. Had he been a fool to contact Mexico? He couldn't have anticipated this development, he told himself sternly.

"Yes," said the Mantis messenger. "The guess is that he will have to make an arrangement with the lands to the north if he loses his assistance from the False Inca of the Green Banner."

"Would he be that reckless? His protector might well gain control over him, and then what would happen to the lands of the False Inca?" Sathale asked, not expecting an answer. "Would *Helaoku* be rash enough to form an alliance with Mexico?" Was Llotl or someone like him holding secret meetings with his second cousin?

"It could mean that your lands, True Inca, would be caught in pincers, if Helaoku has aid from the north," said the Mantis messenger with fervor. "You must strengthen your borders, as I have heard you are doing already. There must be more, as well."

"Soldiers have trouble in these mountains. The roads are few, and with Spiders aloft, they cannot approach any fort without detection. I now have twenty Spiders in the air from an hour before dawn until an hour after sunset. No army can move in these mountains in the dark, not even if they know the way." He gave a quirky smile. "My Ravens have tried it."

"But if they were to come from two directions, True Inca: the north and the east—" The Mantis made a sign to ward off evil thoughts.

Sathale did not respond at once. "Have you seen the jaws of one of the great lizards? They are frightening when they gape. But keep your courage and thrust a stick into the lizard's mouth to hold it open and the lizard will not be able to bite. The Spine of the World is far harder to break than the stick in the lizard's mouth. As long as we have messengers on the ground and Spiders aloft in tethered and untethered kites, there is no doubt that we will prevail."

"How can you mean that? There are many more men in the lands of the False Inca, and if you add to that the men of the lands to the north, it's as bad or worse than foreign soldiers. What can we do with such risks?" asked the messenger. His distress showed in spite of his courtly reserve. "What if the False Inca of the Green Banner sends his soldiers again, as he has sworn to do? What if Mexico accepts Helaoku as an ally?"

"We do not know with certainty that my second cousin has made such overtures." Feeling rigid, Sathale made himself continue. "We can establish treaties with the Maoris. Who knows, the Japanese may be willing to trade with us, now that Yukio Shigemaro and Hisoka Hyogo have taken my invitation to their Mikado to enter into proper arrangements." He saw shock in the Mantis's face. "You are upset because I contemplate alliances with foreigners?"

The Mantis took refuge in a safe answer. "It . . . it is contrary to our teaching. It has never been done before."

"Yes. But the False Inca has never sought foreign soldiers to come against us, and the lands to the north have never been stronger than they are now. Little though we may like it, we cannot hide in the fastness of the Spine of the World and trust that the High Gods will keep us in peace." The Inca put his palms flat on the table. "Perhaps before the foreigners, before the steam engines and these new engines that run on lightning, when Spiders rode only tethered kites and the Whale clan did not venture beyond the Spider sight of land—perhaps before these and the telegraph, we could count ourselves safe, but not now. We are being drawn into the business of the world. One way or another, we will have to deal with foreigners, if not this way, then through war. Or,'' he added with distaste, ''revolution.''

''The Elders cannot permit such arrangements. No one can want foreigners on the mountains,'' said the Mantis messenger.

''I have done nothing against the Elders,'' said Sathale quietly, wishing it were true. ''We hear word of all the world now, and we hear the how the wind is blowing, the Elders and I.''

The Mantis made a gesture of protest. ''And what next? Will you want to use foreign troops, as your cousin has tried to do, and with their assistance, conquer the lands of the False Inca?''

The guess was a little too close to Sathale's ambitions for him to concur. ''No,'' he lied, then gave a brief smile. ''But my grandson might.''

On the morning of the tenth day since landfall, Pallatu declared he was pleased with the repairs on his ships and was ready to resume his journey to the Maoris. He made an elaborate speech, stretching Etenyi's rapidly expanding vocabulary of the Maori tongue to the limit. He thanked the Morioris as profusely as he was able, and took the liberty of presenting one of the ceremonial gifts intended for the ruler of the Maoris to the headman of the Morioris, with the promise of more to come as trade between their countries increased.

''For I truly believe,'' he said with fervor, ''that we cannot have come so far, through such danger, only to fail in the task the True Inca mandated. Already I look forward to the day when we will return again to meet you, when we will be able to sit down as old friends and share our tales of adventure on the ocean.''

Several drums and wooden bells were beaten. The people gathered in the central plaza cheered and whistled. The noise was terrific.

''They are pleased.'' Etenyi said. She had to shout into Pallatu's ear to be heard.

''Good,'' said Pallatu. ''Then perhaps they'll help finish loading the ships.''

The leave-taking continued even after the two vessels were loaded and the small engines fired up to drive the paddlewheels. Morioris came out to surround the ships and give them escort out of the harbor. They sang for the foreigners, and threw flowers into the wakes of their ships.

Only when the Morioris had turned back did Apenimon go aloft in his kite, his tether playing out in the billowing wind in a long, graceful curve. On the deck far below, his twin watched anxiously, though he would not go near the donkey engine that held the tether.

''Tulapa,'' said Iyestu as he came near his older brother, ''you are looking much better now.'' He said it heartily enough, but the truth was in his eyes and he could not change it: Tulapa's body had recovered but his spirit continued to ail, and it showed in the somberness of the boy, and a jerkiness of movement that he had not had before.

''The ocean is calmer,'' he said, looking toward the stern instead of the prow. ''And we are not far from the lands of the Maoris now. What is the name of the city we were told to seek?''

''Rotorua,'' said Iyestu. ''It's in the mountains, due north and a little east of the port of Wairoa.'' He was proud of how well he had remembered what the Morioris had told them the night before. "In fact, it is an arrangement just like the one at home, with the capital inland, protected by forts and cannon. It'll be just like Algoma and Machu Picchu, won't it?"

"We'll take the steam railway to the capital," said Tulapa, as if his decision was final for all of them.

"Oh, you can if you want," said Iyestu, dismissing the notion for himself. "Why ride?"

"I've never ridden on a steam railway," Tulapa said defensively, his face flushing suddenly.

Iyestu shrugged. "They're probably not much different than the funicular cars, except they have wheels and they carry their boilers with them." He sighed, watching the bow-wave break as it curled back from the prow. "Well, you do as you wish, I'll stay with my kite. I want to fly there."

Tulapa's eyes were hard and bright. "You want to shame me, don't you mean? If you think I dishonor our clan, or our family, you say so. Stop this digging, digging, digging at me!" He flung away from his brother and started toward the companionway.

"Wait!" Iyestu cried out. "Tulapa, wait! I didn't mean anything like that. I didn't!" He could hear his brother rushing down the steep ladder, cursing as he went. "Tulapa!" he shouted, but was given no response.

"Don't press him," said a voice nearby, and Iyestu turned to see Pallatu stroll from the main cabin. "I've seen it happen with sailors, too. They have a bad voyage and it poisons the sea for them, as I suspect that storm poisoned the air for your brother. It will pass."

"Are you sure?" Iyestu asked. "He is so different."

Pallatu nodded. "It will pass," he repeated, then deliberately changed the subject. "Ten more days, did they say, if the winds are favorable?"

"Nine or ten," said Iyestu, his worry forgotten. "We will see the Maori islands in two or three days, aloft." He smiled again, this time secretively, relishing his plan.

"If the winds stay with us, yes," agreed Pallatu. He indicated the tether, noting the way it swayed. "The winds are higher aloft, aren't they, when the tether looks like that."

"Usually," said Iyestu, trying not to resent Pallatu for knowing Spider things. "Sometimes it means there are currents moving two different ways."

"We see that on the ocean, sometimes," said Pallatu, then put his hand on Iyestu's shoulder. "Come. Let me have your company for a meal. Your sister will join us," he went on blandly. "Whale ship, Whale rules."

"Of course," said Iyestu with an uneasy glance at Apenimon's tether.

"The deck watch will guard him, Iyestu," Pallatu said gently. "And Tulapa will not have to remember his own dread."

While he was trying to think of a reasonable objection, Pallatu led him away to his quarters.

A bronze-sailed junk limped into Algoma, its pennons flying upside down to signal distress. The Whale and Rat clans sent their men out to her to find out what was wrong. They returned with the first officer, who had assumed captaincy when his superior was killed.

"We were just south of Mexico," the first officer explained to Sathale and the Four High Priests. "We wanted to pick up some of the fine embroidery the women of those little districts do so well." He had a half-healed cut on his cheek and he limped when he walked. "Zhiao Ping, my captain, used all reasonable caution, keeping the cannon on deck and sending the crew ashore with muskets and pistols as well as gold."

"Yes," said Sathale. "Under the circumstances, a very sound practice."

"Not sound enough," the officer said. "We were set upon as we returned to the ship. Two Mexican warships came, flanking our junk while it was still at anchor and while most of the crew was in the rowboats returning from the land." He took a deep, uneven breath. "They didn't want goods or gold, though they took every weapon they could. All in all, they made off with fourteen men, more than half the crew, and they killed or seriously injured five more."

"Leaving you how many to man the ship?" Sathale asked.

"Not enough. Nine of us. We have had to work twice as long as our regulations require. We can't return to China without repairs and more men for the crew."

"The crew, the crew," the True Inca mused. "Men and weapons."

"They're getting ready for a fight," said Akando, adding, "You don't have to be a Raven to see that."

"No," said Dyami shortly. "Well?" He listened as Sathale promised aid to the foreigners.

"Thank you, Glorious Ruler, for aiding this insignificant person in a time of unanticipated need." The Chinese officer bowed and saluted, then left the room with a Crane escort.

"What do you think?" asked Sathale, when the Chinese officer was gone.

"I think," Akando said, "that our neighbors to the

north are getting restless. I think they want to go to war with someone. The question is: who?''

''Seizures like that one will serve to put us on notice,'' said Dyami. ''What reason do they have to issue warning?''

''Yes,'' said Akando. ''An unwise move. Unless they intended to deliver a message.'' He met Sathale's gaze. ''It was a desperate thing, True Inca.''

''And there is no excuse for desperation.'' Sathale slowly made a gesture of resignation. ''You must do what you must do.''

Akando rose, still looking at the True Inca instead of the other High Priests. ''They'll kill us together, no doubt: you for your treason and me for protecting you.''

''I am sorry about the ships.'' Sathale was speaking only to Akando, and there was a calm in him that was new. ''If I had thought there was another way, I would never have sent them to their deaths. If I hadn't needed a plausible diversion, I would never have mandated so hopeless a voyage. I want you to believe that.''

''I believe it, but it changes nothing,'' said Akando, and began to explain to the others.

Yesterday afternoon Apenimon had caught sight of the Maori islands in the distance before his tether had been reeled in, and now that he was aloft and his spectacles strapped in place, Iyestu saw them clearly. He grinned, testing the foot controls on his kite. The others might think it too radical a design, too hard to operate, but he loved it. He nudged his left pedal and rode the swoop laughing. All it took was another gentle nudge and the kite was once again sailing steadily on the wind.

As Iyestu looked down and back at the *Whales' Breath* and the *Black Dolphin*, he felt a surge of pride.

How astonished they will be, he thought, when they discover what I have done. He felt for the knife in his belt and was reassured to find it, though he had checked it frequently since he went into the air. All the way across the ocean he had been perfecting his plan, and now he told himself that he was ready. The wind was right, the islands lay ahead: with any luck, he would arrive two days ahead of the ships below. And they, who would be grieving for his loss, would have him doubly returned. He would bring fame to the Spiders; he would fulfill the True Inca's Mandate. Imagining his welcome, first from the leaders of the Maoris, and then from his own people as they were reunited, Iyestu drew the knife and caught up the hasp of his tether. The cable was thick and for all its lightness, it was persistently tough. Iyestu sawed at it, sweating despite the cool wind that rushed by him.

And then, impossibly, finally, he was free. The tether plummeted away from him, down to the shine of the distant ocean. Iyestu watched, but could not see where the tether fell. Then he looked ahead, to the distant peaks of the islands of the Maoris. He gave a little kick and the kite soared; another and he hovered as readily as a gull. With the tether gone he picked up speed, racing up the sky toward the splendid, distant mountains and glory.